JB CAINE

RUSH TO JUDGEMENT

Dedication

My sincerest thank you, as always, to Buck and Haley for being my lights and for supporting me through the countless hours of writing, promoting, and editing.

Thank you for gently pushing me when I needed to be pushed, and hugging me when I needed to be hugged.

Thank you, also, to Barbara and Kelly, for your tireless hours poring over my work and helping me to grow it into stories I can be proud of. Your expertise, cheerleading, and counsel are worth everything. I wish everyone had a girl tribe like mine.

I'd also like to thank my parents (Jean and Ron) and extended parents (in-laws, Katie and BB) who, though I don't think they are particularly drawn to my subject matter, never fail to give me the encouragement and parental validation that we all crave, even when we are old enough to have teenagers of our own.

And for my sweet Chopper boy—my most dedicated and attentive writing buddy—see you on the other side of the Rainbow Bridge.

More by JB Caine

Also in the Arcana Trilogy:
Rise of the Moon
Strength of Will
The Ironshield's Shadow Series
The Manifest Destiny Series (with Betsey Kulakowski)
The YOUR STORY Series

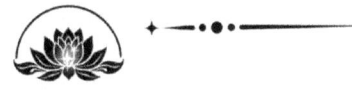

*T*he Great Mage extended his arms over the bubbling pot and stretched forth his fingers.

Energy harnessed and blood to blood.

The droplets of blood that had landed on the sheets of parchment encircling the pot came to life and began branching out, etching lines in seemingly random directions. The circle of mages watched in breathless silence as each design began to take form.

Elige speciem tuam. Choose your form.

Each mage stepped forward in turn and spooned a small amount of the bubbling mixture onto one sheet of the parchment. It was absorbed instantly, and began filling more lines and color into each. Each mage on the Council lifted their individual parchments and stepped back into the circle.

Chapter 1

I f you've ever wondered if it's possible to control time, the answer is yes. I know this because my World History teacher Mrs. Gaither literally managed to slow the passage of time as twenty-eight of us Lockridge Academy sophomores sat in her classroom, willing away the last torturous moments of the period, the day, the school year. I was fairly certain that Her Heftiness had actually sold her soul so that the remaining five minutes would never pass.

Even after we had turned in our final exams, she'd demanded silence. I looked wearily around. Erick had fallen asleep with his forehead on the desk and Rachel had been reduced to doodling on her suitcase. It was Mrs. Gaither herself who finally broke the silence.

"One final thing before you all traipse out of here toward your respective summer destinations: Lockridge's junior history course, as you know, is American History with Dr. Jameson. In preparation for that course, I have been asked to present you with this ... " There was a smug satisfaction on her face as she brandished a set of canary yellow handouts and began distributing them to the front student in each row. Rachel kicked Erick's desk, and he jolted awake, sporting a bright red sleep-strawberry on his freckled Irish forehead. A wave of indignation started in the front row and flowed backwards as students read the sheets.

"Homework over the summer? You've got to be kidding!" Erick was incredulous and, it seemed, personally offended. "Is there going to be a grade for this, or is he just trying to ruin my summer?" Rachel and I exchanged glances and snickered as Erick blurted out the class' silent sentiments.

The teacher held up her hand to silence Erick's (and anyone else's) protests. "Save it. It's neither my course nor my assignment. I'm just the messenger. If you have questions, comments, or complaints, Dr. Jameson's email address is at the bottom of the page."

However unwelcome it may have been, the distraction of the summer assignment had served to eat up the remaining class time. As the year's final bell sounded, a roar of relief rose from the classroom, a roar echoed from each and every classroom in the building. Students poured into the hallways and Rachel, Erick, and I were carried out with the tide. Once outside, we pulled over to let the crowd pass.

"So, you gonna do this assignment, Ree?" Rachel teased me.

"Of course she is. Ree ALWAYS does her work. Even if it's a stinking summer assignment." Erick's yellow paper was already mangled and hanging out of one of the fantasy novels he was always reading.

"Unlike some of us, eh, Erick? Look at this." I pointed to the tattered yellow remains. "You are *hell* on paper. Oh, and look, your mommy's already here waiting for you."

"She was here at eleven-thirty," he groaned. "I had to hide at lunchtime. But at least she went and got my bags from the dorm so I don't have to go all the way back there to get them. Where's your stuff, Ree?"

"I put it in Logan's car this morning. Now that he's graduated and finished his exams, he wants to burn a trail out of here as soon as I can get across the parking lot." Logan was my cousin, best friend, and perpetual chauffeur.

"You're lucky you only have an hour-and-a-half drive," Rachel muttered. "It takes four hours for me to get home. That's four hours in the back seat with my nitwit stepbrother. Speaking of which, there's the MomMo-bile. I gotta go. We'll Skype, okay?"

"You bet. See ya, Rach."

"I'd better go, too," Erick said, seeing that his mother had noticed him and was waving enthusiastically, "before she starts calling me. 'Yoohoo, Erick, sweetums ...' I might die of embarrassment. Bye, Ree. Talk to you later, Rach."

Brief hugs were exchanged and I watched my friends trot toward the parent-pick-up area. As I watched them greet their parents (more affec-tionately than they would dare to admit), I felt a pang of loss. Their familial complaints had been for my benefit, I knew, since there would never be a parent waiting for me in that circular drive.

I scanned the student parking lot, now dotted with huddled groups of students hugging and weeping their summertime farewells. Scenes like that made me feel awkward and uncomfortable, so I gritted my teeth and made a beeline for Logan's hard-top Jeep, hoping none of the fluttery girls who would want to bid my cousin *adieu* had spotted it parked at the very back of the lot behind the elm tree. I arrived to find him mob-less and hunched low in the driver's seat.

"C'mon, Ree, get in! Let's get the hell out of here! If I have to deal with one more sappy goodbye from someone I'm hardly going to remember ten years from now, I'll puke."

"I hear that. I can't get away from all the gooey farewells fast enough."

"Think Rachel might come visit over the summer?" Logan asked as the engine roared to life.

"I don't know," I shrugged. "It's my own fault really. I try to be a good friend, but I really am not great at staying in touch with people."

"Why's that? You're pretty social here at school."

I shrugged again and stared out the window. "I'm not sure. I think I'm not good at feelings that go beyond the everyday superficial ones." I wanted to say, *I'm just afraid to get close to people because it hurts when they aren't there anymore.* But as if to demonstrate the point, I couldn't get the words out. Somehow, though, I think Logan knew, because he reached over and playfully shoved my shoulder.

We screeched out of the parking lot, ready for summer to begin. Within a half hour, we were cruising down highway 64 on our way home, windows down, blasting AC/DC into the wind. We had hardly said a word since we'd left, each settling into our own world of unwinding nerves and dissolving stress. My elbow rested on the window sill, and my eyes were distant and unfocused as the trees sped by.

Out of the corner of my eye, I saw a shapeless form moving in seemingly slow motion. I felt Logan tense up beside me and heard him shout something that my brain couldn't translate into words. I started to turn toward him, also in slow motion, and it was then that I saw the SUV. Through the fog of panic, I heard car horns blaring and the amorphous sound of Logan's voice. Our car veered sharply off the side of the road to avoid the oncoming vehicle.

Spinning, falling.
Like Alice down the rabbit hole.
Whirls of colors.
Flipping, flying.

I heard a high shrieking noise from somewhere in the distance, and only in the hours that followed did I realize that it had been my own voice. There was the sound of shattering glass, creaking metal, and a *shhhhh* of the car sliding on the grass. The world was upside down ... literally. My breath came in painful gasps and sobs; the images of my parents floated through my mind as all the colors faded to black.

Chapter 2

The rest of that day passed as a series of broken images. Even now I'm not sure how many of them were real, and how many are the twisted visions the concussion wove into my brain: Logan's voice (*"Hello? We need help..."*, *"Highway 64"*, *"cousin"...*), sirens, bright lights like pinpricks in my eyes, the sensation of being lifted and plopped down again...sharpness in my side, and then a sudden one in my arm, then darkness again.

I floated through a hazy plane of existence, unaware of the passage of time. I heard voices that I recognized as Logan and my Aunt Pam; I heard the cadence of official-sounding voices that I assume were doctors and nurses. And I heard other voices...ones I had not heard for many years...their words lost in the haze, but their tone soothing and reassuring. I struggled to open my eyes, and yet I wanted to stay in this real-seeming dream.

"Mom?"

I felt so groggy, like my head was full of cotton balls. For an instant I'd forgotten that my parents were dead, just like in those first few weeks after the plane crash. The therapist had told me it was normal, that my brain was still *processing*.

But now it felt like she was here, her presence comforting me like a fuzzy knit afghan. It wasn't real. It couldn't be real. Unless...but no, I wasn't dead. Death doesn't come with headaches.

I pushed my eyelids open a crack and could make out the outlines of a hospital room, dimly lit from the hallway lights. Hushed conversations from the nurses' station whispered across my ears, and I searched for the source of the voice that had motivated my wakefulness. Still bleary-eyed, I focused on a chair by the window; in it, a familiar silhouette moved against the curtain. I strained my eyes, willed my brain to push away the cobwebs so I could focus.

I was distracted by the sound of approaching footsteps. A pale light flipped on above my bed, and I shifted my eyes to a woman in soft, pink hospital scrubs. She leaned over and checked the numbers on the machine which was beeping softly next to my bed. Her eyes flicked from the machine to my face and, seeing me awake, she smiled broadly.

"Well, well...hello, Sleeping Beauty! You've had quite a little nap. There are several people who will be awfully happy to see you back in the land of the living!" She patted my shoulder and bustled off to find the attending doctor. I turned my eyes back to the chair, which was now bathed in anemic light from the small fluorescent bulb over my bed.

The chair was empty, as I had known it would be.

***

After two days of observation to assess the severity of my concussion, I was released from the hospital with a sprained wrist, a black eye, a few cuts and bruises, and warnings to keep an eye out for headaches or other signs that my noggin had taken a more serious hit than it appeared. I was lucky, everyone said, and Logan was even luckier. Aside from some minor scrapes, he'd come out of the accident unscathed thanks to the airbags and seatbelts in his Jeep. His greatest injury was that his Jeep was totaled. It could've been so much worse for both of us. I'd spent a total of four days in the hospital, even though I could only remember two of them, and I wanted nothing more than to get home.

Logan took great pleasure in insisting that I let him push me in a wheelchair all the way to the hospital exit despite my objections. Aunt Pam was uncharacteristically quiet, and tearfully watched us as we bantered in the way close cousins do.

"Are you okay, Aunt Pam?"

She smiled weakly. "I will be. I could have lost you both in that accident, you know." There was a beat of silence as we wheeled through the hospital-beige hallway. "I don't know if I could have gone back to the Glen if I had. It was bad enough when we lost MJ, but you all were young, and the Glen has been in the family for generations. This would've done it, though. I couldn't have lived with all the memories."

"But you didn't lose us, Mom." Logan let go of the wheelchair and put his arm around his mother. "We're okay. And we're going home. ALL of us."

He realized that I was still rolling down the hall, leaving them behind, and jogged to catch up and grab the chair's handles.

"Assuming you don't get me killed on the way out the door," I quipped.

"Look, if you were to have an *unfortunate* wheelchair mishap, at least you're already in a hospital."

"I feel so relieved now, thanks." I looked over my shoulder at my aunt. I didn't like conversations about feelings, but I didn't want to brush her emotions off entirely. "Don't worry, Aunt Pam. I'm sticking around. And you can't leave the Glen. If you did, I'd just have to live in the attic with whichever relative moved in after you. I'm never leaving. I'm going to live there *forever*." I said it with humor in my voice, but I wasn't really kidding. I was never moving out of my attic with its collection of antique furniture that I'd arranged into a bedroom when I moved in six years earlier. They'd have to take me out on a stretcher, in a straightjacket, or a bodybag.

***

I spent the next 24 hours doing as little as possible, and with the exception of a mild headache and the nagging feeling that season 3 of the show I had binge-watched was a complete waste of time, my brain seemed to have avoided serious damage. Rather than more bad TV, I opted for one of my favorite pastimes: daydreaming while staring out at the darkening sky. That night was filled with heat lightning, which is very unusual in Virginia, but there are few things I love more than an eerie night, so I wasn't complaining. The painkillers I'd been given by the hospital were starting to kick in, and I stared out of my bedroom window into the rumbling darkness and shivered in delight as a jagged fork of light sliced through the sky. When I was younger, I'd scramble onto my window seat every time there was a night-time storm, hoping to catch a glimpse of one of the ghosts fabled to roam the grounds of the estate. I had lived at Sheffield Glen for five years now, and *not once* had I spotted any of them, but after my hospital experience (which I had to admit was probably the result of the concussion, but hope springs eternal), I stared intently at the grounds, hoping tonight would be different. So far, it wasn't.

A drizzly rain had begun to fall, heralding the approaching storm. I turned to survey my large attic room, where my suitcases and their contents still littered my bed and every flat surface in the surrounding area. Yep, I was never leaving. My eldest cousin Paul was jealous that I'd taken residence up here, largely because he hadn't thought of it first.

I strained my eyes, trying to see as far into the yard as the light would allow. I could just make out the cobblestone path that led through the woods toward the chapel, and then to the surrounding woods. At least it used to be a chapel. Now it wasn't much more than an overgrown, run-down pile of stones and glass. *Guess the family lost their faith a long time ago*, I thought.

The place held a strange fascination for me, and had for years. Whenever we went for hikes in the woods or down by the creek, we had to walk past the ruins, and I always felt compelled to stop and look. At first, all you could see was a waist-high pile of weed-infested rubble, but on closer inspection, stones with shaped edges became visible, and hewn wood beams and iron window frames make strange silhouettes under the kudzu. In all the years I'd lived here, I'd never ventured closer than maybe 20 feet. Gramps' warnings and Logan's fears had kept my curiosity at bay. Somehow, though, my almost near-death experience made me feel like putting off such adventures might mean they would never happen.

"Hey, Ree! Whatcha doing?" Logan's voice rang out from the doorway that led up to the attic. "Can I come up?"

"Hey, Logan. Come on up. I'm by the window."

He tromped up the stairway, weaved through the present disaster that made up the half of the attic that was my room, and made his way across to where I was sitting. "You just sitting here in the dark?" he asked.

"Yeah. I was looking out toward the chapel path and thinking about the ghosts. What are you up to?"

"Nothing. I'm bored to death. Mom won't let me play on the computer during a storm and I'm sick of all the games on my phone, so I'm just wandering the halls. Makes ME kinda feel like a ghost. Did you see anything yet? Didn't take you long to start looking." He was referring to my on-going quest to spot the spirits of William and Anne Sheffield.

I gave him the side eye. "No, nothing yet. One of these days, though, it's going to happen. You saw one once."

"Yeah, Paul has, too. But don't try talking to Mom about it. You know she doesn't like ghost-talk. Not since Dad..." His voice trailed off, and he followed me over to the wardrobe on the far side of the room. I threw it open and took out the few jackets hanging within. On the back panel of the wardrobe, I had tacked up a fairly sizable family tree, created two generations ago by my grandfather, and added to by my uncle and, well, me. It was littered with sticky notes containing random thoughts and questions. Here and there, a photograph of a family member was taped beside their entry on the diagram.

"This thing always gives me the creeps. It makes you look like a stalker," Logan said. "And it's super super weird that you keep it a secret from everybody except me. Makes me feel like an accessory or an enabler or something."

"Everyone needs a hobby."

"You're deeply disturbed. You haven't been home from the hospital for a day, and you're already obsessing. It's bad for your concussed brain."

"Can I help it if I'm fascinated by the family history?" I retorted.

"You're fascinated by the family haunting, not the family history."

I shrugged. "Fair enough. But you and Gramps are the only ones who will tell me anything at all, and I guarantee Gramps knows more than he's telling me. His family's been groundskeepers here since the 1870's. Most of the modern information I've added to this chart came from him. He literally knows more about our family than any of us do." Gramps wasn't our real grandfather, we all just called him that. But as the custodians of the estate, his family and ours had been close for generations.

"Looks like you're catching up, though."

"Working on it. But he doesn't want to talk about the ghosts either. It's frustrating. All he'll say is, 'Stay away from the chapel ruins ... ' and 'There's a lot of pain in them two spirits. Mebbe that what keeps 'em here...'" I did my best impersonation of Gramps' Appalachian accent, earning a smirk from Logan.

Though the details were sketchy, I had been able to learn a little bit about the ghosts of Sheffield Glen. I had figured out that William and Anne Sheffield were cousins. (I had gotten Gramps to confirm this, though he had added, *Don't dig up the past, Little Miss; it ain't resting comfortably as it is.*)

I'd also learned from the chart that both of them had died in 1876, presumably at the same time. I theorized that perhaps they had died in some horrible accident, and that's why their souls had never moved on. According to many of the books I'd read about ghosts, it was common for a person to be unaware that he or she had died if the death was sudden and unexpected. I wondered if that was what had happened to William and Anne.

"I was thinking of going out to the chapel tomorrow. Maybe I'll take the EMF meter." Logan had gotten me an electro-magnetic frequency meter for my birthday in April. EMF meters are one of the tools of the trade for ghost hunters, and I had the standard ghost-hunter-starter-kit meter: a black handheld device about the size of a small walkie-talkie with five colored lights—blue, green, yellow, orange, and red—and a range of numbers from 0 to 20+. It was widely believed in the "spectral fetching" community that spirits altered the electro-magnetic field in an area, and could even manipulate these fields as a method of communication.

"Yeah, right. You always say that, get within fifty feet, and chicken out." He sat down facing me on the window bench. "Not that I blame you or anything. I've never gone back there after that one time Paul and I went when we were kids. It's creepy. It's not even that interesting to look at. All overgrown with moss and animal crap."

I thought for a minute. "Let's both go out there tomorrow. It won't seem so bad if there're two of us."

"Ree, are you nuts? You know if Gramps finds out we went out there, we'd never hear the end of it. Besides, do you think it's an accident that I haven't been there in eight years? There is something messed up about that patch of land. Besides, aren't you supposed to take it easy or something?"

"Come on, Logan. Just for a little while. I just want to LOOK at it. You know, just poke around a little, and I'm too scared to go by myself. Gramps has warned me away from it so many times that THAT's probably why I freak out and avoid the place. If you go with me, I might just last five minutes. Pleeeeease?"

Logan looked at me in the dim light of the attic. "Okay, jerk. But if you have nightmares for a month it's not my fault. And we're only going for FIVE minutes. I'm bringing a watch."

"Five minutes," I agreed. I looked back toward the path, only barely visible in the light from the house. "What do you think makes that place so creepy? I mean, it's a rundown *church*, for heaven's sake." I giggled at the thought of my pun. "Why would a church feel so spooky?"

Logan shrugged. "I dunno. I can't ever get a straight answer out of anybody either. I think Paul knows something, though, because he goes out there sometimes and it doesn't seem to bother him. Weird how it would bother everyone but Paul, huh?"

"Well, Paul has a different personality, too. Sometimes *he's* almost as creepy as the chapel." I paused, thinking about my older cousin and his characteristic mood swings. "You want to go watch a movie or something?"

"Mom won't let us use the TV or computers when there's lightning, remember? She swears it'll blow up or electrocute us or something. Such a Luddite. What about some cards—gin rummy?"

"Yeah, okay." I wasn't particularly enthusiastic about the idea, but playing cards with Logan was always entertaining, if nothing else. He routinely ended up impersonating a bizarre cast of old movie and TV characters, from Spongebob to Batman. Besides, my mind wasn't on cards anyway; it was on the chapel, and how I was finally going to get the nerve to explore it—at least for five minutes.

Chapter 3

I wasn't sure what it was that awakened me, but from the amount of light creeping into the attic through the window, I estimated it to be around ten o'clock in the morning. I struggled to shake off the remnants of strange dreams of getting lost in hallways which were supposed to be my house, yet were unfamiliar. I yawned audibly, and by the time I opened my eyes, the sense of wandering, searching, and being confounded by the twists and turns of the narrow halls was little more than a vague impression.

I rolled slowly over to look at my alarm clock. 9:47. Pretty close. I wiggled into several different stretching positions, hearing my back and neck pop. The ache in my head and limbs from the accident was minimal, and that set me in a good mood right off the bat.

God, I loved summertime. No schedule, almost no responsibilities, pretty much the opposite of how I spent the other three seasons. During the past two years of high school, both Logan and I spent our weekdays at Lockridge Academy, a boarding school about sixty miles away, coming home to the Glen on some weekends and most holidays. My school life was a busy one, mostly because I was so heavily involved in extracurricular activities. Not because I was overly full of school spirit, mind you, just to avoid the brain-numbing boredom that goes with living at a school. I studied just enough to keep a B-average, and then spent the rest of my time singing with the Glee Club, snapping photos for the Yearbook, working with Stagecraft to build theater sets, and generally goofing off with Erick and Rachel. Occasionally, I'd volunteer to decorate for this festivity or that, anything to fill the empty time I had so that I wouldn't have to hang around the girls' dorm listening to the seemingly endless stream of idiotic gossip of the local debutantes.

I rarely saw Logan at school. He spent most of his time with his rugby and crew buddies, talking about women (if you can call most of the Lockridge girls that) and lifting weights. Unlike most of the guys in his group of friends, Logan was nearly a straight-A student, though I had never known him to study a lick, except maybe during exam week. In the summer, though, we were frequently inseparable, even when friends came to visit. We both relished the lack of commitments, and wallowed in laziness as much as was humanly possible. With Logan packing off for George Washington University in the fall, I wanted nothing more than to drag this summer out as much as possible.

I groaned, gave a final stretch, and dragged myself out of bed. Grabbing a pair of shorts and a tee shirt, I trudged down the attic stairs to the bathroom and proceeded through the morning ritual of washing, brushing, and dressing. My mop of thick brown hair was straight, but unruly, so I wrapped it into a very loose, very messy bun on top of my head, a genuine feat with a sprained wrist, by the way. All I could think about was getting down to the kitchen and downing a Pepsi so that the caffeine could get my brain working. Then I remembered the purpose of today's mini-adventure.

"Holy cow, I almost forgot!" I chided myself aloud, and trotted back upstairs to the wardrobe where all my family ghost-hunting research was stored. I had almost left the EMF meter behind! At first, I couldn't find what I was looking for, and I started feeling that frustrated panicky feeling you get when you know you just saw something, but now it's disappeared.

"Where the heck is it?" I demanded of the empty room. And then I remembered that Logan had given it to me at school, and I'd measured EMF at the library, the dorm, anywhere I could get to that wasn't full of students. I grabbed my school backpack off of my desk chair and dumped its contents onto the bed.

The EMF tumbled out onto the comforter and I exhaled with relief. Holding it gingerly in my injured hand, I turned it on to check the batteries. The green light glowed cheerfully, which meant the numbers registered somewhere around 2.0, which is pretty normal for an attic with slightly old wiring. No unusual EMF to speak of here.

I headed back down the stairs and past the second floor bedrooms. All the doors were wide open, except Paul's of course. He was sort of an odd duck, almost neurotic about his privacy.

I retrieved my caffeine fix from the pantry, and heard a strained grunting and huffing coming from the basement. Logan doing his morning workout, I deduced. Noticing that the door to the basement was partially open, I stomped loudly down the stairs in order to alert him to my arrival. I had surprised him once and he had nearly been crushed under a barbell.

"Hey," Logan grunted between reps with the curl bar.

"Need a spot?"

"Sure," he grunted again.

I took my place standing in front of him with my fingertips of my non-injured hand lightly touching the underside of the bar. "How many? And keep in mind that I can only give you a one-handed spot. Mostly I'm here to call 911 if you get stuck."

"At least three more. Hurpth!" He strained with exertion as his biceps flexed.

"Don't lean back. Come on, PULL!" I bullied him through three more reps.

After setting down the bar, Logan took a deep breath and shook his arms out. "All I have left to do is flyes," he said. "Do you still want to go out to the chapel today? It's going to be gooey out there because of the rain last night." I knew he was hoping I'd change my mind, and was probably regretting that he had agreed to go. Unfortunately for him, my curiosity won out over my empathy.

"Yeah, I still want to go. Soon, too, before it gets too hot since there's no shade over there to speak of," I replied.

"Five minutes. I'm not kidding. F-I-V-E."

"I know, I know. Do you want to walk around the woods a bit afterwards? I don't really feel like bumming around the house all day, and your mom won't be back for probably three or four hours."

"Yeah, that's cool, but you'd better wear hiking boots and high socks," he advised. "The snakes and stuff will be out looking for dry ground. Better find the bug repellent, too." He sat down at the pec deck and placed his forearms on the vinyl pads. I stood by, giving a coach's brand of moral support while Logan flexed his pectoral muscles, bringing the arms of the machine clanging together in front of him. When he finished, we walked up the basement stairs, intending to grab a quick breakfast before our hike. We were greeted by the sight of Paul heating a bowl of ravioli in the microwave, his mop of brown hair (the only family trait we had in common) falling into his eyes as he stared out the window into the yard.

"Power breakfast, huh, Paul?" I grinned. It was Friday morning; apparently, Paul's early summer term classes had been canceled, or at least his attendance in them for today had. "I didn't hear you come in last night. Get in late?"

"Of course you didn't hear me. You live in the *attic*. You wouldn't hear a Sherman tank if it drove through the front door."

I considered this, and at first I was rankled by his confrontational answer. Then I realized he was quoting our family's favorite Christmas movie in an attempt to be funny. I smiled, appreciating the effort. Funny didn't come easily for Paul. "Good point. Anyway, Logan and I are going for a hike.

Want to go?" I kinda hoped he would say no, but I thought it would be especially rude not to ask.

"Nah. Too hot. I'm going to try to get some reading done. I have a paper to do this weekend." The microwave beeped, and he pulled the ravioli out with a potholder. "See you later." I watched his white tee shirt and brown plaid jammy pants disappear up the stairs as he shuffled out of the kitchen and back to his room. Paul's moodiness was sort of his trademark. He might be cheerful and chatty one minute, quiet and contemplative the next. He did seem to take a genuine interest in the family history, and for a while, I'd tried to engage him for information about my ghost-hunting hobby. The problem was that you could never tell if he'd rattle on endlessly about it or snap your head off for bringing it up.

"Always the charmer," Logan commented. He pulled out bowls and the two of us split a cantaloupe.

I spotted a piece of paper taped to the refrigerator handle. "What's this?" It was a note from my aunt. *Gone into town to run errands. Will be back early afternoon. How about a family movie/pizza night? Love, Mom*

I showed the note to Logan. The signature made me feel suddenly sentimental, which I attributed to my recent brush with disaster. Notes were always signed *Mom*, never *Aunt Pam*. She wanted me to know that I was one of her children now, not her niece.

"Ah, our regularly-scheduled family bonding time," Logan commented, his mouth full of melon.

"You love it," I laughed. "And so does Paul, even if he would rather have teeth pulled than admit to such a thing."

"Yeah, I guess we all do. After Dad died, we all had to learn to stick together. I think she needed it even more than we did."

"I can't imagine what it must've been like, waking up with him next to her ... you know ..."

"Dead," Logan said with uncharacteristic bluntness. "She hasn't really been the same since, you know? I mean, do you remember how kind of flighty and silly she used to be? Now she's still nice, but the silliness is kind of gone."

"I remember. And we never talk about Uncle MJ much, just like I don't talk about my parents. For a family who has had to deal with so much death, you'd think we'd be better at it."

"Ah, but silent understanding amongst us, and general avoidance of the topic is our way of coping, right?" Logan was trying to be funny, but it was really just poignant. He wasn't wrong. We all buried our grief, and we knew the others were doing it, too. "C'mon. Let's get this over with."

Several minutes later, after fetching heavy socks, hiking boots, bug repellent, and a couple bottles of water, we emerged into the mid-morning sun, heat, and humidity. We started across the driveway, and I was startled to see our 14-year-old neighbor, Lazaro, sitting on the stone step of Gramps' cottage. He watched us approach, and I couldn't quite read his expression.

Laz had been Gramps' shadow for as long as I'd been living at the Glen. He was brilliant, but he didn't like school much, and he'd been known to miss the school bus on purpose so that he could stay home and help Gramps with the garden, or pressure-washing, whatever was on the menu for that day. Gramps always dutifully let Laz's parents know, but since they were gone at work, he'd let the boy stay and help out. I imagine Laz got in trouble later on, but his parents' hands were tied, and he ended up getting his way. Clever kid.

"Hi, Laz," I greeted him. "I don't think Gramps is home right now. He should be back in a few days."

"Yeah, I know," Laz replied with a half-smile. "I'd heard you were in an accident, so I wanted to see if you were okay. I came by yesterday, but you were resting."

"Oh, uh, thanks. That's very thoughtful of you. I have a little bit of a headache and a sprained wrist." I brandished my bandages. "And I can't be on electronics too much for a little while, but I'm okay." I shot Logan a look, wondering if that's how Laz knew I'd been injured.

"Okay, good." He stood up awkwardly, sort of cat-stretching his back as he rose. He started to walk back down the driveway toward his house, rubbing his lower back a little, as though his sitting position had been uncomfortable.

"Laz?"

He paused and turned back over his shoulder. "Yeah?"

"How long were you sitting there waiting for us to come out?"

"Not long," he shrugged. "Maybe an hour. See you later!"

Logan and I watched him walk down the driveway in silence. Once he had crossed the street and begun walking up his own heavily-wooded drive, we looked at each other in confusion. "He is an interesting kid," Logan finally said.

"That he is," I agreed, and we turned toward the back of the property, where our morning adventure awaited us.

Chapter 4

The chapel ruins came into view. It was evident from the size of the footprint (about the size of a large living room) that at one time, the structure had been intended to house around twenty people. The walls had been constructed of gray limestone bricks, now mostly overgrown with various types of fungi and ivy. No trace of the roof was visible except for a structure that had once been a small steeple, and of that, only a frame of rotting wood and a rusty iron bell remained. The walls had collapsed, maybe due to some storm over a century ago. What had been a building of worship was now little more than a shoulder-high pile of rubble that had become home to countless varieties of lizards, insects, and rodents. Had the clearing not had such a dark aura clinging to it, we might have played there as children, searching for a small flash of shattered stained glass glittering like a jewel among the stones.

Logan and I stood on the cobblestone path, staring at the ruins from a "safe" distance of about thirty feet.

"Well, you wanted to come here. I'm starting the timer. Five minutes, Sherlock. Get going." Logan tried to sound witty, but his voice was tense.

"You're not going all the way up there? I thought you were backing me up," I whined, fighting the inexplicable rising panic that filled me every time I neared the spot.

"I agreed to come OUT here, not poke around. Don't worry, I'll be within a few feet if anything happens."

"What do you think might happen? What happened when you were out here eight years ago?"

Logan shifted nervously, and began to pace a little. "The meter's running. You won't be dragging me out here again, so whatever you're looking for, you'd better find it in the next four-and-a-half minutes."

He looked to me like he might bolt back toward the house at any second. He wasn't lying—there was no way I would get him to escort me again. I took a deep breath and turned to face the object of my curiosity. I pulled out the EMF meter and switched it on. Its light glowed amber with a reading just into the yellow at approximately 3.0. Out here away from electricity, that was a little unusual. Not impossible, mind you, but unusual. I wished I could convince Logan to hang around the area long enough to establish proper baseline readings, but there was no way that was going to happen. My skin prickled with anticipation.

"Okay, here goes." As I moved forward and away from Logan, the fear I felt was almost a tangible presence. I forced myself to keep breathing deeply, all the while telling myself that my emotional state had been brought on by years of conditioning, much like the child afraid of the dark who grows up into the adult who cannot sleep with an arm hanging off the side of the mattress for fear that some unknown ghoul in the night will reach out from under the bed.

Despite the desire to turn and flee, my willpower propelled me, and I at last closed the distance between myself and the chapel. At the end of the path, I could make out small chunks of rotting wood that had made up the door. Slowly, I stepped off the path and into the thick weeds and grass (Gramps refused to tend the grounds of the chapel). The light on the EMF jumped to the high end of orange, putting the reading at about 16.5. My heart began to thud against my ribs, and my concussed head began to pound in harmony.

I circled the perimeter, and the EMF readings danced around in the orange range, implying that this whole area had high electro-magnetic activity. I reminded myself that the metal in the pile could be conducting some sort of electric charge, and I shouldn't get overly excited, but it was hard to contain my enthusiasm. I tucked the meter in my pocket as I began to pull at the kudzu that had grown over most of the structure. The stuff was like living webwork, and I regretted not having brought gloves along.

"Thirty seconds, dork," Logan called. I was just starting to make progress! I side-eyed him in irritation, and started plotting to come back out here on my own, safety be damned.

Spying the edge of a stained-glass window, I screwed up my courage and moved around the pile to what had been the east wall. My panic began to subside, and I examined the iron frame out of which the colored chips had fallen. I raised my free hand to touch the metal, and was engulfed by a wave of intense emotion that knocked me off balance.

Screaming pounding trapped let me out I'm hungry so HUNGRY

I cried out and jerked my hand back as if I'd been stung. I staggered backward and landed squarely on my rear end, panting and staring from my hand to the window. The reading on the EMF had jumped up to 17.4.

"What's wrong? What happened?" Logan called from his spot on the path. "Are you okay?"

I struggled to find my voice. How could I explain to him what I had just experienced? "I—uh—it—" I couldn't even think of what to say, much less spit the words out. Still shaking and not taking my eyes off the iron I had touched, I crawled a few feet toward the front of the ruins before finally struggling to my feet.

"I told you we shouldn't have come here! Are you hurt or what?" Logan's voice was filled with anxiety, and I knew he was only a few feet away, yet he made no move to help me. He seemed glued to the cobblestones. "Say something, dammit!"

I had made my way back to the path and was backing unsteadily toward him. "Cold!" I breathed. "It was icy cold!"

As if possessed by the sound of my voice, Logan shot out an arm, grabbed me around the waist, and hauled me down the pathway until we were back in sight of the house. He dumped me on the manicured grass, where we both collapsed into heaps. My headache began to subside, and I concentrated on calming my breathing.

"You want to tell me what the hell happened?" Logan asked, sounding annoyed, yet extremely relieved that we'd survived the experience.

Noticing for the first time that I was soggy all over from the weedy puddles near the chapel, I stretched out on the lawn as if the heat of the sun could erase the memory of the unnatural cold I'd felt. "Logan, it was so freaky," I began, "I went to touch that window frame, you know, and it's like ninety degrees out here, so I thought it would be warm. I mean it's *metal*. But it was freezing, just like it was wintertime. If I'd licked it, my tongue would've stuck, I swear. And then I felt this—this—*rush*."

"Rush? Like wind?"

"No, it was like feelings. All bad ones. Not just the panicky feeling I always get there, but anger, sadness, pain, and this profound *hunger*. It was awful! I've read some books that say that stones and metal can record strong images and emotions. Something terrible must have happened there! Do you think that William and Anne Sheffield were in that chapel when it collapsed?"

"Who knows? But I know exactly what you're talking about. When I was ten, Paul and I went out there and had a sort of a similar experience. I was going to climb to the top of the rockpile, and when I put my hand on the stone, I felt this *rage*. Just pure hatred, and it was directed *at me*. It scared the crap out of me. Now you see why I didn't want to come back here. I can't imagine why Paul still comes out here. I know he felt it, too."

I heaved a sigh, feeling my pulse begin to slow enough that I was sure the heart attack I expected had been averted. I sat up slowly and turned to my cousin. "What do you say we go down by the creek? The sound of the water will do a lot to calm my nerves. Somehow I doubt going inside and seeing Paul will have the same effect." The EMF was back into the high green range, so I switched it off and slipped it into my back pocket.

"Yeah, okay," Logan agreed.

He seemed as shaken as I had been by the disturbing events of the morning, and we made the half-hour hike to the creek in silence. I forced myself to focus on the beauty of the terrain. Most of the path took us through a wood that was primarily composed of pine trees and brush. Butterflies flitted among the flowering weeds, and I felt certain I had caught a glimpse of a white rabbit on the path behind us. Several times I glanced back and caught a flash of something—a bunny ear, maybe? or a cottontail disappearing among the flora? *How odd to see a white rabbit*, I mused, *and how odd that he seems to be following us rather than running away. It's almost like Alice in Wonderland, except backwards. Curiouser and curiouser.*

When we reached the creek, I untied my hiking boots, stripped off my socks and submerged my feet in the cool water. "Hey, bud, you okay?" I asked Logan, who still seemed pensive.

"Yeah, I guess," he replied. "I shouldn't have let you talk me into that. You'd think one experience in the Twilight Zone would be enough." He shook his head, studying a spot on the toe of his boot.

"Look, I'm glad we went, even if I did get a few years scared off my life. At least now I know that it's not my imagination, and that there is something weird about the place."

"Hmph," he grunted. "I could have told you that. It's just that I feel like maybe the first time I went there was a warning, you know? And now I'm wondering if something will happen because I went back."

"Why would you think something like that?" "This may sound crazy, but in light of what happened to you, maybe it won't. I don't know. What you described sounds different than what I felt when I went to the chapel with Paul all those years ago. I didn't feel the sadness you talked about. I only felt hatred, like whatever was there wanted me dead. Wanted to kill me, maybe." He shuddered, but continued. "I don't want to sound like a big baby or anything, I just can't tell you how afraid I was. I slept with either my parents or Paul for a month because I was so scared that something would kill me in my sleep. I thought I'd gotten over it, but . . ."

"But you didn't touch anything today; *I* did. And I didn't feel anything like that at all. Hey, don't worry about it. Everything's fine. C'mon. Take your shoes off and let's walk upstream a ways. Maybe we'll see some trout."

Half-heartedly, he joined me. We waded upstream to where the woods were denser, where there was no sign that humans had ever existed. We reached a place where the creek joined a much larger stream, the junction creating a small hole where Uncle MJ had taught us to fly-fish. Logan had once caught a beautiful brown trout here. His father had been so proud that he had measured and photographed the fish before Logan released it, and then he had had a taxidermist make a fiberglass replica of it as a Christmas gift. The fish still hung above Logan's bed, and this spot had always brought back that memory. I had hoped it would cheer Logan up to come here, but it only seemed to make him feel worse.

"Look, Logan, I'm *sorry*. I had no idea that this was such a big deal for you. I just wanted to satisfy my curiosity. I didn't know it would totally freak you out." I studied my cousin's faraway expression. I felt like a jerk for upsetting him, and the weight of the guilt was making me cranky.

He stared blankly into the water. "I know I'm being a dork. This place always makes me think of Dad, you know? I guess it's because I'm so creeped out, but no one ever really figured out how he died, and I wonder about that sometimes. The doctors said heart attack, but he never had heart problems. He was in great shape. I mean, who has a heart attack in his sleep?"

I laid my hand on Logan's arms, which were crossed over his chest. "Don't do this to yourself. I know your mom was never really satisfied with the doctors' answers, but that doesn't mean they were wrong. You hear about pro athletes having heart attacks all the time. Out of the blue, too, no prior history of heart disease. Just *boom*. What happened to your dad was terrible, a freak tragedy, but that doesn't mean the same thing will happen to you. You can't live with fear like that. Believe me, I know. Remember how scared I was to get on that plane to go to Mexico for that trip with the Spanish class last year?"

"Yeah, I remember, Ree. But this isn't the same thing. I just can't explain it. Aw, forget it. I'll be fine. Let's just go home."

***

B ack in my room, I pulled a chair over to my "Ghost Wall", as Logan called it, and switched the EMF back on. The light glowed amber with a reading of about 3.0. I moved it around, holding it in different locations while watching the numbers go up, down, up, down. After a moment, the reading returned to zero and stayed there, punctuated by the blue light. I switched the meter off and placed it in the wardrobe. *Curiouser and curiouser indeed,* I thought.

I retrieved a pad of large sticky notes and wrote down a quick account of what had happened at the chapel. I tried to focus on facts, quantifiable observations, but the events of the morning were beyond mere numbers and data. After a moment's hesitation, I added some of the questions that were nagging at me.

Where did that feeling come from?

WHO did that feeling come from?

Was it Anne and William?

What happened there to make it feel that way?

Hungry for WHAT?

I tucked the note behind the corner of the family tree. If Logan saw this note, it might upset him even more. Here he was, reliving trauma, and I was still on my ghost-hunting expedition. I should be empathizing more, trying to help, but somehow thinking about death from 150 years ago was a lot easier than dealing with grief within my own lifetime. Curiosity was easier to feel than pain.

Logan's mood improved very little over the course of the day. He had bowed out of the "movie/pizza night", claiming he wasn't feeling well, but I knew it was really because he wasn't up to seeing the horror movie Aunt Pam had chosen. No problem, she had said, we had the movie streaming for three days and could watch it tomorrow. The pizza was good, though, and we had all eaten together. Both of my cousins were sullen and quiet. Logan was still twisted from the days' events, and Paul was watching him like a hawk. An almost predatory look shadowed Paul's eyes throughout the meal. Plagued with guilt and unable to witness any more of Logan's moping, I trudged up to the attic shortly after 9:00 and went to bed. I was tired anyway, lingering effects from the car accident and the concussion. Besides, sleep is the universal cure for all things uncomfortable.

Chapter 5

"*But I LOVE you! How can that be evil? How can love ever be evil?" I am pleading with someone. But who?*

"Do not argue with me. You KNOW we cannot tell anyone. You know we cannot leave here until we have money to go. How would we live?" The man before me turns to face me. Sandy hair, blue eyes, and an angelic dusting of freckles–Logan, but not Logan, just Logan's face. I cover my eyes and weep. He steps closer and puts his arms around me, kissing my hair and whispering that he will find a way to get the money. Despite my tears, the feeling of his arms around me fills me with warmth and love—and desire, though I would never admit it, not even to myself.

"Don't you cry, little Annie. We'll not have to hide from her forever. You'll see. Just you be patient. Someday soon we will be able to speak out loud that which we have already sworn before God. Patience. We'd best be getting back. The sun will be up before long."

Then he leads me out of the chapel, and suddenly I am in a bedroom, which is supposed to be my aunt's bedroom, but isn't. It actually looks more like Paul's, but with my own bedroom furniture. I am lying on the bed, and then the pain comes. The horrible, searing pain, as if my stomach would burst. I dig my fingernails into the bedpost and scream.

***

I woke with a start, and a strange feeling in the pit of my stomach, no doubt as a result of my disquieting dream. I was about to roll over and look at the clock when I became aware of the strange smothering feeling you get when you're being watched. I lay stock still, barely breathing. Opening my eyes just a slit, I surveyed the small area I could see without betraying myself with movement. I was facing the stairway that led to the rest of the house, which meant that I could see through the entire parlor area of the room. I could feel the other presence behind me, by the picture window I loved. My heart pounded in my chest, and I tightened my grip on the sheet that covered me. I forced myself to breathe deeply, slowly, and to try to think rationally. *You're just spooked because of that crazy dream and what happened at the chapel. Stop being stupid. There's no one in the room with you.* But I just couldn't shake the feeling. I could almost hear the disruption in the air, feel the electricity of another body.

After what seemed like hours (but was only a few seconds), I took a deep breath and pretended to be rolling over in my sleep. I kept my eyes closed at first, but then slowly, imperceptibly raised the lids. The air caught in my throat.

Silhouetted against the deep blue of the nighttime sky was the figure of the man in my dream, holding his head in his hands, then slowly raising his eyes to look at me, then turning out the window to gaze into the yard below.

For an instant, I thought I would scream, but foggy reason stopped me. "Logan?"

The silhouette visibly jumped. "Geez, Ree, you scared me! I didn't mean to wake you. Sorry."

I almost wept in relief at the sound of his voice. "I scared *you*? What are you DOING up here?"

"I—couldn't sleep," he mumbled.

I started to rise from the bed, but the memory of the strange feelings from my dream made me stop. I certainly felt no desire for him now, but the fact that I had dreamt of feeling such passion for my cousin made me uncomfortable.

"Are you still freaked about this afternoon?" I asked him. He said nothing, just turned his face back toward the window.

I reached over and flicked on the stained glass lamp on my bedside table. The light cast a pinkish-orange glow over the corner of the room, and I could see the tired expression on Logan's face. Sisterly love conquered the discomforting remnants of the dream, and I threw one of my pillows to the foot of my bed.

"Come on, scaredy cat. Come get some sleep and I'll watch out for the boogeyman." My words were flippant, but my tone was soothing. He turned back to me with a grateful smile.

"I know I'm being a baby, but I can't help it."

"Shut up and get in bed."

He crawled onto the bed so that we were stretched out head to foot, upside down to each other, the way we had sometimes slept as kids. I grabbed an afghan and threw it over him, and he flipped onto his stomach. "Thanks, Ree. Just this once, I promise. I'll see a shrink or something tomorrow."

"Yeah, whatever, just don't kick me in the head like that one time," I said softly. "It's all my fault anyway. But it's a good thing for you that I have a queen-sized bed." I reached across his feet to turn off the lamp but stopped before my fingers reached the switch. My eyes were locked on the bedpost. There, though carefully stained over, were three very distinct ragged scratches in the smooth wood.

Chapter 6

The next day was a strange one, capping off the bizarre week since we'd gotten out of school. Paul was uncharacteristically visible all day, seemingly following Logan and me around, yet insisting that he "wanted to be alone" every time we asked him what he was up to, or if he wanted to join us in an activity. When we all finally settled down to watch the movie (which turned out to be campy enough that Logan was able to enjoy it), it seemed to me that Paul's eyes were rarely on the screen. Instead they darted from person to person in the room, as if he were expecting one of us to turn on him or spontaneously combust.

As I lingered on the edge of sleep that night, my mind sifted through some of the last few days' strange occurrences. A feeling of uneasiness had settled over Sheffield Glen. Logan's nervousness had persisted, Aunt Pam was tense and jumpy, Paul was secretive and paranoid, and as I tried to fall asleep, my dozing dreams were filled with disturbing images: dreams of running around the house searching for ... something ... desperately, dreams of being buried under the chapel ruins and trying to dig my way out ... and *hungrysoHUNGRY* ... As much as I wanted to tell Logan about the insane dreams, particularly the dream about what I guessed was being in labor and the scratch marks I had found in the headboard, I feared that the creepiness and the coincidence would be enough to push him over the edge.

I struggled to remember the details of the visions that had been haunting my sleep. I knew the dreams were all connected somehow, and I felt certain that they had all centered on William and Anne Sheffield. Though the particulars were hazy at best, the moods of the scenes had ranged from terror to shame to intense passion. I wondered vaguely if I was actually dreaming about details of my ancestors' lives, and I lamented the fact that almost none of it remained in my memory when I awoke. What little I could remember, I jotted down on sticky notes to add to the Ghost Wall.

This night was no different. I tossed and turned, in and out of sleep. I dreamt of my parents sitting in Logan's ruined Jeep and started awake. The clock read 3:42. I sighed in frustration and flopped over onto my stomach. My mind was working overtime, and sleep seemed evasive at best. As I wriggled around, searching for that magically comfortable position that would allow me to drift back off, I became aware that the temperature in my room had dropped several degrees. I cursed inwardly, suspecting that Paul had been fiddling around with the air conditioner, which he'd been known to do on occasion. Getting out of bed now, even to check the thermostat in the hall downstairs or to get an extra blanket, would guarantee that I'd be up and wide awake for the next couple of hours. I was in a genuinely foul mood as I sat up in bed and decided to both adjust the thermostat and wring Paul's moody little neck. My eyes darted to the stairway as a faint illumination passed the door below. Straining to listen, I heard padding footsteps pass by and continue down the hall.

"Caught you red-handed!" I hissed, and hopped quietly out of bed. I tiptoed to the stairs, avoiding the inevitable creaky boards, and vowing to scare the daylights out of my elder cousin. I crept as softly as I could down the steps, and the footfalls ahead of me continued to fade down the hallway. By the time I stepped into the passage, my target had disappeared around the corner and into the area of the house that used to be servants' quarters, where Paul had moved his room years ago, because that area of the house was more private, even if the rooms were a little smaller.

I turned the corner and could now see light flickering from underneath Paul's bedroom door. I raised my hand and prepared to bang loudly enough to wake the dead. That's when I noticed the smell. A faint, sickly sweet odor wafted out of his room, stopping me in mid-pound. My jaw dropped open. Paranoid behavior, lack of interest in school, mood swings, and now this odd aroma emanating from Paul's room? It all began to make sense to me now. In disbelief, I strained to listen, hoping to hear something . . . some clue that would prove or disprove my theory. I could hear Paul mumbling to himself . . . singing, in fact . . . but couldn't make out any words clearly. I thought I heard a sigh and then Logan's name, but I couldn't be certain.

He's totally stoned, I thought. *Stoned and singing to himself.* I continued to stare at the door, and reconsidered my original plan to confront him. What should I do? Facing Paul now would probably be both stupid and counterproductive, but I had to tell somebody. I made my way back down the hall and down the stairs to the second floor of the house. Seeing that Logan's lights were off, I hesitated, but then slipped quietly into his room. Half asleep or not, he'd be able to come up with a good plan for talking this out with his brother.

The temperature in Logan's room sucked the air right out of my lungs. The windows were coated with a thin layer of condensation, like when you pull a soda can out of the fridge and it sits on the table for a while. Turning my attention to Logan, I noticed that his breathing was raspy and the occasional whimper escaped his throat. Apparently, I wasn't the only one having bizarre nightmares. I moved to his side and shook him gently.

"Logan, wake up," I whispered. "You're having a nightmare. Logan, it's Ree. Wake up." The only result of my attempts to wake him seemed to be increased panic on his part. I reached over to his bedside table and flicked on the lamp. When I looked back at him, I let out a yelp of horror. His eyes were wide open, and his face was a mask of utter terror.

I felt panic welling up within me as flashes of Uncle MJ's death passed through my mind. I looked around desperately, not knowing what to do to save my cousin.

"Aunt Pam!" I screamed at the top of my lungs. "Help! It's Logan! He can't breathe!" Somehow, though, I knew that even if Aunt Pam heard me (which was unlikely since she nearly always took something to help her sleep), she wouldn't have any better idea of how to help Logan. I had to act quickly.

Maybe his air passage is blocked, I thought. Remembering something I'd seen in Health class, I decided to turn him onto his side—-maybe I could dislodge whatever was stuck in his throat. I started to reach across him, but was halted by an invisible obstacle hovering over Logan's chest. Blinking in disbelief, I tried again, but with the same results. It was as if there was an invisible rock on his ribcage, crushing him. Tears of helplessness filled my eyes, and reason abandoned me. With a scream of frustration, I heaved my full weight against the phantom object.

And it moved. A little.

Logan's panicky stare shifted to me, and a shade of recognition crossed his pallid face. A pleading sob escaped him.

Hardening with resolve, I thrust myself at the object again. It was like trying to move a block of ice that's been frozen to the wet ground. Again. Again. And with my fifth heave, I toppled, weeping and wheezing, across my cousin's torso.

The crushing presence gone, Logan sucked in air like a man saved from drowning. As he struggled to sit up, I threw my arms around him in relief, shaking and trying to assure myself that the danger had passed.

After several moments, he asked in a hoarse and trembling whisper, "Did you see it?"

"No. I just felt it. And your room was freezing, just . . . like . . . mine . . . ." I said with a tremor, my heart thudding in my chest.

"What?" He pulled back and looked worriedly at me. I related the events that had led to my ending up in Logan's room. He rose shakily from the bed. "Let's go see Paul."

"Now?"

"Yes, now. And your nose is bleeding." His jaw was set, not in concern for his brother, but in anger. I could see that Logan had a whole set of suspicions about Paul that were different from my own.

"I feel like I missed a chapter somehow," I commented as I padded down the hall after him. I raised my hand to wipe the trickle of blood. Had I whacked my face against the phantom object, or when I fell across Logan? I shrugged. It wasn't important. Figuring out what had happened was. "What's going on? What was that thing?"

"I don't know what it was, but I remember that feeling. That was the same rage, the same anger I felt when I went to the chapel as a kid. I *knew* going there was a bad idea. And I'll tell you who else knows something: Paul. He still goes out there and talks to himself ... or maybe to that ... whatever it was. Paul's not on drugs," he replied simply. "I think you smelled incense."

By the time we reached Paul's room, Logan was literally trembling with fury. He was clearly disappointed when we found the door open and his brother gone. I suspected that he had really been looking forward to kicking the door in. Paul's room was dark and vacant, and the strong aroma of incense hung heavy in the air. Logan switched on the light and began rifling through the disaster of Paul's belongings.

"Are you okay here for a minute?" I asked Logan, who nodded grimly. While he conducted a search of the room, I slipped stealthily downstairs and confirmed that Paul's gray Toyota was no longer in the garage. Logan, apparently frustrated, was shuffling out of Paul's room as I returned.

"Paul's car is gone," I reported. "Whatever he was doing, it looks like he hightailed it out of here. He's probably headed back to Richmond. What did you find?"

Logan shook his head. "Not much. He cleared out of here pretty quickly. But I did find this bundle of stuff tucked into a cloth in the back of his desk drawer." He spread his hands, showing me the items he had confiscated. A small black pot with ashes inside (a quick sniff confirmed that this was the incense I had smelled), a black candle (with the wax near the wick still slightly soft and warm), a decorative knife, and something that looked like a playing card. I took the knife and examined it.

"It looks like an old-fashioned dagger," I commented. The blade itself was shiny and silver, sharpened and straight-edged on both sides. The hilt was a duller, heavier gray—probably pewter, I surmised. It was molded into the shape of a fierce dragon, and it bore a clear crystal sphere between its jaws. In circumstances other than these, I might have found it enchanting, even beautiful. Now, however, it filled me with dread.

I set the knife down and picked up the card. I recognized it as a tarot card, though I'd never actually held one before. It had a Roman numeral on it: XX ... 20. The card was called Judgement, and showed a shadowy winged figure blowing into a heralding horn while people cringed below. The image of a golden scale hovered in a stormy sky. I felt drawn into the image.

Logan grunted and retrieved the dagger, and wrapped it back into the cloth with the pot and candle. I tucked the card into the pocket of my jammie pants so I could study it more later. "I don't think I'm going to get any more sleep tonight," he said. "How about you?"

"Seriously doubtful," I replied. "Logan, what are we going to do about this? This isn't some sort of Dungeons and Dragons cosplay thing. This looks like actual witchcraft."

"I don't know, but we have to do something. To be honest, the only thing I can think about right now is beating him bloody. I don't know what that thing was that attacked me, but it looks to me like Paul summoned it or controlled it or something. He has to come home eventually."

As if by instinct, we started toward the kitchen. "Somehow, I doubt that kicking his ass will help much," I responded. "I agree that he was doing some sort of spell or ritual here, but he's your *brother*. He wouldn't try to hurt you."

"Look, we don't know that. Whatever he was doing here, it was connected to that thing. It can't be a coincidence. He can't chant spells or summon things if I rip his tongue out," Logan growled, "but you're probably right in the long term. I need to know what he was trying to accomplish and why."

"I don't think we should jump to conclusions, but I have to admit that Paul definitely looks guilty of something. But summoning a demon to attack you? I still think it's a stretch, but it would probably sound crazier if I hadn't been living here the past week."

Logan turned to me, trembling in anger. "And not only that, I think it succeeded in getting my dad. Aria, what if Paul killed my father? Our father? Oh, God, and he was trying to kill me!" He stopped walking and steadied himself by holding on to the kitchen counter. His eyes filled with tears born of both anger and fear. "What is he? Why would he do this?"

My heart wrenched. This was a possibility I had not considered. Paul was definitely weird, even spooky, but a killer? Surely not. But how else could this be explained? Was he hunting down the family one by one? "We need to talk to your mom, Logan. She needs to know what's going on."

Logan nodded abstractly, and then fixed wide eyes on me. "Ree, she was in the room when my dad died. What if she knows? I mean, what if she's been protecting Paul all along?"

"You can't think like that. She wouldn't ... She couldn't."

"Couldn't she? He's her son. Mothers are always doing crazy stuff for their kids. Remember how that one mother in Texas was killing off the other cheerleaders so that her daughter could make the squad?" He leaned his forehead against the wall.

I grabbed Logan's arms and turned him to face me. "Let's not go off the deep end here. Let's just talk to your mom. Maybe she'll know what to do."

Still shuddering at the shadow of this new prospect, Logan silently nodded.

"Look, the sun doesn't come up for another hour or so. Why don't we grab a couple of those cupcakes your mom made yesterday and go upstairs to my room and talk about this? Maybe we can put together a few more pieces before she gets up. There's no need to drag her out of bed with a bunch of crazy accusations and ghost stories."

"I can't believe you're so calm about this, Ree."

"I'm not. I'm just trying to be rational because I don't know what else to do."

"Well, forget that," Logan huffed, "I'm waking Mom up right now. I want some answers, and I'm not waiting until dawn. Paul was trying to kill me!"

"You can't be sure about that," I began, but even I had to admit that things weren't looking too rosy for Paul. He was smart to run, I thought, because otherwise Logan would have put him in the hospital.

Shaking his head as if clearing the cobwebs from it, Logan resolutely started for his mother's room. I knew better than to protest. Logan was on the edge as it was, and with good reason.

Chapter 7

My aunt rubbed her eyes dazedly and looked again at her son and me. She fiddled with the wad of blanket in her lap.

"Well?" Logan asked at last. He had been waiting several minutes for his mother's response to the frightening story he had told her.

I had remained quiet, letting Logan narrate the series of incidents that had led to our showing up in Aunt Pam's bedroom an hour before the first hint of dawn. I had studied my aunt's face as Logan talked, watching for signs of shock, horror, disbelief, or worse: I had also been watching for signs of guilt, but none of these were in evidence. At first, she had struggled to focus as she shook off the remnants of the sleeping pills, but even once she was awake, Aunt Pam's face had remained placid and distant for most of the account. Only during the part of the story when Logan described the smothering sensation he had experienced had her eyes betrayed any emotion. They seemed haunted.

"Logan, honey, I think we need to stay very calm and rational here, don't you? We need to look at the circumstances and try to come up with a logical conclusion as to what you experienced."

"Logical? Has any part of this story sounded logical to you, Mom? Haven't you heard anything I've said? Anything?" He began pacing the room, shaking his head. "This is not a logical situation!"

"Logan," she began with maternal authority in her voice, "sit down. Being panicky isn't going to help us figure anything out. Sit." Reluctantly, he obeyed, perching himself stiffly at the foot of the bed. "Here's what I think happened. You gave yourself a serious scare by going out to the chapel, and it brought back all of those fears you had when you were small. You started thinking about your father." The haunted look flickered in her eyes again and her voice trembled slightly. "You had another one of those nightmares, just like the ones you had years ago, and it scared you badly enough that you had a panic attack. Think about it, tightness of the chest, shortness of breath, a panic attack. And you know as well as I do that it isn't even slightly unusual for your brother to take off in the middle of the night."

"I can't believe this!" Logan wailed. "You're protecting him! You know what he's doing, and you're protecting him!" Though I remained silent, my heart was pounding. I took a step forward to stand behind my cousin and squeezed his shoulder.

"I am doing nothing of the sort, young man." There was no tremor or grogginess in Aunt Pam's voice now. "Are you listening to yourself? Are you aware how ludicrous these 'theories' of yours are? Your brother used witchcraft or voodoo or some hocus pocus to kill your father? And now he's trying to do it to you? For what? What could he possibly gain?" Her own voice had assumed the panicked, feverish tone of her son's. "And who's next, me? What is his evil master plan?"

Logan sat very still, dumbfounded at his mother's reaction. I squeezed his shoulder again tightly, trying to reassure him that I still believed him, that I knew that what was happening defied scientific and rational explanation.

"I don't know what his motives are, Aunt Pam," I said evenly and deliberately, "but I didn't push a panic attack off Logan's chest, and a panic attack doesn't cause frost on the windows. Both of those things are physical and real, and both just happened. I'm not even sure Paul was trying to hurt Logan, but he's up to something. There's no doubt that something was trying to kill Logan, whether it had anything to do with Paul or not." I was trying to remain calm, but the tension was mounting within me. "And I'll tell you something else; I think that same thing killed Uncle MJ. So whether Paul is behind it or not, you'd better start taking this seriously." And with that, I turned my back on my astounded aunt and cousin and walked out of the room, headed for the attic. I had never spoken so disrespectfully to my aunt in my life, but the rage and fear I felt for Logan wouldn't allow me to stand quietly any longer. I had lost my parents and my uncle; I wasn't about to lose Logan, too.

***

I stood in front of my Ghost Wall, holding the card I'd pocketed. I'd never seen a tarot deck around the house, and I'd never heard Paul mention one, but it appeared Paul had a number of secrets I wasn't privy to. I studied the card, turned it over in my hands. My bloody hands.

"Oh, crap," I grumbled. I'd forgotten to wash up after we left Paul's room. I'd wiped all the blood off my face, but it was still all over my hands. Wiping the card off with the back of my hand and hoping I hadn't bled all over the thing, I tucked it carefully behind the family tree. I pulled a wet-wipe out of my backpack and scrubbed off the dried blood, then went to sit in the window seat and wait for the dawn.

After several minutes, Logan poked his head cautiously into the stair-well. "Ree? Can I come up?" He took my soft mumble for assent, and climbed the stairs into my attic. He crossed the room and sat opposite me on the window seat. "Thanks, Ree."

I sighed and turned to look at him. "Thanks for what?"

"For telling Mom off like that. It really shook her up. It's so not like you, you know? I think maybe she couldn't stay in denial once you laid it out like that."

"What did she say after I left?"

"Not much. Said she needed to think, then maybe we could talk over breakfast. I sort of left it at that. You know," he said as he gazed out at the gauzy glow of dawn, "I thought maybe you didn't believe all this crazy stuff either, because you were being so calm about it. I even doubted it myself a little when Mom was telling me how insane it sounded. But we're not crazy. Something is going on here, and Paul's in the middle of it."

I sighed again and nodded solemnly. "All that time when you were talking to your mom, Logan, I had a strange idea. Once it got into my head, I couldn't shake it. It makes this whole mess even crazier, but ..." I paused, trying to gauge whether or not I was putting my own obsessions into this crazy situation.

"Spit it out, Ree."

"Logan, I think that what's happening is connected with William and Anne Sheffield and how they died. It all started with the chapel, I'm just sure of it."

"You mean you think the ghosts are responsible for the attacks on Dad and me?"

"Maybe," I nodded. "I just have this feeling that it's all part of the same thing, that it can't be a coincidence. I'm thinking about trying to talk to Gramps today. Will you come with me? He knows the family history better than anyone. I know he never wants to talk about it, but this isn't just idle curiosity. He's got to know something that can help us."

Logan yawned. "That's a good idea, Ree, but there's one problem: Gramps went to visit his grandkids or something. He won't be back until Monday, remember? So whatever it is you want to ask him will have to wait two days. I wonder if Paul will be back before then? I'm thinking I might *beat* some answers out of *him*."

I snorted in frustration. "Gah! I forgot about that. Well, we can't just sit around here on our hands for two days. We have to see if we can find some clue about this somewhere."

"I'm not going back out to the chapel, so don't even entertain the thought. Ain't happening. Not in a million years, if I have my way."

"I doubt we'd have any luck there anyway. We don't know what we're looking for. I was thinking that we need to find out how William and Anne Sheffield died. Do they keep that kind of information in public records? Maybe in the City Hall or something?"

"Well, maybe, but that was, like, 125 years ago, and this wasn't exactly a heavily populated area back then. It still isn't. So who knows what kinds of records were kept? And that would have to wait until Monday, too. I wonder ..."

"Wonder what?"

"Well, you already found Granddad Sheffield's family tree. He was really into genealogy and stuff. Maybe he had more stuff. I bet he had all kinds of family information he used to put that tree together. You'd think there would have to be some death certificates, right? Was there anything else in the box with the chart?"

"No, the chart was in a big mailing tube. I mean, I live in the attic. How could I not know about another stash of family papers?"

"Geez, I don't know. But you've kept your little hobby a secret. Mom wouldn't have thought to mention it to you, but she might know where it is, if there is anything. She helped Dad pack up all Granddad's stuff when he died."

"Maybe you ought to ask her. She might be mad at me. I can't believe I snapped like that," I groaned. Even though I felt justified, I still felt guilty for my outburst.

"I don't think she was mad, Ree. Just shocked, you know? Why don't you go shower and get dressed and meet me in the kitchen in about a half an hour? Maybe by then she'll have done enough thinking and we can talk to her about it."

I looked at him skeptically. "Do you really think she's not pissed? I sure would be if I were her."

"Look, even if she is mad, she'll get over it. You did what you had to do to get her to listen to us. Now get going. I want to get started looking for this stuff so we can get some answers."

"Or at least try to," I replied doubtfully, but dutifully plodded off toward the bathroom.

***

The three of us sat in oppressive silence around the breakfast table as the sun rose higher into the sky. We all nibbled thoughtfully on our waffles, not sure what to say or how to approach the 800-pound gorilla in the room. Finally, Aunt Pam heaved a sigh and spoke without looking up from her empty plate.

"I don't know how much of the 'Paul-conspiracy-theory' I'm buying into, but I can't deny that something strange and scary happened this morning. I hope the two of you will forgive me, but I need some more time to think, and I'm just not ready to discuss all of this yet. Some of the things you said this morning brought back memories I wasn't quite prepared to deal with. I'm not trying to cut you off, I just have to get myself together a little more before I can really talk to you about it."

"What memories?" Logan asked quietly.

"Logan, I told you I'm not sure I'm ready to deal with this. I need to talk to Dr. Gruber in town. Just trust me on this one, okay?"

"Dr. Gruber? The therapist you went to after Dad died? Mom, you're starting to scare me. Why do you have to talk to him?"

Aunt Pam's eyes were filled with tears and the haunted look I had seen earlier. "Logan, please."

"Aunt Pam, I know this is hard for you, but I can tell you know something. You know that what happened to Uncle MJ and what happened to Logan are connected. I can see it in your face. You have to talk to us about this. Logan could be in real danger here!"

Logan was staring at his mother in disbelief. "You saw it back then, didn't you?"

Chapter 8

Aunt Pam looked up with a jolt. "Saw what? What did you see?"

"That thing! The thing that was on my chest! You saw it kill Dad, didn't you?" Logan was nearly shouting, his own eyes filling up with bitter tears.

"Oh, God," she whispered. Bursting into sobs, she threw her arms around her son, muttering incoherently.

I was stunned. I wanted to ask what it was that they had seen, but I was afraid to speak. There was no question now that Aunt Pam would help us, and I felt relieved about that, but I also felt a pang of grief watching this emotional mother-son moment unfold before me. The loss of my own parents gripped me, and I felt their absence more than I had in years. I suddenly felt very alone and angry, and couldn't bear to sit still and watch my aunt and cousin. Needing something to do, I rose and cleared the breakfast dishes as I fought back tears of my own.

"Logan, I thought I was dreaming or maybe hallucinating, trying to somehow make sense in my mind of what had happened to your father," Aunt Pam wept. "I was lying there beside him that night, and I woke up because his breathing was raspy. And it was so cold in the bedroom! I turned my head, and I looked at him and—oh, God—" She broke down into sobs again. "There was this horrible grayish thing on his chest. At first, I thought an animal had gotten in, maybe a small dog or a possum or something. But when I tried to get up to shoo it away, I couldn't move! It was like I was paralyzed from the neck down! I tried to scream, but I couldn't. I tried; I swear I tried! And then the thing turned toward me ... looked at me, I think ..." She was crying so hard now that she couldn't continue speaking. Logan clung to her, realizing the true horror of his father's death, and remembering his own brush with the creature only hours before.

My back still to them, I myself dissolved into silent tears. The panic I had felt when I'd seen Logan's stricken face was still fresh in my mind, and so was the momentary terror I experienced when I thought I couldn't help him. As they clung to each other, I was consumed by how alone I felt. Part of the family, yet apart from them at the same time. Story of my life. Multiple levels of suck.

It was Logan who collected himself first.

"We can fight it now. I don't know what that thing is or why it wants me, but I know we can beat it. We just have to work together." He cleared his throat and wiped his eyes on his sleeve. "Mom, Aria thinks this is related to the Sheffield ghosts somehow. We need to look through Granddad's genealogy stuff and see if we can find out how William and Anne Sheffield died. Maybe we can put some of the pieces together if we go back to the beginning."

"What? Oh, I think the papers are in the basement somewhere. It's in a cardboard box marked *family*. I'll help you look."

Still plagued with loneliness and fear, I was certain that my weeping had gone unnoticed, and I wanted to keep it that way. "I'll run and look!" Without turning to look at Logan and Aunt Pam, I bolted out of the room and down to the basement, grateful for something to do and for a moment alone to rein in my emotions.

By the time I reached the basement, I was half out of breath, and my head had started to pound slightly. Switching on the light that illuminated the storage section of the basement, I began scanning the multitude of boxes stacked amidst the extra furniture. I concluded that the *family* box would probably be toward the back of the mess, since it probably hadn't been touched for over twelve years. I started moving boxes aside, and I coughed as the air filled with the dust of years of neglect. I considered rifling through the *family* box before my aunt and cousin had a chance to look at them, just out of sheer curiosity, but I felt a little bit like I was invading someone's privacy. Even though it was my own family, it seemed like it wasn't my business to poke around.

"Let me help you with that," Logan said, startling me. He grabbed a particularly heavy box and moved it off to the side. He squeezed my shoulder comfortingly and continued to help me in the search. Looking over my shoulder, I saw that Aunt Pam was digging through the stacks as well. Within minutes, we had found our prize and dragged it over to Logan's workout bench.

"I was just sure that the family tree was in here ..." my aunt began.

Logan looked at me out of the corner of his eye.

"Um, yeah, about that," I began. I told her about my little Sheffield Family Shrine, and when I finished, her mouth hung open just a little bit.

"Do we need to have a conversation about this? How long have you been collecting information about the ghosts?" she asked.

"Um, no, I don't think so. It's just something I've been interested in for a while."

"How long is 'a while'?" she pressed.

I shrugged. "Three years?"

She seemed to decide something. "Okay, well, I'm not sure how I feel about the fact that you've been hiding this, but I'm glad you told me now. I could have helped you gather information, you know. Historical stuff."

"I wasn't sure how you'd feel about it," I confessed. "But we can work on it now. Maybe it's important." I felt a strange relief that she knew my secret and wasn't preparing to have me committed.

"Hold on, I'll go take a picture." Logan darted up the stairs, and we could hear the *thump, thump* of him running up the next set, his footfalls quieting the higher up he went. After a couple of minutes, he returned with his phone and numerous photos of my Wall and sticky notes.

Aunt Pam nodded. "We'll work on it together." She put her arm around me in a half-hug, then turned back to the box. "Give me five minutes. I'm going to try and reach Paul to get his side of things. But then let's get at it." I suspected she was going to try and locate Paul using his phone, but if I knew him at all, I was sure he'd turned it off to make sure he couldn't be found.

I couldn't help feeling sorry for her. She was trying to hold it together, but it had to be a lot of strain. As a child, I had been fascinated with her mane of ash-blond hair and piercing eyes the color of a stormy sky. But Uncle MJ's death had taken a toll on her. In the past five years, her hair had become heavily streaked with gray and the lines around her eyes had deepened. She was still beautiful, but her eyes seemed more haunted than stormy. As protective as she was of us, there was an underlying detachment that comes with profound loss. I knew that feeling only too well, but it seemed neither of us knew how to talk about it, at least not with each other.

***

After nearly two hours of rooting, reading, and sorting, we were distressed to find that the box held little information that would be of help. Aside from what I already had on the family tree itself, in fact, there was no mention of William and Anne in any of the family's documentation. There was, however, a Civil-War-era tintype showing the original Sheffield family shortly before their immigration to the United States from Scotland. The tintype had the year 1870 scratched into the corner, four years before the family had come to America, and only six years before William's and Anne's deaths. The faces were small and faded, but Logan immediately recognized one of them.

"There! That's Anne Sheffield!" he cried, pointing.

"How can you be so sure?" I asked.

"Because I saw her once. Or her ghost, rather. She's much younger in this picture, but it's definitely the same face."

"You saw her? When? How have you seriously never told me this?" I punched him in the arm.

"Ow. I honestly didn't remember it until I saw her face just now. I was about nine, I think. I was helping Dad and Paul move some of Paul's stuff into his new room. Well, there wasn't much in some of those back rooms then; they used to be servants' quarters and were sort of small, so we didn't really need them except sometimes for storage. Anyway, I was kind of poking around in some of the empty rooms. I was always running around, pretending to be a knight in a castle, looking for a dragon or something. Anyway, I walked into this one room, and it was kind of dark and completely empty except for a chair with a drop cloth thrown over it and a wooden crate. Well, I heard this kind of humming sound, and when my eyes got used to the light, I saw that there was this girl sitting in the corner sort of behind the closet door. It looked like she was writing something, and she was wearing really old-fashioned clothes. She was humming a lullaby, I think. I tried to talk to her, but she didn't seem to hear me. I asked her who she was, why she was in our house. Then I looked away for a second, because I thought I heard Dad coming, and when I looked back, she was gone."

"Did you tell Uncle MJ about it?" I asked.

"Yeah, you remember, right, Mom?" Aunt Pam nodded. "I told him about it and I talked about it at dinner, too. Dad told me I'd had my first official ghost sighting, and that I had seen a ghost, and that she was one of my ancestors, a distant cousin or something. He'd seen her before, too."

"But you didn't feel that anger and hatred like you felt at the chapel?"

Logan shook his head. "No, she seemed kind of sad. But I didn't even realize she was a ghost when I saw her. She didn't glow or anything, and I couldn't see through her. She just looked like a person in old clothes. If she was even aware of me, she sure didn't show it."

"Could she have been trying to write a message to you?" Aunt Pam asked.

"It sounds like she was a residual ghost," I chimed in. Both of them turned to look at me as if I'd just started speaking a foreign language. "There are three basic types of ghosts," I continued. "A poltergeist, which is an active haunting that affects its environment and causes various levels of mischief; a sentient ghost, which is aware of those in the living world and sometimes tries to communicate; and a residual ghost, which is sort of like a memory replaying itself over and over. I think that's what Logan saw. A residual."

"Riiiiight," Logan replied. "And you know this, how?"

"I've binge-watched every single episode of *Ghost Hunters*," I shrugged.

"Of course you have."

"Okay, guys, back on mission," Aunt Pam interjected. "What was Anne writing, Logan?"

"I couldn't really see what she was writing. It looked like she was writing in a book or something. I wasn't at an angle where I could see. In fact, I kind of got the impression she was hiding, because she didn't want anyone else to know she was writing either. Maybe I'm just inferring that because she was on the floor and sort of behind the closet door, though."

"Do you remember which room it was? Could you show me?" I was tingling with excitement.

"Yeah, I guess. It's that weird back room off the Jack-and-Jill bathroom. But don't get your hopes up; don't expect to see anything. We've all been in and out of that room for years. Hey, Mom, do you think Town Hall would have death certificates for William and Anne that would tell how they died?"

"I don't know, but they might. Want me to try to call around while you and Aria check out that room? The records room at Town Hall might be closed, but the library might have copies of some of the documents."

"Would you? I mean, I don't know if they would still have those types of records, but it might give us some helpful information. We clearly aren't going to find much more here," Logan sighed, looking in disappointment at the contents of the *family* box.

"I'll call, but I want you two to promise me you'll stay together. I don't want to take any chances with your safety. Deal?"

"Deal," Logan and I said in unison.

***

Logan and I made our way to the second floor and through one of the guest bedrooms. At the back of the room was a small chamber which seemed to serve little purpose in modern times, but probably served as a dressing room or nursery when the house was built. This room was connected to a bathroom with a door on either end. The far side of the bathroom connected to Paul's room.

"See—she was sitting right here ..." Logan pointed, "and then I looked back at the door, and then she was just gone. Hadn't seen her before, haven't seen her since. The guest room next door used to be Paul's," he added.

I chewed my lip as I studied the spot where Anne had been sitting. *What had she been writing, and why was she hiding?* I shrugged. The room was empty now except for a card table with a small box of wallpapering tools. "Well, I don't know what I expected to find. Probably nothing, which is exactly what I got." I shrugged again. "Logan, can I see that photo of the family tree for a second?"

"Yeah, sure." He handed over his cell phone.

I sat cross-legged on the floor and opened the photo he had taken. I had an idea, and I used my fingers to enlarge different parts of the chart, examining them closely. At the bottom of the chart, I located my own name, Logan's and Paul's names, and the names of several other cousins I barely knew or had never met.

"Hey, look at this ..." I traced first my line, then Logan's line with my finger. "You're a direct descendant of Anne's parents. Like, strangely direct. I don't know why I never noticed that."

"What about you?"

"No, I'm not a descendent of Anne's or William's. Look." I pointed to a spot near the top of the chart. "1874. That's when the original family immigrated to the United States. Eugenia Sheffield, her three sons, and their wives and children. You and Anne come from Robert Sheffield's line. He was the oldest brother. And then I come from Baxter Sheffield's line ... and then here ... whoa! The youngest brother was Daniel Sheffield, William's father. It looks like that line died out with William."

"Geez, look how far you and I are removed on this chart! Baxter's line spreads out and covers like two-thirds of the paper! So you and I are, like, fifth or sixth cousins? Twentieth cousins, twelve times removed? I knew our parents weren't siblings, but I don't think I realized we were this far apart on the family tree. I don't even know how to calculate this. It's amazing that our families are even still connected. There are cousins on here I've never even heard of."

"I guess the Glen has always been sort of the center point that brought at least some of Baxter's descendants back. But that's not the point. The point is that William's death ended his line. And according to this, he was only 18."

Logan sat and studied the series of lines, dates, and names. "Wait a minute. Anne died the same year as William, and she was only 17. I guess you might've been right about them dying together."

"But that's not all. Look at Anne's line—your line. Notice anything? This is what I was saying about 'strangely direct.' It looks like only one person in every generation since the family came to America had kids. And then there's this mark," I pointed to a symbol, like an underlined Greek letter Omega. "Doesn't that seem weird?"

"Wait, what? Let me see that." Logan grabbed the phone and navigated over the enlarged images. "Okay, Anne had two brothers: Gordon and Wallace. Wallace died three years after Anne, when he was 17, so no kids. But Gordon got married and had four kids. Three of them died young, but one, Harry, got married and had three kids. Two of them died before they were 20. And basically, that happens every generation. My dad was an only child, but he had Paul and me. Ree, I don't think I like where this is going."

"I don't either. It's definitely a pattern. There's nothing like that in my line. But if your line's pattern continues ..." My voice trailed off.

"Then either Paul or I have to die before we're old enough to have kids. Whatever attacked me and Dad has been killing us off for four generations or more ... at least since William and Anne died."

"Do you think it could be their angry spirits?"

"I don't know. When I saw Anne, she didn't seem scary. But I've never seen William. I think my dad did once, but as far as I know, no one has seen William for years and years."

"We have to figure out how they died. That's the key; I just know it," I said resolutely.

"Hey, you two!" Aunt Pam's voice called. "Come on down here. We're going to the library."

"Why the library?" Logan yelled back.

"Because that's where all the public records over 50 years old are kept. Guess what ... they haven't been digitized. Let's go!"

"Alrighty, then," Logan smirked. He pocketed his phone and we trotted downstairs.

By the time the library closed, hours of rifling through deeds, tax records, birth and death certificates had yielded very little information and three blistering headaches. We found real estate records and wills that showed that Baxter Sheffield had moved his family to Arkansas in 1873, only one year after arriving on American soil.

We also found death certificates for William and Anne Sheffield dated 1876. Both teenagers' deaths had been attributed to "natural causes."

Chapter 9

My own research didn't end once we returned home. The card I had taken from Paul's room was pulling at the edges of my thoughts, like I was missing something important. I pulled up a browser on my phone and looked up the tarot card for Judgement. *Self-awareness, placing blame, insight, karma, self-evaluation, forgiveness.* The Web seemed to have a variety of opinions about what this card meant, but the general meaning was more or less contained in the name. Was the creature hunting down the members of Robert Sheffield's line exacting some sort of revenge? For what? It seemed to me that the answer to that question, and the question of what happened to William and Anne, was at the center of everything.

I went to the wardrobe and retrieved the card from its hiding place. I flipped it over in my hand, studying each detail. The pictures, in many ways, were frightening. The naked people with their arms uplifted ... were those graves they were standing in? Some of their faces were filled with ecstasy, some with fear. I focused on the winged herald above them. Weren't angels supposed to look serene? This one had a furrowed brow, as if she couldn't decide how she felt about the scene before her. Wispy images, which at first I'd thought were sound waves from the angel's trumpet, now revealed themselves to be something else, something rising from the graves. *Ghosts?* I shuddered. And above them all, the scales of Judgement.

The symbolism was unmistakable. The deeds we do in life catch up with us one way or another.

***

N ever before had the nighttime sounds of Sheffield Glen seemed so ominous. The house-settling noises, the switching on-and-off of household appliances, the chirping of frogs outside, the occasional screech of an owl—all were sounds that had greeted my ears on a hundred summer nights, but now they took on magnified and threatening proportions.

And then there was the sound of two other people breathing in the darkness.

Believing there was safety in numbers, Aunt Pam had suggested that we all sleep in the master bedroom. I wasn't sure how that made Logan any safer, but it made him (and my aunt) feel better, so I kept my skepticism to myself. There had been no word from Paul, which set my aunt even more on edge, but it wasn't unusual for him to ghost us for days. It's just that the circumstances this time were alarming. Aunt Pam had taken one of her pills to help her sleep, because her nerves were shot. Logan, on the other hand, could sleep anywhere, anytime. Me? I doubted if I'd be able to sleep at all. Again.

The low rumbling of summer thunder heralded another powerful storm and lent an even darker atmosphere to my thoughts. I sighed. If my mind was going to be in overdrive anyway, I might as well give it something useful to focus on. I slipped silently out of the king-sized bed where my aunt continued to sleep, checked to make sure Logan was snoring peacefully on the air mattress he'd tossed on the floor, and tiptoed out of the room.

As I passed the dresser, I snagged the photocopies of the documents we'd found at the library. There was something so obvious here; I just knew it. I flipped open my phone case to reveal the Judgement card tucked safely inside. I made my way back to the room where Logan had seen Anne years before, and pulled up the photo I'd had Logan text me of Granddad's meticulously-recorded family tree. There were no lamps in the room, so I switched on the bathroom light and then blinked in the stark light from the naked studio bulbs that surrounded the mirror. Indirect and wan light spilled out into the small and empty room.

There has to be something here, something we're missing, I mused, spreading the papers out on the floor and sitting cross-legged in front of them, careful not to block the light.

Outside, rain had begun to fall, and the drops pelting the window sounded like a hypnotically irregular clock ticking away a time of its own. I sat in the doorway that led to a tiny closet, and held the copies of William's and Anne's death certificates up to the light. I had been right, I was certain—they had died together. Both certificates were dated October 4, 1876. There was just so much here that didn't make any sense.

I closed my eyes and leaned back against the wall, resting my temple on the doorframe. What was Anne trying to hide in this room? Did that secret somehow lead to her and William's deaths? And how did that connect with the demonic creature that seemed to be stalking Robert Sheffield's bloodline? Had Anne and William been the source of this family curse, or its victims? As the questions swirled around in my brain, the rhythmic drumming of the rain achieved what the rhythmic breathing of my family could not, and I drifted into a troubled sleep.

***

I'm running, or at least trying to. The panicked flight up the stairs causes my ankles, knees, and back to hurt even more than usual.

My thoughts are filled with panic as I struggle to escape discovery. Must ignore the pain, the fear. Must not let Nan see it … where? Where to hide?

Elizabeth's room? No—can't explain why I'd be in there when she's not. Wait! The sitting room! The closet! Yes! Must reach the closet! Quickly, behind the coats—close the door! Not all the way; that might look suspicious, and I wouldn't be able to see out. She's coming! Must quiet my breathing ... she's here! Oh, please God, don't let her see me. I peek out between the woolen garments.

She stands at the door looking in, stern as always. She mumbles quietly to herself, and is clearly displeased. Probably with me, as usual. She takes one more visual pass of the room, then turns to look into the hall.

"Anne! Where has that girl got to?"

Her footsteps fade down the hallway.

Deep breath. She's gone. That was far too close. I must be more careful. I creep slowly from behind the coats, making my way over to Elizabeth's writing desk and pull out the drawers that hold the ink and paper, setting the drawers quietly on the desk. I feel around in the empty space behind the drawers until my fingers find the tab they seek. With a gentle tug, the panel slips free, revealing a small compartment. I quickly stash the small book I'm carrying into the compartment and replace the panel and drawers. I heave a sigh of relief.

I should probably destroy the book. Nan must never find it. Then she would know the truth.

***

A crack of thunder woke me up. I wasn't sure how long I'd been dozing, but I thought it couldn't have been that long, since the storm was still raging outside. I struggled to hold onto the details of the dream. Hiding again, the book, the desk ... wait! The desk! Suddenly, I was wide awake, all my nerves on fire. I stood up and rushed out of the room so quickly that I barely registered the spicy scent that filled the air.

I didn't even remember running up the stairs that led to my room, but as I stood there facing my desk ... *Elizabeth's desk* ... the blood pounded in my ears. Panting more from excitement than exertion, I reached out and ran my fingers along the dark wood of the drawer that had, in Anne's time, held bottles of ink. I grasped the small handle and pulled the drawer completely out of its track, then followed suit with the one below it. My breathing quickened as I reached into the space the drawers had occupied. Feeling along the back panel, my fingers quickly found the satin-y tab I'd been seeking. I pulled gently, and the loose panel gave easily.

And with a soft *fwump*, the book ... *Anne's book* ... fell forward into my waiting hands.

Chapter 10

It was exactly as I had seen it in my dream—small, barely larger than my hand, with a faded red cover, slightly tattered on the corners and binding. It was tied shut with an uneven strip of brown leather. I gingerly untied the strip and opened the cover.

I couldn't believe that the journal I'd seen in my dream was actually in my hands.

Here at last was the silent voice of the woman who had haunted my waking and sleeping moments for the past several days. I began to skim the entries hungrily. It was evident that Anne had been keeping the journal before the family's immigration, and at first, the passages were intermittent, yet typical of any teenage girl: gossip, frustration with the demands and rules of her family, excitement about a gift or a visit from a friend, a chronicle of Anne's view of the move to America. The tone of the journal changed, however, with an entry from the spring of 1875.

April 13, 1875

The most startling of things has happened today. Uncle Daniel and William have returned from their trip to Charleston, and naturally, the entire family was excited to have them home. I personally thanked William for the kind letters he had sent during their two months' absence. In reply, he said not a word ... he simply smiled at me. In fact, he kept GAZING at me for what was unquestionably an inappropriate amount of time. I should have been offended, I suppose, but I was not. In fact, I caught myself gazing back—wholly ill-bred behavior on my part. In my embarrassment, I looked away and laughed, and told him I thought he had perhaps grown taller, and that the hint of a mustache that he was attempting to grow did not suit him yet. He seemed more amused than insulted at this, and then departed to assist with the horses. I must admit that I am quite flustered, and I do not know what to think about this interaction.

June 15, 1875

It has been evident to me for some days that William has begun trying to talk to me alone. I have been disquieted, not because he wishes to speak to me, but rather because I am so eager at the prospect of being alone with him. Since his return from Charleston, I become fluttery whenever I am in his presence. Surely it is wrong for me to feel this way, and even more wrong for me to hope that he should feel the same.

June 17, 1875

He was finally able to corner me this evening after dinner as the men were retiring to the main parlor. He asked me to meet him at the chapel tonight after everyone is abed. I told him that was abominable behavior for a young lady of my breeding, but he must have sensed that I was only partially in earnest. He told me he would wait for me until the first glow of dawn shone on the horizon. I have not yet decided what I will do.

June 18, 1875

I believe that I must be weak-willed. I slipped out of the house the very instant I thought it safe, and true to his word, William was there waiting for me. I am not sure if I should be horrified or elated, but he told me that in the two months he was in Charleston with his father, he thought of nothing but me and could not bear to be parted from me. Sentimental creature that I am, I confessed everything regarding my feelings since his return. I am disgusted with myself for being so totally shameless, and I told him so. I told him that under the best of circumstances, such a conversation was unseemly. And these were certainly not the best of circumstances.

He told me that it was not terribly uncommon for cousins to be married, and that since reading in a magazine that the brilliant writer Edgar Allan Poe himself had been married to his first cousin, he had dreamt of presenting such a proposal. I told him Nan would never hear of such a thing, and I fled to the safety of my own bed, or so I believed. But thoughts of William chased me even there, and I am loath to admit that the suggestion of becoming his wife was the very thing I had hoped to hear from his lips. I shall pray doubly hard tomorrow, but shall I pray for forgiveness or God's blessing in delivering my heart's desire?

***

The sun was just beginning to paint the horizon pink, and my eyelids felt like they were lined with cotton. My lack of sleep was making it hard to focus, even though I was fascinated by what I was reading. It was like some twisted show on an independent TV network, and I wasn't sure if I was rooting for William and Anne's relationship or not. On the one hand, *ew, gross.* But on the other hand, I had to remind myself that the social rules of the 1870's were very different from those of modern day. An 18-year-old girl was expected to be on her way to being a wife and mother at that time, often to a man twice her age. And in well-off Victorian-era families, marriages were still quite often arranged for the benefit of social ladder-climbing. At least William and Anne seemed to love each other, and were making their own choices.

I had a feeling, though, that I had stumbled upon what was the beginning of their end.

If I was going to keep reading, I was going to need caffeine. I crept down the stairs and peeked into the first-floor master bedroom where Logan and Aunt Pam were still sleeping. I waited long enough to see both of them reposition themselves in their sleep; I didn't really relish a rematch with the specter I'd encountered the night before. Then I made my way to the kitchen and popped open a cola. Sugar and caffeine ... just what the doctor ordered. Well, maybe not. I doubted this is what the doctor would recommend when trying to heal from a concussion.

I settled myself in the solarium, which was really just a fancy term Aunt Pam used for a large enclosed porch off the formal living room. The dawn had already given the room a rosy glow, and I could see the misty fields of distant neighbors out the large windows that paneled every side of the room. I curled up in a lounge chair to finish Anne's story.

The next several entries were brief, but it was clear that she and William had surrendered to their feelings and were trying to figure out how to be together. It was also clear that there was no way their grandmother (the woman Anne had referred to as Nan throughout her narrative) was going to accept their union.

I guess I couldn't really blame Nan ... what grandmother would embrace a relationship between two of her grandkids? But I also knew teenagers. Has anyone EVER convinced a teenager in love that she doesn't need the person she believes she loves? Nope.

My instinct proved to be correct.

July 12, 1875

We are one now, at least in God's eyes. I know it. We met in the chapel, and recited our wedding vows before God and each other. Is there any earthly bond that could be stronger than this? I think not. No marriage could be more sacred. There were no trappings, no presents, no material gain. Only the most heartfelt of promises before the only Judge who matters ... God Himself.

I am William's true and loving wife now, in body and soul. And yet, we must keep our secret until we can sneak away and begin life anew together, away from Nan's heavy hand and disapproval.

I am filled with joy to be his, and yet filled with sorrow that we are still parted. We must be even more careful now, William says, lest our loving eyes or lingering touches give us away. He told me that he would go to Richmond next week to inquire about an apprenticeship as a county clerk. I can not bear to be parted from him, and it is tearing my heart apart.

His words and his arms were a comfort, and he says that if he can establish a job where he can at least make enough money for us to live, we will leave together in the dark of night if we must.

My concentration was broken by the sounds of kitchen cupboards opening and closing a couple of rooms away. I rose from my lounge chair and shuffled through the living room and into the kitchen, and was greeted by the rear half of my aunt poking out from behind the refrigerator door.

"Hey," I mumbled in my typically eloquent fashion.

Aunt Pam yipped, startled by my sudden appearance, but quickly recovered herself. "You're up early," she observed. "I was wondering where you'd gone. Didn't sleep well?"

"Didn't sleep at all, really," I replied. "But I did discover something!" I held up the faded book. "It's Anne Sheffield's journal."

"It's WHAT?" She nearly dropped the eggs she'd been pulling out of the fridge.

"It's her journal. It was hidden in my desk in the attic." I gave her the Cliffs-Notes version of how I'd come into possession of the book, and what I'd learned so far about William and Anne's relationship. Her jaw was open and her eyes were as big as dinner plates by the time I finished my summary.

"I'm ... I ... I don't know what to say about all of this. Aria, what you've found is very important. It might well be the key to everything that's been going on."

"Right? I was thinking the same thing. What are the odds that there was this weird relationship between them, and now there's a family curse?"

"I hesitate to guess. Can I read it?"

"Yeah, sure. I think I'm going to go lie down in my room for a little bit anyway. I'm super tired." I looked at the clock. It was just before 7:00 a.m. "Will you come get me at 11 if I'm not up? I want to talk to you guys about all of this once Logan is awake."

She took the book from me and held it like she was afraid it might bite. "Of course. I have a feeling we're all going to have a lot to talk about."

"Thanks." I gave her a quick hug and dragged myself up two floors worth of stairs. I was fast asleep before my head hit the pillow.

Chapter 11

*H*aze. Fog. I'm not alone, but I can't see who's here.

    I hear a sound. It begins in a low growl, and I can't tell where it's coming from. It rises to a whine, a high-pitched shriek filled with pain and rage. Then it is quiet.

    Now a skittering, scrabbling sound, like something is circling me, but it doesn't attack. It doesn't like how my blood smells. I don't know how I know that.

    I spin around, trying to see whatever it is. It's small, I can tell. But it's everywhere and nowhere, and I need light to pierce the mist. I feel something brush my leg. I'm terrified, but I don't scream. I close my eyes, count my heartbeats, trying to squash the panic.

    It's growling again. It feels my fear. It wants, it needs, it hungers.

    I think of my parents, and grief washes over me, replacing the fear. It builds, and the pain and rage in me mirror the pain and rage in the creature. Here in this misty world, I don't hide it, I don't push it down. The creature begins its piercing scream again, but this time I'm not afraid. This time I raise my face to the sky and scream with it. The emptiness that can't be filled with anything but anguish rips out of me until I can't even hear the creature anymore.

I scream until my voice is ragged and I fall to my hands and knees. I feel grass beneath me.

'Shhhh,' says a female voice in the distance.

***

A clatter of footsteps like horses on the stairs woke me. "Ree? Are you okay?" Logan burst through the open door, looking sweaty and panicked.

I was sitting bolt upright by this time. "I'm okay … I'm okay …" I replied, but I wasn't sure if I was trying to reassure him or myself.

"You were screaming."

"I know. I had a nightmare." My throat was killing me. I needed water. "I think the past couple of days are getting to me."

He stared at me, not sure what to do or say. "Why don't you come downstairs? Gramps is back from his daughter's house. He's in the kitchen."

Gramps' family had been caretakers on this property as long as it had been owned by the Sheffield family. He KNEW things … maybe even things that could start tying together all the scattered bits of family history and family drama that had been surfacing for the last few days.

"Yeah, okay, I'm coming." I untangled myself from my nightmare-sweaty sheets and followed Logan down the stairs, making a quick stop in the bathroom to brush my teeth and throw my hair up into a messy bun. When we walked into the kitchen, Aunt Pam and Gramps were huddled together over the journal.

"… so it's clear that they considered themselves married and continued their affair in secret while William tried to save up money for them to run away, and … oh, hi, guys! I was just telling Gramps about everything that's happened."

"Did you tell him about that thing that's been stalking our family?" I asked.

"I done heard the legend all me life, Missy. But them's just stories. Gotta be. I don't doubt that there's some angry haint out there, but one what kills people? I don't buy it. I think Mr. Paul believes it, though."

"What do you mean?" Logan asked. No one had mentioned Paul or what we'd found in his room.

"Well, when he was a boy, I told him about the restless spirits 'round here. Right after he visited the chapel, it was. He was always pokin' 'round out there, even though I told him not to. And then once his father passed, I reckon he got it into his head that the family was cursed."

"What makes you say that?" asked Aunt Pam.

"Well, as he got older, he weren't pokin' the place anymore. I'd just see him out there, pacin' around and mutterin'. I asked him 'bout it once, and he told me his father'd been marked, and now he was, too."

"What is this 'marked' business?" my aunt demanded.

Gramps shrugged. "I dunno exactly. Mr. Paul wouldn't tell me much more. Just said somethin' like, 'it was my father's and now it's mine, but it's cursed.' I asked him what he was talkin' about, what object he got, but he clammed up good."

"What object?" I asked. "Got it how?"

"I told ya, I dunno. But I know it's not very big, because Mr. Paul kept it close. But he wouldn't let me see it or tell me what it were. I think mebbe that ya just finds it when it's s'posed to pass to you." A sense of recognition came over me. I knew exactly what the small object was.

"None of this makes any sense! This is ludicrous!" Aunt Pam threw her hands up. "I've heard enough of this foolishness about curses. Whatever is going on, it can't be this nonsense! Ghosts are one thing. But curses?" She snapped the journal shut and slammed it down on the counter. "There has to be another explanation, a slightly less INSANE explanation, and I'm going to find it!" She stormed out of the room and up the stairs, leaving Logan and me with Gramps and a very awkward silence.

The thing was, I felt in my bones that Gramps was right about everything.

"So ... do you think it's William's ghost?"

"Mebbe. I ain't seen it. I felt it, though, by the chapel, where they died."

"Wait, what?" Logan asked. "William and Anne died there?"

"That's the story. How they died, ain't no one knows. Ain't no evidence one way or t' other. That secret went to the grave generations back. I have a suspicion now 'at they killed 'emselfs there when their love was exposed."

"And I thought my family was messed up," came a voice from the back door. We all jumped, and I recognized Laz's shape in the side window, standing just outside the door.

"Laz? How long have you been standing there?"

"I came over when I saw Gramps pull into the driveway. I've pretty much been standing here the whole time. That's a crazy story."

We all exchanged looks. Finally, Logan shrugged and opened the door. "It's kinda rude to eavesdrop, Laz," he said, ushering our neighbor inside.

"I didn't mean to eavesdrop, I was just waiting. And then the story pulled me in, you know? And I didn't want to walk away and miss part of it." His brown eyes were wide with innocent excitement. "William and Anne must have really loved each other to risk everything like that. And you know," he continued, "I can see why they didn't think it was so wrong. Morality is such a fluid thing. What's taboo in one time and place is common in another."

We all stared at him with our jaws hanging open.

"What grade are you going into again?" Logan asked.

"I'm starting high school next year," Laz grinned. "But I'm wise beyond my years. At least that's what my mom says."

It felt a little weird having this extremely private family conversation with the kid across the street, wise or not. But there was no putting the toothpaste back in the tube, as it were. I shrugged and picked up where we had left off.

"I feel like if we can find out what happened to them, we might be able to break the curse," I said. Laz nodded emphatically and took a banana from the fruit basket on the counter.

"I 'spect Mr. Paul thought the same. But I don't think he had any luck."

"I don't know about that," Logan chimed in, watching Laz eat. "But whatever was after him, I think he offered me up instead."

Gramps raised a comically bushy eyebrow. We told him about the presence that had attacked Logan, and had also likely been somehow responsible for my uncle's death.

"Well, now, that does sound like a curse, but I think ya better talk t'yer brother b'fore ya jump ta conclusions. Yer father was a good man, God rest his soul. I'm right sorry to hear that unnatural causes mighta been involved. I'll be back around here in a little bit, children, but I'm gonta have to take my leave for a bit. I need to take my things up to the caretaker cottage and unpack. You keep me apprised if ya learn anything, will ya? Laz, my boy, why don't you come help me?"

We nodded and he and Laz ambled out to Gramps' pick up truck.

"Logan, we need to finish reading that journal. Maybe we can figure out some more information that can help us."

"I think my mom did finish it. Should we ask her?" "No, she's not really dealing with this very well. I think she's afraid of the possibilities. Let's go back out to the solarium."

We grabbed drinks and went back out to the lounge chairs. I found where I had left off and began to read aloud.

August 1, 1875

William has been gone for a week now, and I am so heartsick that I cannot bring myself to eat more than a morsel at each meal. I cannot even write about it, lest I am overcome with grief.

August 16, 1875

The family received a letter from William today, and he says that he has secured a temporary apprenticeship with a patent clerk, and must stay for two weeks so the man can ascertain if William is suitable for a more lengthy appointment. This is glorious news, for though I hate to be parted from him for so many more days, I fear that my sickness may be more than grief at William's absence. If my suspicions are right, then we must flee together shortly after he returns, or our secret will surely be exposed.

August 27, 1875

William has extended his stay in Richmond for a month, and I am filled with despair. I am quite certain that I am with child, and I will not be able to hide that fact for very long. I feel I must try to send a letter to William somehow so that he will come for me. Surely if I can reach him, he will come home or give me direction as to what to do. He would not leave his wife and child in danger.

September 20, 1875

I am not certain if today brought disaster or deliverance. I attempted to mail a letter privately to William, but Uncle Daniel intercepted me and demanded to know why I was acting in secret. When I remained mute, he did the unthinkable. He tore open the letter I had written and perused its contents.

To say that he was shocked does not do his reaction justice. He railed at me for several minutes, and I was grateful that there was no one around to hear. I would have given up hope at that very moment, but at the end of his rage, he told me that he had suspected William's feelings, though he had had no inkling that I felt the same.

Uncle Daniel said he has not yet decided what he must do. He claimed that he had a "higher duty" to do what was right. I am not sure what he meant by that, but I hope that it means he will find a way to help me.

September 21, 1875

Uncle Daniel spoke with Aunt Sarah, and they have agreed to help. While they do not support the choices William and I have made, and they do not believe that God would bless our marriage under the circumstances, they feel that the higher duty is to protect the innocent babe.

It is their hope that they can find a way to remove me from the Glen and secret me off to William. He is not able to support a family as yet, but Aunt Sarah believes we can easily hide my belly for another two months, and hopefully in that time, William will be able to secure a position sufficient to support us. In the meantime they will wait to tell William, lest he acts foolishly and jeopardizes his opportunity for employment.

Uncle Daniel tells me, though, that Nan and Father will unquestionably disown us as soon as the truth comes out. There will be no avoiding it. William and I will have to sacrifice the family we know for the family we have created.

I am deeply grateful that God has touched their hearts. They may not think that He recognizes our union, but their willingness to protect me proves to me that He does. Uncle Daniel is widely known as a man of infinite fairness, but also as one who believes in judgement and consequence. Surely such a man would not hide so desperate a secret unless God's hand had touched his heart.

That was the last entry in Anne's journal.

"Holy crap," Logan breathed. "There's no way in a million years I would've imagined all of that. It's freaking creepy!"

"Honestly, I don't know how to feel about it," I agreed. "It's disturbing, but I'm kind of rooting for them, too. Kind of like *Romeo and Juliet.*"

Logan rolled his eyes. "First of all, *Romeo and Juliet* isn't a real love story. Romeo just wanted to get into her pants, and back then you had to marry a girl to do it. Secondly, Romeo and Juliet weren't cousins."

"Okay, Judgey McJudgenstein. I get your point. But I have to admit, now that I know she was pregnant, I'm really hoping they ran away together and didn't actually die in that chapel." Even as I said it, I knew better. I remembered my dream about giving birth, and I knew it had happened in this very house. I thought about mentioning that, but I didn't want to sound like a complete nutjob.

"I'll give you that one," he relented, "but it's still disgusting."

"Yeah, okay. No argument. But I wonder what happened to them? I hate that it ends there. Worst cliffhanger of all time."

Logan was silent for a moment, his mind clearly turning the family mystery this way and that in his mind. "Ree, what are we going to do about Paul?"

"To be fair, Logan, we don't even know his side of the story. We don't know what he was doing. Maybe it isn't what we thought." I recalled the card I'd found in his room. "So, you know that card I found in his room? Judgement? I bet that's what he was hiding from Gramps. Do you think it's a coincidence that this curse might be a punishment placed on the family?"

"And if it was," he added, "was it a punishment for what William and Anne did, or for what happened to them afterwards?"

"I hate to say it, but we really need to talk to Paul and find out what he knows."

"Screw Paul."

"Look, Logan, I understand why you're upset. I do. But as much of a jerk as Paul is, I just can't believe he'd try to kill you."

Logan thought for a moment, then stood abruptly. "I don't know what I believe. I'm going to go upstairs for a little while. This is all just ... a lot. I need to think."

I nodded. "I'll come check on you later."

"Thanks, Ree." He started to walk away, but when he reached the living room door, he paused without turning around. "I really appreciate you being sort of the voice of reason in all this. After Dad ... and now Paul ... well, Mom's trying, but I think it's more than she can process. Maybe me, too. You're the youngest, but you're dealing better than we are. We need you." Then he passed through the doorway and out of sight.

I was taken aback by the rawness and sincerity of his statement. Tears stung my eyes. Even though every effort had been made to make me feel like I belonged in the Sheffield household, I'd always felt like an outsider. It wasn't their fault. My aunt and uncle even offered to adopt me legally, but I had declined. I was Aria Rush, not Aria Sheffield, and a legal piece of paper wasn't going to change that.

And yet now, in this moment, I wasn't an outsider. I was the rock. I was the glue. I was NEEDED.

And I wasn't going to let my family down.

Chapter 12

If I was going to solve this and be there for my family, I was going to have to bring my A-game. And I wasn't going to be able to do that if I was running around in a state of exhaustion, so I told Aunt Pam I was going to sleep in my own room tonight.

"But, honey, it's dangerous ..."

"Not for me. Whatever this thing is, it's not after me. I'm not part of the bloodline it wants." I couldn't really explain how I knew that, but my dream stayed with me, and I knew it was true. "Here," I said, handing her a large bell I'd found in the living room curio cabinet. "Keep this beside you in the bed, and I'll wake up and come if I hear it ringing."

She took the bell out of my hands. "MJ bought this for me in Prague ..." She turned it over and over in her hands, lost in her reverie. I patted her arm and headed upstairs, leaving her with her memories.

I made my way up to my room and crawled into bed. I must have been more exhausted than I even realized, because almost instantly, I fell into a deep and blessedly dreamless sleep. I woke up the next morning full of energy and raring to solve our family mystery.

Unlike a lot of kids my age, I didn't tend to spend a lot of time on my phone, but it was time to get to the bottom of things. I took a deep breath and scrolled down to Paul's number.

Paul, we need to talk. This is a crazy situation, and we need answers.

I figured it would be a long time before he got back to me, but the conversation needed to be had. We had to know what he was up to, and I still couldn't reconcile the idea that Paul was trying to kill his brother. To my surprise, a response came almost immediately.

You have no idea what's going on.

We know more than u think. We know about the curse.

I knew that must have shocked him because he didn't respond for several minutes, but I kept seeing the telltale flashing dots revealing that he was typing, then erasing, then typing again.

What is it that you think you know?

2 much 2 type. Call me.

Again, a pause.

Later. Can't talk now.

Make time. This is important.

After a few minutes with no reply, I set my phone down. I was interested in what Paul had to say, but I also wasn't going to sit around waiting for Prince Less-Than-Charming to decide to enlighten me about the family secrets. I was going to have to do my own research, my own way. We'd likely found out all we were going to find in books.

I packed a drawstring bag with the Judgement card, my phone, the journal, a bottle of water, and my EMF meter. I was still a bit tired, but the day was young, and there were answers to be had.

I slipped down the stairs and back into the room where I'd had the revealing dream about the journal. I bundled up the wallpapering tools, closed the card table, and put them into the guest room so that the small chamber was completely empty. I closed the adjoining door, as well as the door to the bathroom, and drew the shades.

"Anne?" I called, pulling out my EMF. "Anne, I don't know if you can hear me, but I'm Aria. I'm, well, a distant cousin of yours, I guess." I switched on the device, and it glowed green. "Anne, I know that whatever is happening here isn't your fault. I think you've been trying to tell me that. Please, let me help." I waited and watched the light. It was still green. "I think you've been showing me the past because you want me to help." Green. I don't know what I expected, but maybe I hoped she was just waiting for me. Of course, ghost hunters don't usually do their schtick at 11:00 in the morning, either.

I emptied my bag. I felt like a little bit of an idiot, but I was doing what felt right based on all the shows I'd watched and books I'd read about ghosts. And besides, there was no one here to see me, so there was nothing to lose.

"Anne," I repeated, laying down the EMF and picking up the tarot card, "I want to protect my family. I think that's something you understand. I know what it's like to feel like an outsider, even with the people you love. I'm listening. What do you want me to know?" A blip caught my eye. I glanced at the meter, which was flickering back and forth from green to amber. "Come closer to this device with the yellow light, Anne. That's how I'll know you're here." The numbers on the meter climbed slightly, but the light stayed yellow. "What do you want me to know?" I rubbed my finger over the card again, and found a rough patch of dried blood I had missed earlier when I'd wiped it off. I scratched at it with my fingernail. "Talk to me, Anne."

The light on the meter didn't change, but something felt different in the room. A floral smell I couldn't quite place—maybe lavender?—filled the air, and everything felt *heavy*, like when you take cold medicine and you feel a thickness in your consciousness. I knew I wasn't alone.

I watched the meter carefully and with a mix of anxiety, excitement, and determination as the numbers on the EMF started climbing again. My phone screen flashed on, and I watched in fascination as the image of the family tree popped up. Something was zooming in on the image, closer and closer, navigating around the chart. It stopped on Uncle MJ's name and zoomed even tighter on the strange symbol to the left of his name.

Then the screen panned down to Paul's name. I expected it would move to Logan's name next, but it didn't. The screen blinked and my own name appeared. Then it zoomed in on the empty space before my own name and for an instant, the same symbol, the one that looked a little like an underlined Greek omega, was clearly visible. Then the screen went dark.

"What? What does that mean? Talk to me!"

But the EMF meter was green again, and I knew I was alone.

Chapter 13

A few minutes later, I found myself knocking on the door to Gramps's cottage. I felt like he was holding back on a few things, maybe always had been. But it was time for everything to be out in the open. The curtain on the door window pulled back, and the caretaker of the estate regarded me sternly. After a moment, there was a click and he opened the door.

"Well, there, missy. You spent the last coupla years searchin fer ghosts, and now I speck you've got yer wish, eh?"

"You could say that, Gramps, but there's more to this than just ghosts, and I think you know that."

"Huh," he responded noncommittally.

"Come on, Gramps. No one knows more about this family than you, and I bet that's been true down your family line. I don't want anything to happen to Logan ... or Paul, for that matter."

"That may be beyond yer doin', Aria." He waved me in to sit down at his kitchen table, and sat down across from me.

"What does that mean?"

"The Sheffields is a complicated family, girl. Lotsa secrets over lotsa years. My own father, he knew more'n I do. Yer uncle, he told me once he wanted ta get away from some of the old family traditions."

"What traditions? What are you talking about?'

"Aria, love, I don't really know how much I kin tell ya. There's an oath and an understandin' atween yer family an' mine. An' there's some bits I'm not sure if yer allowed ta know. I need to speak ta young Paul."

"Paul?" I demanded. "Why do you need to talk to him before you can tell me my own family history?"

"Ah, it's not the history ..." Gramps was clearly struggling to both explain and keep his word. "It's more the legacy, miss. The legacy that, if you'll pardon my bluntness, ain't part o' yer line."

"You mean because I'm not descended from Robert Sheffield."

Gramps seemed surprised that I'd caught on so quickly. "Well, yes, exactly so.

My family is bound to his line, ya see."

"No, I don't see. But I bet it has something to do with that symbol on the family tree, doesn't it?"

He narrowed his eyes at me. "What symbol ya be talkin bout?"

"This one." I pulled out my phone and opened the photo of the family tree. I zoomed in on the strange symbol by my uncle's name.

"Hm. Yes, I guess it might be related."

"Paul should have that symbol, too, shouldn't he?"

Gramps's eyes widened. "What do you know about that, now?"

I wasn't sure how much I should reveal, but if I wanted information, I had to give up a little. "I think a ghost showed me that Paul was next in line to have that symbol. And then she showed me that I should have it, too."

"Now yer talkin nonsense."

"You know I'm not." I was pushing my luck, but I didn't really want to tell Gramps about the card. If Paul kept it a secret, so should I.

"I'll tell ya this, miss. Yer right that Paul should have that symbol now, but ghost or no ghost, there's no reason why you'd have it."

"Because only one person in a generation has it?"

"Sumpin like that, yes. And if Paul's got it, then you don't."

Unless Paul no longer had the card. I did. Somehow that symbol was connected to the card. Whoever had the card got that notation next to their name. But Gramps didn't know that.

"Okay, well, maybe you're right. But do you know what the symbol is?"

"Oh, yeah, sure. Ye can look that one up fer yerself. It's the symbol for Libra."

"Libra? The sign?"

"Yep. I really can't tell ya more'nat, Aria. I'm sorry."

I could tell I wasn't getting any more out of him right now. "Okay, Gramps, thanks anyway. I AM going to figure this out, though. I'm not letting anything happen to my family."

He looked at me with sad eyes. "I don't want nothin' to happen to 'em, either, Aria. I hope ye know that."

"I do. Sorry, but I've got to go. I've got some things I need to do."

He nodded slowly, and I left with my head a jumble of thoughts.

Libra. If memory served, Libras have October birthdays, which none of us in the household did. But I knew something else about Libra. It was symbolized by the scales. The scales of balance ... and judgement.

***

It seemed to me that I was going to have to keep thinking out of the box for answers. As crazy as it sounded to most people, the ghost angle was really the only one I'd been successfully working lately. That meant going to the source. The chapel. Alone.

Not gonna lie, I didn't relish the notion of going out there alone, but somehow it seemed less scary now that I knew that whatever was stalking the family didn't have me in its sights. Even moreso, it appeared that Anne Sheffield wanted to help me find the answers in whatever limited way a ghost could do that. I took one more look at the house, and then set out for the chapel. If that little room upstairs led me to answers, I was pretty sure the chapel would, too.

As I approached the pile of rubble, I pulled the EMF out of my bag. The light glowed amber and the numbers kept going up the closer I got. By the time I stepped off the path and was an arm's length from the stones, the light was red, and the machine was beeping like crazy.

"Well, this is what you came out here for ..." I told myself, trying to fight that familiar fear that crept over me everytime I came near this place. I turned off the EMF and slid it back into the bag, and pulled out the Judgement card. As I approached the iron window frame that had affected me so strongly—was it only four days ago? five?—my head began to throb slightly. "Anne, if you're here, help me out. Show me how to help my family."

I grabbed the iron like I had done before, and nothing happened. No cold, no *whoosh*, no anything. I sighed in frustration, but then remembered the terror on Logan's face the night that *thing* had tried to kill him, and I remembered my own fear and desperation when I thought he might die in front of my eyes. Failure was not an option here.

"All right. Fine," I complained to no one in particular. I stepped a little closer to the pile, holding onto the iron frame for stability. I hesitantly raised one foot, as if I expected to be knocked down by an invisible force at any moment. When nothing happened, I stepped firmly on one of the larger stones and climbed up a few feet. Still nothing happened. I spotted a fairly flat-looking section of rubble and side-stepped so I could sit on it, but as I did, the rock I had been standing on shifted slightly, causing me to lose my balance and my grip on the iron. I scrambled desperately holding the judgement card over my head to protect it, but gravity prevailed, and I plopped awkwardly onto my behind, scraping my empty hand on the stone.

"Gah!" I snorted in frustration and pain. The resulting injury looked like the road rash you get when you fall off a bike or a skateboard, and I was just grateful that it hadn't been my injured wrist. I'd really been putting my body through the wringer this summer.

Transfering the card gingerly to the fingertips of my now-slightly-bloodied hand, I swung the bag off my shoulder and pulled out the water. I laid the card carefully on the stones and rinsed the blood and grit off my hand. As the water hit the pile of rubble, I heard a rushing sound in my ears like I was being pulled underwater. Dizziness overcame me and my vision went dark. All I was aware of was darkness, the sound of my breathing, and the stinging in my hand.

Emotions swirl around me. The hunger is here, always here. Always under everything. But there's fear. And sadness. And longing. Despair, so much despair.

But now there is something else, something apart from the anguish of this place. There's a voice whispering underneath it all. It's whispering to me, and I know it. It's ... SHE'S calling me, waiting for me. I listen, but I can't make out the words. She wants me to hear her, but the interference is too strong.

And then the Hunger returns. It is a thing of rage, sniffing around me. It wants to come for me, I know it, but it's confused. I'm the wrong blood. It doesn't understand why I'm here, why I'm not too afraid to seek it out. It is primal, but it is something else, too. It is Hunger, but it is also lost.

It doesn't like that I know that. It doesn't like ME. But it can't figure me out either, so it doesn't know what to do. It's close to me, vibrating with all its hate, and a shriek pierces the veil of wherever this is. I am startled by the sound, but in this place where everything is detached, I am blinded by darkness, but not fear. The thing shrieks again and this time I am not startled. The sound is jarring.

But it's also human.

There was a popping sound in my ears, like when a plane lands. I sat on the pile of stones, and the strange darkness that had engulfed me was gone. I was glad to be back in the real world, but the darkness had left me knowing something now that I didn't before. I knew that the thing hunting my family wasn't William or Anne. It was the third person who had died that October day so long ago.

Their child.

Chapter 14

I put the card and water back into my bag and climbed down off the pile of rocks. I pulled out the EMF meter, and it was flicking back and forth from amber to red as the number hovered around 4.5. I wasn't alone, but I also wasn't scared anymore. Now I had a direction, a lead.

"I'm going to figure this out," I said to the lingering presence, and then I walked back toward the house. The farther away I walked, the lower the numbers on the meter dropped until they held steady at a yellow-glowing 2.0. I was being followed, but at a distance. I had evoked something other than rage in this ghost. I had evoked its curiosity. That, in itself, was progress. And I was hoping that also meant that Logan was safe for the moment.

Still, I needed to know more. I sat in the shadow of an oak tree, placed the meter on the ground next to me, and pulled out my phone. Research time.

I opened a browser and typed "baby ghost" into the search box. What came back was initially disappointing. Movie and TV plots, urban legends, creepy costume photos (which really made me shudder, given the reason I was searching) ... none of it was useful. So I added the word "myth" to my search terms, and there I struck gold. There I found an entry for something called a "myling".

I read the page eagerly, then backtracked and searched for more lore on these spirits. The more I read, the more I knew that I had no doubt found the key to what was stalking our family tree, even if it was a little different in our case. But now I had to find out how to end the haunting, end the curse.

Plus, knowing about these poor spirits made my heart hurt.

Just then my phone buzzed. I stopped reading for a moment and found myself shaking. It was a text message from Paul.

Where are you?

I'm at home. Outside.

Where outside?

Are you here? I'm out past the back patio by the big oak.

No response, but I suspected Paul was carefully avoiding the rest of the family and making his way out here to me. A couple of minutes later, my suspicions were confirmed.

He strode toward me with purpose, almost menacingly, and as he approached, the EMF reading started rising, creeping solidly into the red and beeping like an alarm. I switched the meter off because I didn't want that to be the conversation starter here.

"I'm glad you're here. We have a lot to talk about," I began. I was hoping to sound non-confrontational. If I wanted him to tell me what he knew, I was going to have to play this carefully.

"Do we? You don't understand what's happening here. You all think I'm the bad guy, but I'm not."

"Why don't you explain it to me, then?" I pressed.

Wrong thing to say, I guess, because Paul tensed up immediately. "Why don't you explain what you think you know first?"

I considered pushing back, but if he was already defensive, I was going to have to lay my cards on the table, pun intended.. "I know the family curse is real. I know that it's stalking Logan and it tried to kill him the night you left. I know some of what happened to William and Anne Sheffield, and why. I know you're up to some kind of hocus pocus, but I don't know what you're trying to accomplish."

He considered for a moment before responding. "You don't know the weight of what I'm up against." His shoulders slumped, and he looked tired.

"You don't have to do this alone, Paul. I've learned so much ..."

"You don't understand, kid. This isn't your fight. It's mine."

"It's not JUST your fight anymore. I know what we're up against now! I—"

"You don't. No one does. And I'm not allowed to tell you."

"But I've—"

"Aria, you have to stop whatever it is you're doing. You're just going to make it worse!"

"If you'd just listen—" I was getting really frustrated.

"This family has a lot of secrets you're not meant to know. It's my burden to bear, and—"

"WILL YOU SHUT UP FOR A MINUTE?" I yelled. Paul jumped, startled by my outburst. I took advantage of the pause. "I know what the ghost is that's been killing the family. Not just WHAT it is, I know WHO it is. If you'll just quit being all King of the Martyrs for a second, I might just tell you something you didn't already know."

That seemed to legitimately surprise him.

"You know WHO it is? What do you mean, WHO?"

"Let's go back to the house and call a family meeting. That way I can tell all of you at the same time."

"You don't understand! The secrets—"

"There ARE no secrets anymore; don't you get it?" I demanded. "If we're going to pull out of this, we need to do it as a family. Now let's go up to the house and talk."

He was about to argue with me, but I pushed past him and made for the solarium.

A few minutes later, the whole family was gathered in the sunny room, and I had managed to convince Logan to contain his rage until we'd all had a chance to talk.

"Okay, so I'm going to go first, and then Paul, you'll have a chance to explain yourself," I began. "I've been working on the theory that this ghost was connected to William and Anne, and I wasn't entirely wrong, but I wasn't entirely right either. I really believe that Anne wants us to solve this and lift the family curse. I think that's why she's been sending me dreams and led me to her diary."

"Led you to her WHAT?" exclaimed Paul.

"Oh, yeah, you don't know about that. After you left, I had this crazy dream. Well, I'd been having crazy dreams about Anne's past ever since I came home from the hospital, actually, but this dream showed me where she had hidden her diary. And I found it. Basically, William and Anne were in love with each other, and of course the family wouldn't have approved. So they swore marriage vows in the chapel, and you know, had a wedding night or whatever."

"Ew. That'd be like you and Logan. That's disgusting," he said, making a throw-up face.

"Yeah, okay, but it happened. And so they kept it secret, and William went off to try and make some money so he and Anne could go start a life together. But Anne found out after he left that she was pregnant ..."

"Aaaagh! Stop! That is so nasty!" I could always count on Paul to be melodramatic. I glared at him. "Sorry. Finish your story."

"Right. So Anne tried to write to him, but Daniel, William's father, intercepted the letter and confronted her. And even though he didn't approve, to say the least, he didn't want to be responsible for anything happening to an innocent baby. So William's parents agreed to help hide the pregnancy until they could find a way to get Anne and William away from the family, and then they'd be on their own."

"So what happened?"

"That's kind of where the diary ends, but I think that Anne had the baby. I had a dream of that, too. And I don't know what the fallout was, but I think the whole family found out about it somehow. All through the diary, Anne is terrified of her grandmother, and what she'd do if she found out. I don't know what happened after that, but I think William and Anne *and their baby* died in the chapel."

There was silence as I finished the summary. This was, of course, the first time that Logan and Aunt Pam had considered the possibility of the fact that the baby had actually been born, and the air around us was thick with the realization of the tragedy.

"Last thing," I said. "We've known for years that William's and Anne's ghosts had been seen on the estate. I think that when they died, the baby became a special kind of ghost known as a *myling*. And I think THAT is what's been killing our family generation after generation."

"Oh, God ..." Aunt Pam whispered, placing her hand over her heart. "That poor child." Her eyes were full of tears.

I nodded. "I feel the same way. But listen to this. The myling is a Scandinavian myth, but lots of other mythologies have something similar. A myling is the ghost of an unbaptized child that dies of exposure. It haunts the spot where it died and follows travelers who pass by because it can't rest in peace."

"I knew we shouldn't have gone out to the chapel!" Logan exclaimed. "Now that thing is after me."

"It's been after you for years," Paul chimed in, and we all turned to look at him, our jaws dropping open at this revelation. "Dad first told me about the thing when I was ten. I mean, he didn't know what ... who ... it was, but he knew there was something out there. He knew that it would come for one of us." He looked pointedly at Logan. "Dad wasn't willing to accept that. So he took us out there one day to try and—I don't know—reason with the thing. But it didn't work. All Dad could do was to perform this ritual, sort of blood magic, to try and stave it off. When

I was about thirteen, he told me about it, taught me how to do it. Told me some of the family secrets." Paul paused here, and I could tell he was holding something back.

"What, Paul? What else?"

"Nothing, really. We kept doing the ritual, feeding it some of our blood to, I don't know, appease it, I guess. But then," Paul got up and walked away from us, looking outside across the property, "then I think it got mad. The blood wasn't enough anymore. Dad did all he could to protect us, and it ended up taking him instead." At this, Paul's voice broke, and he had to stop and gather himself.

"Blood rituals? Magic? How did I not know this was going on? Oh, sweetheart, why didn't you tell me any of this? " Aunt Pam asked.

"Would you have believed it? Hell no, Mom, you'd have had me committed. And who would protect Logan then?"

"Protect me?"

"What do you think I was doing that night, you idiot? That thing was quiet for years, and then you two numbskulls went and pissed it off."

Chapter 15

Paul's revelation left us all stunned. It went a long way to explaining the surliness we'd come to expect from him. We all stared at him, dumbfounded, and the weight of the secrets he'd been keeping seemed to seep out of him while we watched. He hung his head, and suddenly looked older than his 19 years.

After a moment, I felt like it was time to speak up. "Paul, I think it's time we knew everything. Like everything. No more secrets. Gramps has kept your secrets, too, but unless we work together, I don't think we can protect our family. I think that's the only way."

He raised his eyes, resigned. Logan was hard to read, but the anger was gone from his expression. Aunt Pam looked like she wanted to cry.

"Okay," Paul sighed, "I guess you already know a lot, so you might as well know it all. Or as much as I learned before Dad died, anyway.

"The Sheffields are part of an ancient order of families with magical blood. I don't know too much about the history before they came to America, except to say that Virginia Sheffield, who was sort of the matriarch of the family when they immigrated, was a devout Protestant, and denounced the family legacy that came down through her husband's line. Unfortunately for her, blood was thicker than faith, so to speak, and her son Robert was still marked."

"What do you mean 'marked'?" Aunt Pam asked.

"There's a family artifact, a tarot card, that gets passed down through the generations. A bunch of families got them, and then they were scattered around the world. I don't know why. Whoever holds the card supposedly has certain magical abilities, though no one in our family, as far as I know, has had anything but the damn curse."

A chill ran through me. I knew I should return the card to Paul, but frankly, I didn't want to. As it happened, though, I didn't have much of an internal debate, because Logan finally spoke up.

"Tarot card? Aria, is that the thing we found in Paul's room?"

Paul's eyes darted to me. "You have to give it back to me, Aria. It's not meant to be yours."

I felt like I should argue, but somehow *finders keepers* didn't seem to be a good defense. Reluctantly, I fished the card out of my bag and handed it over. He took it from me and held it with his fingertips, as if I'd somehow defiled it.

"Yeah, so anyway," he continued, "as near as I can tell, every generation of Robert Sheffield's line has had a guardian of the card, passed down from father to son, mostly. And only one person in each generation survives to continue the family line. Sometimes it's the one that's marked; sometimes not. But if the marked person dies, then the card becomes the property of someone else in the family."

"And Dad gave it to you?" Logan seemed suspicious, maybe hurt.

"Not exactly. When he ... died ... it sort of just showed up amongst my stuff. I found it under my pillow after the funeral. I don't know how it got there. I thought maybe Gramps put it there, but he swears he didn't. And since then, I've been trying to do what Dad showed me every so often. I was hoping maybe the curse would skip Logan and me, since it killed Dad, and he was the last of the generation. But it didn't last." He hesitated, clearly trying to decide how much he should share.

"Out with it, Paul. No more secrets," I prodded.

He shrugged. "Okay, well about a year ago, I started getting these weird phone calls and texts from an unknown number. Stuff like, 'judgement is coming", or 'You can't run from judgement.' That kind of thing. Clearly, it was someone who knew about the card. Maybe someone who has one of the other cards."

"Did you ever talk to this person?" Aunt Pam asked. " Have you ever seen him?"

"Her."

"What?"

"Her. The voice on the phone was female. Youngish, I guess. I think she had a British accent. She never said much, because it wasn't about information. It was about intimidation. But I don't know why. I guess I got maybe six calls or texts over the past year. I saved the texts." He pulled out his phone and scrolled through his messages, then handed the phone to me.

The first message was from April of last year.

Judgement is coming. You cannot avoid it.

Who is this?

It's coming, and I'm watching. Your bloodline can't avoid it forever.

This was followed by a string of cursing on Paul's part, and no answer from the mystery texter.

Then there was another message from December.

I warned you. It's coming for you, and your brother. Your time is done.

Another string of profanity from Paul.

Curse me all you want, boy. It's time for new blood.

Paul's response was no less colorful, but this time demanded to know what the messages meant. There was no response.

And then one final message ... from about ten days ago, right before we got out of school and returned home.

Time's up, mate. Judgement demands new blood.

Paul hadn't bothered to respond this time.

I showed the messages to Logan and Aunt Pam, and we sat in silence, not knowing what to make of these exchanges.

"What did she say in the phone calls? Like EXACTLY?" I asked.

"Same type of stuff. She called twice. Once she said that my poisoned blood wasn't worthy, and that judgement was coming. The other time, she said she'd be there when we were gone. Both times she hung up before I could say anything."

"What could that all mean?" Aunt Pam wondered.

"Maybe it's referring to the curse," I said. "You said you were supposed to have abilities, but all you have is the curse. Maybe something happened … maybe it's tied to what is happening here. To what happened to William and Anne, and their child. Maybe that's how the curse started." I pulled out my phone and opened the image of our family tree. I looked at Paul's name and mine, and the symbols that had flashed on my phone screen earlier were gone. But it didn't matter. That wasn't what I was looking for. I found the Libra symbol next to Uncle MJ's name, and traced it up his family line to the beginning of the American Sheffields', expecting that Robert would bear the first Libra symbol on the chart.

But he didn't.

Robert's youngest brother Daniel did.

William's father.

Chapter 16

O ur brains were exhausted from trying to process all of the information we'd uncovered in the past couple of days, so we decided to try and talk to Gramps some more the next day. We ordered pizza and read some more about mylings. There was a lot of material online, but most of the sources we read agreed that what the spirit wanted, more than anything, was a proper burial, and that its rage came from never knowing any emotion other than *need*.

This got me thinking about a couple of the dreams I'd had lately. Certainly I'd tapped into the myling's energy, and it had been confused about my blood because I was related, but in a different, *non-cursed* family lineage. What I couldn't figure out was the other ethereal presence, the female voice I couldn't quite hear.

I caught Paul in the kitchen after dinner.

"So, Paul, I have a question."

He eyed me with a mixture of annoyance, curiosity, and exhaustion. Unloading the secret burdens he'd been carrying for years had worn him out.

"Have you ever had, I don't know, visions about the curse or anything?"

"Visions? No, not really. I mean, I definitely felt sort of a rush of power whenever I did the blood ritual, and I could sense the presence of the creature, you know, the myling or whatever. But nothing other than that. Pretty crappy magical legacy, if you ask me."

"So you've never heard a female voice or been aware of another presence?"

"No. But you whacked your head pretty good last week. Maybe it's related to your concussion."

"What, like a hallucination?"

"Maybe, maybe not," he sighed. "Sometimes a whack on the head can alter someone's perception. Or maybe sort of a near-death-experience made you think of your mom."

I considered that, and it was definitely possible. I had half-expected to see my mother when I woke up in a hospital bed. "Yeah, okay."

"You've never had any kind of visions or anything before the accident, right?"

"No, only after."

"So you have to take that into consideration. Something has changed, and it may or may not be supernatural. I've never had any sense of a female presence, but Logan had seen Anne's ghost when he was a kid ..."

"No, it's not Anne's voice. I don't know how I know that, but I do."

He nodded. "Look, I'm not trying to dismiss anything you're saying, but it does strike me as a little weird that I've been the one with the supposed magical connection, and yet you've seen more ghosts and had more paranormal experiences in the past week than I've had in three years. Let me know if something else happens, though. We shouldn't discount anything." He grabbed a soda out of the fridge and shuffled past me toward the stairs. I let him go.

I couldn't be sure, but it almost seemed like he was jealous. He had been adamant about getting the card back from me, and he seemed pretty content to write off at least some of my experiences to my concussion. He might be right, of course, but that explanation just didn't ring true to me. I felt like it had more to do with the curse on his bloodline.

With this in mind, I followed him up the stairs, but when he branched off toward his room, I climbed one more floor to my own. I opened the wardrobe and pointed my desk lamp at the family tree, reaching back through the generations to the beginning of our story.

Daniel had the Libra symbol, but after William's death, there was no one left in his line to inherit the card. Was that why George Sheffield, Robert's only surviving son, had been the next in the magical line? And then every surviving Sheffield in Robert's bloodline that hadn't been taken out by the vengeful myling? Why had the card not come to my bloodline instead of Robert's? Was it because Baxter Sheffield, my ancestor, had left the Glen years before any of the events which cursed the family had occurred, or was there another reason? I felt like there was a piece of the puzzle I was missing, like the whispering voice in my visions that I couldn't quite hear.

***

Despite my protestations that I was safe from the myling, Logan, Aunt Pam, and I were still bunked together in the master bedroom. Paul declined to join us, claiming that the myling had never targeted him, since he was the card-holder for his generation. There was some argument from my aunt on this, but she eventually relented. I, on the other hand, decided not to argue. She was under enough stress as it was: this supernatural being was targeting her children, a terror no parent is prepared for. Paul didn't seem to be too concerned about her feelings, but I was.

I lay on my side of the king-sized bed, flipping ideas through my head like a high-speed slideshow. One thing seemed clear to me, though I didn't relish the thought. We were going to have to excavate the chapel ruins and try to find the remains of the three souls who died there so that we could bury them properly. I wasn't sure how that suggestion would go over, but there was no way around it, if the mythology was correct.

I was just drifting off to sleep when the bedroom door inched open. My heart started to pound, and I held very still, my eyes fixed on the widening crack. After a moment, I made out Paul's figure as he slid through the doorway, dragging a blanket and a pillow. He settled himself on the chair and ottoman by the dresser. At first I was amused by his change of heart, but the more I thought about it, the more disturbing it seemed. Paul was very stubborn, and wouldn't have changed his course without solid reason to do so. I resolved to ask him about it in the morning, and I drifted off to a troubled sleep.

I am standing by the chapel, which stands as it must have looked many years ago. The rest of the yard is unchanged: the pool, the patio furniture, the path leading into the woods which eventually finds the small stream where we sometimes fish. Only this small plot is changed, lost in time, perhaps. I walk toward the open door, and as I cross the threshold, the walls disappear and I am standing on a flagstone floor. A gentle breeze blows my hair across my face, and as I brush my hair away, I look to the treeline maybe 50 feet away. That's when I see her. She is wrapped in a white, sleeveless gown, and her deeply bronzed skin reflects the dappled sunlight. The blackness of her hair melts into the shadows between the trees. She is waiting, as she has been for so very long. She does not speak, but watches me intently. It feels like she is sizing me up, evaluating me. I try to call to her, but I am frozen in place, as so often happens in dreams. She dissolves into shadow, and a moment later, a vulture rises above the woods and soars in concentric circles before disappearing over the treetops. I feel like she has not gone far, though I can no longer see her.

***

The morning sun sneaking through the slats in the window blinds woke me. Aunt Pam and Paul were both gone, and Logan was still snoozing away with his forearm over his eyes. I slid out of the bed as quietly as I could and padded over to the bathroom to shower. I noticed with satisfaction that my black eye from the car accident was largely healed, and only a little discoloration was still visible.

As I stood in the steaming water, I thought about what Paul had said about the connection between my concussion and what appeared to be a significant shift in my perception of the paranormal entities that had been part of my family history for as long as I'd lived at the Glen. Had a brush with death altered my senses somehow, or had something changed in my brain chemistry? And if it was the latter, would my ability to perceive these things fade as my head injury healed? Over the past week and a half, my headaches had decreased significantly, but the events and my ability to see and feel them had not, so it seemed as if these new skills were here to stay.

I dried off and pulled on my fluffy red robe, since I hadn't bothered to grab clothes from my room before my shower. As I opened the door and let the steam roll into the hallway, I heard a ruckus and a lot of swearing coming from Paul's room. I poked my head into his half-open door, and found myself looking at a room that seemed to have housed a small tornado.

"Uh ... Paul? What's up?" I asked, surveying the carnage.

"I can't find it. It's missing. It NEVER goes missing."

"Can't find what? What's missing?"

"The CARD. I can't find the CARD."

His voice betrayed more than frustration. There was an underlying panic creeping in, and the state of his room was evidence of it.

"Maybe I can help. Where did you put it after I gave it back to you?"

He stopped tearing the room apart for a moment. "I put it in my drawer, where I always keep it when I'm at home," he said, gesturing toward his desk. All the contents of the drawers had been dumped out on the floor. "When I went to look for it last night, it wasn't there, and I thought maybe I'd set it down somewhere, but I couldn't find it, and it was so late that I just ... decided to find it this morning. But it's not here. Not anywhere."

"Why did you need it last night? Is that why you came into Aunt Pam's room in the middle of the night?"

He shot me a side glance, clearly displeased that I had noticed his furtive entrance. He hesitated. "It ... well, it ... started getting really cold in my room last night." He paused here, and I went very still, remembering what Logan's room had been like the night the myling had come for him. "I was going to try doing the ritual, you know, because that's the routine when we had some sort of sense that the thing was active. But I couldn't because the card was gone. So I sucked it up and slept on Mom's chair. I didn't think anyone knew I'd been in there. I got up pretty early."

"What did you mean when you said the card never goes missing? That's a weird way to word it."

"I mean that I can't actually lose the card. After Dad died, it just sort of showed up, like I told you. Then one time, I forgot to take it with me to Lockridge during my senior year, but it showed up in my backpack. I can't leave it behind, and I can't lose it, because it follows me after a couple of hours. Except now ..."

"Look, let me go get dressed, and I'll help you look. It's got to be somewhere, like you said. Give me a few minutes."

He nodded, barely registering what I'd said, as he stared at the heaps of his belongings.

I trotted up the stairs into the attic and threw on a tee shirt and yoga pants. I felt really bad for Paul. The more I learned about the fear he'd been living with and the burden he'd been carrying, the more I understood his hallmark stormy personality. I pulled on some socks and sat on the edge of the bed to pull my shoes on, and my eyes were drawn to the ancestry chart that had been such a focus of the past few days.

Peeking out from the bottom left corner, the corner closest to my name on the chart, was the Judgement card.

I retrieved the card and held it in my hand. I knew I should take it down to Paul right away, but somehow that felt wrong. The sensation of being pulled into the image overtook me, as it had the night we found it in Paul's room. I studied the picture and its symbolism, trying to connect it with the curse on the family, and on the series of incidents which led to the curse in the first place.

Some of the people in the image reached up toward the winged figure, while some cringed in fear. What could that mean? My English teacher's voice pricked at my brain, urging me to look at the central idea, and the reactions of the characters. *Central idea: judgement. Some fear it, because they know they've done wrong. Some welcome it because they feel their actions are righteous.* The figure itself was winged, but a silhouette with no features. It could be an angel or a demon, or something in between. *Judgement has two sides: justice and fairness, or jumping to conclusions.* The people in the image appeared to be naked. *In final judgement, all masks and defenses are stripped away, and only the bare soul remains.*

I felt like I was starting to get an understanding for what the symbolism of the card meant. No matter how someone presents himself, who they are on the inside is what the Universe judges. I wasn't exactly sure who or what was doing the judging ... it probably depended on your personal belief system. But as I looked at the people who were afraid of judgement in the image, I realized it wasn't judgement itself that they feared; it was punishment. Could the curse on Robert Sheffield's bloodline be the punishment for the deaths of William, Anne, and the baby? Since William's father was the card holder in that generation, had he somehow placed a curse on his brother's descendants?

"Aria, what the HELL?" I started at the sound of Paul's voice, and looked up to see him brimming with fury to find me holding the object of his search.

"Paul, I swear, I came up here to get dressed, and I found this in my wardrobe. I don't know how it got there. I promise I was about to bring it to you." That was *probably* true, anyway.

"Oh, it just magically showed up in your stuff?" His voice was laced with sarcasm.

"Yes, actually," I replied flatly. "Unless you put it here, which you clearly didn't."

"Hand it over."

I reluctantly obeyed, still feeling like there was something *wrong* about giving it to him. He snatched it from my outstretched hand and stormed down the stairs. It wasn't too likely he'd be interested in discussing my theories now; I was pretty sure he thought I had swiped the card. Nevertheless, we still had a family curse to solve, so we'd all have to work together whether he liked it or not. I closed the wardrobe door firmly and sighed.

It was nearly 11:00 by the time Logan made his way downstairs. Paul had closed himself in his room (probably trying to undo the damage he'd done to it earlier), and Aunt Pam had gone shopping. I was picking at a bowl of cereal and waiting.

"It's about time!" I exclaimed as he shuffled into the kitchen.

"Yeah, good morning to you, too," he muttered.

"You're right. Sorry. I've just been awake for a couple of hours, and thinking about what we need to do."

"Nope ... not even having this discussion until I've had caffeine." He made his way over to the coffee maker, popped in a pod, and stared at the machine as if in prayer. I waited in respectful silence until he'd ingested maybe half of his cup.

"How about now?"

He sighed heavily and plopped down at the table across from me. "Okay, now."

"We have to excavate the chapel."

"Are you out of your MIND?" His eyes widened in disbelief. "Have I not made it abundantly clear that I am NOT going out there again, EVER?"

"Yeah, I know, but every day that passes that we don't find the remains of William, Anne, and the baby, and bury them properly, that's another day where you and Paul are in danger. This thing has been killing your bloodline for generations, and I don't think it's planning on taking a vacation just because we know what —who—it is now."

"Who's to say that won't make things worse?"

"Worse? How could it possibly be worse? It wants you dead!"

"Who's to say it's not just waiting for me to come out there where it's stronger? Forget it. I'll help in other ways, but I'm not going out there. No." Logan stormed out of the kitchen, leaving me grumbling in frustration.

***

I had one last hope: Gramps. Logan and I had been planning on talking to him together, but I didn't really feel like waiting. Gramps hadn't been overly helpful up to now, but maybe now that I knew all about the family curse, he wouldn't feel like he had to hide things. I knocked on his cottage door for several minutes before concluding that he wasn't in. I hoped he wasn't working too far from the house, because trying to find him over a dozen acres could be a challenge. I craned my head, listening for the sound of the riding mower, and gave a small sigh of relief when I heard it faintly from the direction of the woods. I spotted him out past the toolshed, and waved as I approached, knowing he'd never hear me calling him with his huge earphones on. He spotted me and switched the motor to idle.

"Hey, there, Aria girl. Ye looks like ye're on a mission."

He wasn't wrong. I told him, as succinctly as I could, everything we'd learned about the curse, the family, and the myling. I carefully omitted any mention of the card, since it appeared neither my uncle nor Paul had ever told him about it.

"So, it comes down to this, Gramps: I need to try and find whatever remains I can out there, and we need to bury them properly. I really think this might end the curse. Will you please help? I can't get either of the boys to help me."

Gramps stared at me for a long moment, clearly processing what I'd told him and trying to fit it into the reality and information that he'd known about for who-knows-how-many years. Finally, he seemed to come to a decision.

"Missy, I think ye're onto sumpin. Leastwise, no one's ever figured out as much as you, and this is sumpin what's never been tried. Lemme park this beast," he said gesturing at the riding mower, "and I'll grab some gloves and shovels. I dunno if this be a good idea or no, but it's worth a try. I think I might be able to scare up another set o' hands, too."

Chapter 17

If you told me a week ago that I'd be something halfway between an archaeologist and a grave-digger before the summer was out, I'd have told you you were crazy, yet here we were. Gramps and I headed for the chapel ruins, loaded down with gear. We had shovels, gloves, garbage bags, buckets, and a burlap sack. We also had Laz. He ambled up the driveway with a grin on his face; you'd think he was going to a theme park rather than an excavation.

"Hey, Laz. Thanks for helping us out. I know it's hot out here," I smiled.

"My pleasure. I like being able to help your family." I felt like there was more in the undercurrent of his comment, but I was so preoccupied with getting to work on the chapel, I decided to let it pass instead of digging deeper, no pun intended.

It was a huge task we were taking on, but we both dove into it with gusto. We started by creating a pile of rocks out of the collapsed masonry, which we'd add to as we made our way through the debris. We pulled away weeds and moss, and carefully placed any metal bits into the garbage bags. It was slow work, which surprised me because the foundation of the chapel building itself was no larger than our kitchen in the main house, maybe 15 feet by 20 feet. I had thought the whole family would be out here pitching in and making quick work of the rubble, excavating down to the remains of our ancestors in a matter of a couple of hours.

But with the three of us working alone, it was going to take much longer than I'd planned, and the 90° heat was stifling. I had the constant feeling of being watched, but with curiosity moreso than anger. We'd been working for a little over an hour when Gramps called for a break.

"Missy, le's stop for some lunch. Last thing we need is ta be gettin' dehydrated. It's the high point of the day, and I don't think any of us want to be gettin' the heat stroke."

I couldn't disagree. We were making slow and steady progress, but it was clear that we had hours ahead of us. "Okay, you're right," I said, wiping the sweat from my dripping brow. "Let's meet back here in an hour or so." He nodded curtly and he and Laz headed for his cottage, leaving me alone to wander back to the house on my own.

Once back inside, I found myself alone in the house. Paul's car was gone, and I couldn't find Logan or Aunt Pam. My heart and mind were heavy with the task I'd set for the day, and I couldn't bring myself to eat anything, so I poured myself some lemonade and tried not to chug it. Once that was gone, I filled the same glass with water and wandered up to my room to cool off for a little while.

As I passed the room where I'd seen Anne, I paused by the door, hoping to feel her presence, but I was greeted by silence and emptiness. I don't know what I was expecting or why I was disappointed. Did I really think she'd just be waiting there, hanging out to say, "Hey, girl, way to go! You've figured it all out! Nice job! Spectral high five!" Of course not. But given the good fortune I'd had with contacting her in the past week or so, I guess I thought maybe she'd give me some sign. After a moment, I shrugged and made my way up to my room.

I sat in the window seat, not wanting to get my icky sweat on my bed. Staring out the window in the yard, I fixed my mind on how I wanted this to work out. I imagined myself finding the intact (and not at all creepy) skeletons of my ancestors. I'd lay them gently onto a blanket and find a lovely spot to lay them to their final rest. I saw myself digging a wide hole and laying William, Anne, and the baby together, covering them over and saying quiet words of respect. I saw myself planting flowers, maybe lavender.

A cool breeze blew across my back, startling me. I spun around, half expecting to see Anne's ghostly form behind me, but all I saw was my empty room.

And my open wardrobe.

I looked around my room with a mild sense of fear. Had Paul come back up and rifled through my things? What could he have been hoping to find? I rose from the window seat and crept carefully across the room, my eyes darting side to side, half expecting someone to jump out at me. As I approached the wardrobe and peered inside, I was shocked to see the Judgement card poking out from behind the ancestry chart, just as it had been this morning.

Paul's words came back to me: *I can't leave it behind, and I can't lose it, because it follows me.* What did this mean?

I reached out slowly for the card, only this time I was almost afraid to touch it. Something was different this time.

Now *I* couldn't leave it behind. Now it was following *me*.

I swallowed hard and retrieved the card. It felt warm, almost like it was vibrating. I looked at the images, which were now so familiar to me.

The time has come. There it was, that voice, faint but unmistakable. *Her* voice. Not Anne's. The other *her*.

"What time?" I asked aloud.

Your time. I am waiting. Finish your task. It was barely more than a whisper in my head, but it rang through me like the school bell that had released me from my annual bonds just a week ago.

"My task? You mean the burial?" I awaited a response, but this time, it didn't come. If I'd been waiting for validation, though, now I had it. With renewed energy and purpose, I chugged the remainder of my lemonade, grabbed a hat and a towel, and fairly flew down the stairs, only stopping long enough to refill my water bottle. I knew I was on the right path, and I had to see this task through.

I knew it would be awhile before Gramps and Laz came back from their lunch break, but I had no intention of waiting around. Anything I was strong enough to do by myself was going to get done. We had cleared enough of the surrounding debris to begin to make out the shape of the original building, and I set myself to work trying to find and clear the doorway. What we had cleared was vaguely rectangular, and it stood to reason that the door would have generally faced the house. That narrowed it down to two sides, so I picked one and began using a garden hoe to scrape away more than 150 years of growth. After about 15 minutes, I was gratified to get my first glimpse of stone, and kept working along the side, hoping to find a break that signified the chapel entrance.

At some point in my work, Gramps and Laz had silently rejoined me and returned to hauling potentially dangerous rusty metal out of the ruins and into the scrap pile we had started. Every once in a while Gramps would stop and watch my fevered efforts, but he said nothing, and I barely noticed him. Laz, too, worked in silence, save for grunts of exertion and the occasional chugging of water.

I was grimy and sweaty, but eventually I found what I'd been seeking. The stone wall ended in one spot and picked up again four feet later. Surely this was the door! Any wood had long ago rotted, but as I dug into the earth between the two stones, I saw a piece of curved metal poking through. Could this be the handle? The shape looked about right. Without regard to the risk of tetanus, I reached down to pull it out of the dirt and inspect it.

Crying. She hears a baby crying, and her head is so foggy. Whose baby is crying? She struggles to open her eyes, struggles to wake. It's dark. And then the baby cries again, and she is aware that it's her baby. Her son.

She fights through the fog and uncloses her eyes. She's in the chapel. How did she get here? She sees a form lying a few feet from her. It's William, and it looks as though he is sleeping as well. The baby lies between them, struggling and crying, wrapped loosely in one of her shawls.

She forces herself to sit up, though it feels as though she's moving through mud. She lifts the baby and loosens her bodice so she can feed him. He quiets, content that he is finally getting what he's been demanding for who knows how long.

"William! William, wake up!" She can see that he is breathing, but he doesn't wake when she calls him. She slides her leg over and jostles him with it. "William!" He grunts, but then drifts away again.

"Laudanum," she says aloud. "They must have slipped us laudanum." She looks around the chapel, and though she is still not clear-headed, she can see that something looks amiss. The light isn't coming through the few narrow windows as it should. She cannot see the colors of the stained glass, but she can see sunlight coming from under the door. She begins to panic.

"William, you have to wake UP!" This time she kicks him as soundly as she can from this odd angle and he snorts and begins to revive.

"Wha—what? Where am I?"

"William, we're in the chapel. I think we're trapped."

There are voices coming from outside, and an irregular scraping sound she can't identify.

William drags himself up and shakes his head to clear it. He stumbles toward the door in the dim light. He tries the handle, but it won't budge, so he begins to pound. "LET US OUT!" he cries, and the voices outside quiet. The scraping grows louder. "I said, let us out!"

"You're an affront to God, the both of you," Nan hisses from outside, "and that whelp of yours is an abomination. You've dishonored the Almighty and this family in the most heinous of ways, and you must be purged from our bloodline."

Anne holds her son closer and starts to cry. William stares at the door in disbelief. He begins looking around for tools, candlesticks, anything sharp that he can use to try and make an escape, but there's nothing to be found. Nothing remains but the benches and the Bible.

"My father will never allow this!" William yells.

"Your father won't know about it until it's far too late," Robert Sheffield sneers in his deep baritone voice. "He's not the only one around here who can pass Judgement."

William pounds on the door furiously, in frustration as much as fear.

He knows now what the scraping sound is. It's the sound of a trowel as his uncle seals up the door with mortar and stone.

***

"Aria! Aria, girl, speak to me!" I came to with Gramps shaking me vigorously by the shoulders.

"Huh? I'm okay, I'm okay!" Gramps stopped shaking me, and was looking at me with great alarm. Laz handed me a my water bottle, his eyes wide. I drank down a few gulps, trying to process what I'd just experienced.

"Yeh din't look okay! Yeh yelped like you'd been bit an' gripped onta that piece o' iron, and then yeh fell down twitchin' an' mumblin'! I think yeh better stop fer today an' go sit in the cool air."

"No, no, Gramps, it wasn't a heat stroke. It was a vision. I know how William and Anne and the baby died ... and it's more horrible than we could possibly have imagined."

Chapter 18

As much as I wanted to complete the entire excavation in a day, it was just impossible to do so. By about 4:00, I was sweaty, exhausted, and sore, and Gramps, as tough as he was, had neglected all of his other duties to help me all day. Laz patted me on the shoulder before heading home.

"I have to clean up before dinner," he said, "but I'll be back here to help tomorrow. You're doing the right thing; I can feel it in my bones. Your family needs you ... not just the living ones, but the dead ones, too. Every family needs someone they can count on to do the hard things. In this family, that's you."

I was taken aback by his words. It was always hard to remember that Laz was only 14. "Uh, thanks, Laz. And thanks for helping, too. I appreciate it. This isn't even your fight."

"It is now," he answered, and he was beaming. Somehow, he seemed as determined as I was to see this through. I guess he liked feeling needed, too.

***

I showered off and made myself a sandwich, finally replacing some of the calories I'd been burning all day long. Logan was playing video games, and Paul was back, though I had no idea what he was doing, because he'd shut himself up in his room. My aunt sat at the kitchen table, reading through the diary again. I sat across from her and nibbled my sandwich while she read.

"It's such a dark story," she said at last, closing the book and setting it on the table.

"Darker than you think," I replied, and told her about the vision I'd had at the chapel. Her eyes grew wider, but for once, she didn't question my certainty about what I'd seen.

"My God," she whispered. "That's the most awful thing I've ever heard."

I nodded, not sure what else to say. I was haunted by what I'd seen, and by what had likely happened afterwards.

"I could really use some help out there tomorrow. Logan refuses to help, and Paul's mad at me—for something that's not even my fault—and Gramps and Lazaro helped me all day today. Laz said he'd be back, but I know Gramps has other responsibilities besides digging up the chapel. I feel like the clock is ticking, and we need to work faster."

Aunt Pam gave me a long look. "You're right. We should all be pitching in. This is too important for anyone to sit out. I'll handle it, and we'll all be out there with you tomorrow."

"Thanks, Aunt Pam," I replied, feeling a weight lift off my proverbial shoulders. With all of us working together, we'd be able to make twice as much progress as the three of us had today.

***

I'm not sure what she said to the boys, but they sullenly agreed to help with the work the next day. Dinner was sullen and quiet, with only a little bit of small talk interrupting the awkwardness. We cleared the table and Paul immediately made tracks toward his room. I wanted to catch him before he closed himself in again, so I chased him up the stairs.

"Paul," I panted behind him, "we need to talk."

He paused outside his bedroom door, but didn't turn around. "About what?"

"You know about what. Did you put the card back in my wardrobe for some reason?"

"Of course not," he replied, but he didn't sound surprised at my question.

"I didn't take it, I swear."

He sighed heavily and turned to face me. He didn't look angry, he looked defeated. "I know."

"Why does it keep showing up in my stuff?"

"Because," he began, but then paused, struggling for the right wording, "because it chose you. I've been *replaced*," he added bitterly.

I wasn't sure what to say. "I feel like I should apologize, but I didn't do anything to make this happen, Paul. I don't know why it's happening." I could tell he felt like he'd been robbed of something that set him apart, something that made him special, even if it was nothing but a legacy of loss and pain, and a curse that threatened to kill either him or his brother.

"You know what? Who cares!" He started to turn away, but then took a deep breath and reconsidered his anger. "Look, I know it's not your fault, it was just a connection I had with my dad, you know?" I nodded. "Truth is, I think it's because you can do what I can't. It's because you're not part of the curse."

"I just want our family to be okay."

He thought about that and nodded. "Yeah, I get it. But I don't want to talk about it anymore, okay?"

"Okay."

He stepped into his room, closing the door behind him, and left me alone in the hallway.

W e got up in the morning and were ready to go. Or we would have been, had the skies not opened up and decided to rain for most of the day. I was furious and frustrated, but there was nothing to be done. Gramps said he'd let Laz know, and we'd pick up again when it wasn't so wet out.

After checking the weather radar and confirming that today was a no-go, Aunt Pam suggested we pile into the car and head into Harrisonburg to the Farmers Market and maybe pick up some nice plants for the memorial area we planned to build for our fallen family members. It seemed like a pretty good alternative, and at least I'd feel like we were making some sort of progress. We drove down Mt. Clinton Pike in silence, listening to what Aunt Pam called "chubby rain" splatter on the windshield. We tried listening to music, but the mood in the car was just too somber for us to enjoy anything we could tune in.

It took us about half an hour to get there, but we arrived just before 11:00. Turner Pavilion was a covered open-air market which, despite the soggy weather, was bustling with many dozens of people purchasing food and a variety of organic products. Paul and Aunt Pam wandered off in search of kale and cucumbers, and Logan and I headed for the tables where a variety of plants and flowers were being sold by a woman who looked a bit like she never made it out of the 1970's.

The selection was not as varied as a big-box store, but she had the lavender I wanted, as well as daisies and a spicy-smelling plant called lantana. They were a little wild-looking, but somehow, that felt right. I was inspecting each plant, trying to make sure they weren't infested with random insects, when I got this tight feeling at the base of my neck, like the feeling you get when you know you're being watched, but multiplied times twenty.

I raised my eyes slowly, pretending to look for my aunt and elder cousin, and I scanned the crowd for anyone who seemed out of place. It didn't take long to spot a pair of people who sure didn't look like they were from Harrisonburg. About thirty feet distant from me, a pair of decidedly NOT central Virginians made an elaborate show of inspecting soy-based candles and soaps. He was a good-looking man of about 45, I guessed, with a neat, dark haircut and closely trimmed dark mustache and beard. He was wearing crisply pressed tan slacks and a designer polo-style shirt. I recognized the brand from school, with its tiny whale insignia. Way too fancy to shop for veggies and soap.

His companion, clearly half his age, was even more striking, standing shoulder-to-shoulder with him at nearly six feet tall, and with skin that seemed to absorb light and reflect that glow outward. She had black and gray microbraids trailing down to the middle of her back with tiny silver crimp beads at the tips. Wearing camouflage Zumba pants and an orange crop-top tank, she looked like she was dressed more for a fitness photo shoot than a Farmers Market. I moved around to the side of the plant table so I could face them, and it wasn't long before I caught the Fitness Queen shooting a sneaky look in my direction.

She leaned over and muttered something to Mr. Country Club and they turned and walked together to the next booth farther away, which sold organic dog biscuits. I kept an eye on them as he bought a small bag of treats for large dogs.

"What are you looking at?" Logan asked.

"You see that pair of people over there?" I used my chin to point. "I think they're watching me—or us—I'm not sure."

"Why would they be watching us?"

"I don't know. It's a gut feeling."

"Well," he replied dubiously, "your gut has been working double-time lately, so I'm not going to question it. You want to get out of here?"

"I have an idea," I said, and gestured for the proprietor to total up the plants we'd chosen. I paid her and we gathered our purchases in the large cardboard boxes she gave us. "Let's start hauling these to the car so they don't get wet since it's drizzling. We'll see if they follow."

We moved slowly, which seemed quite natural, since we were heavily laden with plants, but it really just allowed us to make a really obvious exit: easy to follow if someone were so inclined. Which they were.

I cast furtive glances behind us by pretending to turn to talk to Logan, and it was clear that they were trailing us from a distance, moving in our direction one booth and kiosk at a time.

"What do you want to do about it?" Logan asked me.

"I'm not sure. Maybe nothing, if they don't make a move. But it's really weird. I can *feel* them, even when I'm not looking at them."

"Why can't our family just be NORMAL?"

"I don't know what to tell you, bud. It is what it is."

We reached the SUV and Logan opened the door with his fob. We started loading the plants in. "So do we head back to the market or not?"

"Yeah," I replied, "I think we kind of have to. It'd look weird if we didn't." So we locked the car and headed back, all the while keeping our eyes peeled for our new "friends".

We didn't see them upon our return, so we went to collect Paul and Aunt Pam, who we found checking out with several insulated cooler bags of fresh produce. As we made our way back to the car, I told them about the strange pair who'd been watching us.

"Aria, I'm not saying you're wrong, because you've been right about a lot lately, but it would be prudent to at least entertain the possibility that you might be a little on-edge with all that's happening. Maybe they're just tourists who stopped through for lunch." Aunt Pam darted a glance at me in the rearview mirror and Paul turned around to look intently at the traffic behind us.

"Yeah, maybe," I grumbled, but I wasn't convinced.

***

One of the great things about living in a college town is that there are literally 100 places to eat, and nearly every kind of food you can imagine. And we were all about ready to do some stress eating. We cut across on Market Street and targeted a Japanese steak house where we could eat ourselves into a coma.

We sat in the cool, dim light of the restaurant, sipping our drinks and waiting for the signature ginger salad and clear soup that precedes every meal at this kind of restaurant. There were a significant number of people here even at lunchtime, probably because it was so close to the interstate. I was a little salty at the fact that Aunt Pam had seemed to dismiss my concerns about the strange duo we had seen earlier. Rationally, I knew she was probably right, but my gut told me there was more to it than the obvious.

Paul and Logan were making small talk about college life, since Logan would be starting at James Madison in the fall. He'd decided to live at home and commute for his freshman year, and as Paul ribbed him about being a mama's boy, my attention was drawn away from their banter by a gnawing feeling that I had left something in the car. *The Judgement card ... I'd left it in the car. But wait, I hadn't brought it along, had I?* I didn't remember taking it out of my wardrobe, and yet I couldn't shake the feeling that it was in the car, and that I should immediately go and get it.

"Aunt Pam, can I borrow your keys for a minute? I think I left something in the car."

She looked at me curiously, then fished her fob out of her purse and handed it over. "Don't forget to re-lock it."

I nodded and slipped away from the table and out of the restaurant. The car was around the side of the building, and as soon as I was within sight of it, I hit the "unlock" button on the remote. I whipped the back door open and began looking through the seat pockets where I'd been sitting, but there was no card, only an umbrella and a first-aid kit.

"Looking for something, sis?" came a velvety British voice from behind me.

I started and looked over my shoulder. The Fitness Queen from the market was standing over me, smiling a strange mix of amusement and intimidation. My heart thudded in my chest, but I stood and looked up at her.

"Who are you, and why are you following me?"

She chuckled. "Well, for the first part, my name's Zora. That's probably all you need to know about me for now. But I think you know the answer to the second part."

"Let's pretend I don't," I replied, unwilling to give voice to what I suspected.

"Zora, dear, don't tease your sister." The man in the expensive casual-wear came around the rear of the car and joined his companion. "Hello, Aria. My name is Dorian Blair. Perhaps you've heard my name mentioned in your family?" His voice carried the same accent as hers, though he spoke more slowly and crisply.

I shook my head, aware that I was cornered and almost certainly out-matched.

"Ah, well, no matter. I might have thought it would come up at some point, but that's not why we've come to speak with you. You've had a rather eventful summer so far, haven't you?"

"What do you know about me, or my summer?" I tried to sound brave, defiant. But the fact that they seemed to know quite a lot frightened me.

Zora stepped aside slightly and Dorian came closer. "I know all about you, my girl. I know about the cards, for instance." Here he paused and watched for my reaction. "It's changed to your hands by now, I take it?"

I had no idea what to say. A few weeks ago, no one in our household knew about the cards except Paul. Now some stranger was targeting me with questions about it in a parking lot.

"What did Paul tell you?"

At this, Zora and Dorian both laughed. "Do you think yours is the only one? Cards come in a deck." Dorian's cloud-gray eyes twinkled with amusement, and I could tell that there was, indeed, a powerful storm behind them.

"You ... have a card?"

"Cards, love," Zora replied. "I'm Strength. He's the Magician. And you, I believe, are now Judgement. How did your cousin react to that?"

I was increasingly uncomfortable with their familiarity. "What do you know about us?" I demanded, "and why are you hassling me?"

"Now, now, my girl, don't be impolite. We weren't sure how many of your family members were aware of your ... unique situation. It wouldn't be prudent to go chattering about such things in front of your entire family if they weren't aware of their magical heritage, now would it?" Wait. Back up a minute. Sis? *Sister?* Because we both had cards? Paul had mentioned that there were several magical families. What had I been pulled into?

I hated that he was making logical sense. "I suppose not."

"There, now," Dorian continued smoothly, "we simply wanted to introduce ourselves. All of this must be overwhelming for you just now. But you'll want our support soon enough, and we'll be waiting." He handed me a black business card printed with even blacker ink. It displayed a phone number and a strange symbol.

"We'll be seeing you around, sis," Zora smirked, and they turned and walked away.

Chapter 19

Logan met me at the door as I was heading back into the restaurant.

"What the heck did you go out there to get? And what took you so long? I was getting worried!"

"Actually," I began, not sure how much to tell him, "I don't think I needed to get anything. Guess who met me at the car?"

"Who?"

"Those people from the market. Turns out they were looking for me after all. They know about the cards."

Logan's eyes grew wide. "They what?"

"Yeah, I think we need to have a serious family chat in the car after lunch."

"After lunch?"

"Yeah, I don't think this is the kind of conversation you have at a table when two other families are within earshot, you know?"

"Oh, right. I see your point."

"Besides, I'm not sure what to make of it yet, and I'll think better after I've had my stir fry."

***

An hour later, we were on the road heading back home, and Aunt Pam was lamenting having left the plants in the car at midday.

"Honestly, I thought that since it was rainy and we parked in the shade, it wouldn't be quite so bad, and there was nothing we could do about it because the Farmers Market closes at 1:00 ..."

"Aunt Pam?"

"... and it's so gray out that it wasn't even that hot outside ..."

"Aunt Pam."

"... and now the car smells like wet soil and lavender ..."

"Aunt Pam!"

"What, Aria?"

"I need to tell you guys something. I couldn't talk about it in the restaurant, but now that we're in private, there's something you need to know."

Paul was sitting in the front passenger seat and turned to face me as best he could. "What is the big deal?" He was trying to sound flippant, but I could tell that he was concerned.

"So, you know how I mentioned that I felt like those people were following us at the Farmers Market?"

"Yeah."

"Well, they were. They were following me. And they cornered me at the car when I went out to the parking lot at lunch."

"They WHAT?" Aunt Pam jerked the wheel a little.

"Don't wreck us. I've had enough of that for one summer, thanks. But yeah, they were waiting for me to come out. They just wanted to talk to me, they said."

"How did they know you'd come out to the car?" Paul asked.

"I'm not sure about this, but I think one of them maybe put the idea in my head that I left something in the car."

He raised one eyebrow and looked at me like I was losing my mind.

"I know how it sounds. But they know about the cards. And they have cards, too. Different ones."

That got his attention. "What did they say?"

"Well, not a lot, really. They introduced themselves, for starters. Her name is Zora, and his name is Dorian Blair."

"Dorian Blair?" Aunt Pam gripped the wheel tightly.

"Yeah, do you know him?"

Her jaw tightened slightly. "I might have heard the name."

"He actually mentioned that. That I might have heard of him. Why is that? Who is he?"

"I'm not sure," she said cryptically. "Go on with your story."

"Anyway, they said that she was Strength and he was the Magician. And that they knew that I was Judgement now." I looked sympathetically at Paul. His face darkened, but he didn't comment. "They said I'd want their support, and they gave me this card. They were both British, I think. I think it's a good bet that she's the one who's been calling Paul."

I handed the card to Paul so he could look at it. "Do you know what this symbol is?" he asked. I shook my head. "It's the symbol for Mercury."

"The god?" Logan chimed in.

"No, well, sort of. More the planet, I think. It was in this book I read on tarot."

"So kind of like the Judgement card is represented by the Libra symbol? Maybe that's the sign for the Magician?" I was on the edge of understanding something, I just knew it, but I couldn't quite work it out.

"Yeah, maybe." He handed the business card back to me. "You think one of them put an idea in your head?"

"I think so. I was sitting there at the table, and I got this idea in my head that I'd left the Judgement card here in the car. I knew I hadn't brought it, but I felt like I had to come and check."

"That's one heck of an ability for someone to have," Logan commented. "It's scary that someone can get in your head and make you do something or believe something."

We pulled into our driveway. "I hadn't really thought about it that way. But you're right," I said. "Look, I don't want to think about it right now. Let's get these plants outside and us inside before it starts raining again."

We lugged everything over toward the shed where Gramps kept his equipment, then brushed ourselves off and headed inside. Paul had headed upstairs, and Aunt Pam was in the kitchen putting away the veggies she'd bought and trying not to look at me.

"Aunt Pam," I began as Logan and I sat down at the counter, "who is Dorian Blair? I could tell you recognized his name."

She stood with her back to me and stared into the refrigerator with a head of broccoli in her hand. "It's a name I hadn't heard in a long time. Not since before you were born. I think he's someone your mother used to know."

I could tell that she didn't want me to keep asking questions, and that made me afraid of the answers. But there was some connection between this man and me, and I needed to know what it was. "Used to know HOW?"

"I'm not really sure how they met. It was a long time ago. I think she knew him in college, maybe. She brought him here once. Your uncle and I had been married for maybe five years at that point. I was pregnant with Logan at the time."

"Brought him here? Like they were dating?"

"If he's the same person I remember, yes. I don't know that I ever knew his last name. But he was English, and your mother was rather smitten with him, as I recall. He was quite charming."

The words were pleasant enough, but there was something underneath her voice that told me there was more to the story. "What aren't you telling me?"

She finished putting the vegetables in the fridge and closed the door. Slowly, she turned to face me. "I can't really put my finger on it now, and I couldn't then either. He seemed very nice, and was lovely to your mother.

He was polite enough to us, too. But there was something about the way he looked at Paul that made me nervous, and he asked a lot of questions about my pregnancy, which also made me uncomfortable. He didn't say or do anything wrong. It was just a feeling."

"Did my mom date him for a long time?"

"Well, I don't know exactly how long, because she wasn't living here, you know. She was working on her Masters and living in Santa Fe at the time. But I only met him that once. The next time I saw her, she and your dad had fallen madly in love, run off to Vegas and gotten married, and she was pregnant with you."

"So I guess it couldn't have been that serious, right? If you only met him once? So why is he popping back up? Did my mom know about the Judgement card?"

"I really couldn't say. I didn't know about it, so I don't know if she did. I'm sorry I don't have more to tell you."

I heard the rain start to splatter against the windows, and I had the random thought that I was glad the new plants would be getting a little water. My aunt was right; she wasn't going to have any more answers to my questions. Only one person had those answers, and the cloak-and-dagger way he went about introducing himself made me highly suspicious of his motives.

"I guess I'm going to go upstairs for a while. This has been a weird day." I started up to my room, and Logan was close at my heels. A part of me wanted to be alone to think, but the bigger part of me needed to give a voice to the thoughts knocking around in my brain, so I let him follow. We sat down opposite each other in the window seat and stared out at the rain.

"What's going on in your head?" he asked.

"I don't know if Paul already told you this," I began, "but the Judgement card isn't Paul's anymore. It's mine now."

"He told me."

"And I know he's not happy about it, but I think it had to switch hands because your bloodline can't break this curse, but mine can. And after that, I don't know what it means. Maybe nothing. But then there's this whole thing with Dorian Blair. He has a card, too. And so does that girl who's with him. And they know the card is mine now."

"How could they have known that?"

"I asked myself the same question. When I first noticed them at the market today, I felt something first. Kind of like when you know you're being watched, but stronger. Maybe people who have these cards can feel each other somehow."

"So what now? Are you going to call him?"

I hesitated. "I don't know. I feel like I'm not getting the whole picture with him. Like there's something sinister under that smooth surface. Like I shouldn't trust him. But at the same time, he seems to have a lot of knowledge about the cards, and I have a lot to learn. But I feel weird about him."

"Then you probably shouldn't call."

"Yeah, but no one else can shed light on what it means to hold a cards. I have questions."

"Like what?"

"Like how do the cards work? What does the Judgement card do? How did he know that our family had one?" I couldn't share the question that was nagging at me the most. I was afraid of the implications, even if I only said it to Logan.

Why had he referred to Zora as my sister?

***

Something about all of this wasn't sitting right. I felt strongly that Aunt Pam knew more than she was telling me. I wasn't sure how I knew it, but I did. After Logan left, I opened the wardrobe and stared at the ancestry chart. There was no mention of the last name Blair anywhere on the sheet. I pulled it off the back of the wardrobe and spread it out on my bed and laid the Judgement card next to it. After staring for a moment, I grabbed a pencil from my desk and drew a tiny Libra symbol next to my name.

As I examined my own tiny section of the family tree, I noticed something I hadn't before. When I looked at my cousins' family, a line connected Aunt Pam and Uncle MJ, and then a line dropped down from the center of that connection and split into a bracket with Paul and Logan listed on either side. When I looked at my own family, my parents had a similar line connecting them, but the line that dropped down to my name didn't come from the bar between their names. It dropped down directly from my mother's name.

The realization of what that meant hit me like a truck. The man I had known as my father was not, in fact, my biological father. And worse yet, other members of my family had known that was the case, and had kept that information from me. If it was noted here on the chart, then Uncle MJ certainly had known. And if he knew, probably so did Aunt Pam.

She had stood there in the kitchen with this knowledge and hadn't told me, even when I asked about Dorian Blair. The way I saw it, that was basically lying by omission. The sadness in my heart grew into rage. Nothing was as it seemed in this family! Hadn't I already lost enough?

I whipped out my cell phone and fished out the card with Blair's phone number. Did I really want to call this man, this *stranger*, who might well be my father? I stared at his number until my eyes began to blur with the tears that were threatening to fall.

How could they do this to me?

Slowly, I dialed the number on the card. Blair picked up on the second ring.

"Aria, dear. That didn't take long at all."

I tried to choke as much emotion as I could out of my voice.

"Are you my father?" It was an unwise question, I knew. I could feel in my gut that it wasn't a good idea to trust this man, even if we did share common genetics.

"Well, well. This is unexpected," he sounded pleased, and I wasn't sure that was a good thing. "I take it you've had a rather awkward conversation with your aunt?" When I didn't answer, he continued, "I imagine this must be a very difficult revelation for you. My guess would be that you never knew that Steven Rush wasn't your biological father, probably never even suspected it, since you're nearly the spitting image of your mother, God rest her soul."

"And that girl, Zora, she's my sister?"

"Well, half sister, technically, but yes, I have several children. You have quite a few brothers and sisters, my girl. You don't have to feel alone anymore; you have an entire family waiting for you."

"And our whole family has cards?"

"That's a much longer conversation, I'm afraid. Why don't we get to-gether? I'd be happy to come pick you up and answer all of your questions." My gut twisted. He wasn't being entirely honest with me, I could tell. I stared at the Judgement card. I could feel the danger lurking beneath his smooth and comforting words.

"I don't think that's a good idea right now. We've got a lot going on around here."

"Is there any way I can help? I do have a rather unique set of skills, as does Zora." He seemed really sincere, but the issues I was dealing with at this exact moment were Sheffield family business.

"Thanks, but I don't think so."

"Well, the offer stands, my girl. People like us need to stick together. We can accomplish so much when we set our minds to it."

"Can I call you if I have questions?"

"Of course. I know this is terribly awkward and probably also very emotional for you. I won't presume to just swoop in and take over your life. But just know that I am here, and I very much want to get to know you. And I want you to get to know your siblings and me."

"Thanks. I'll be in touch." I hung up the phone, feeling very conflicted. I wasn't sure I was ready to confront my aunt with what I knew, and I also wasn't ready to trust this total stranger who just so happened to maybe be my biological father. It was all too much.

Chapter 20

T he next day was another yucky weather day. I didn't want to talk to my aunt, because I felt like I would lose my temper with her. I didn't want to talk to my cousins, because I wasn't ready to share what I'd learned, and besides, I was really rotten company at the moment. I was stuck in the house and cranky.

I passed the time streaming mindless teen dramas on my computer, a favorite pastime at school that I hadn't had much time for during this upheaval of a summer. It was early afternoon when my phone rang. I didn't recognize the number, but I really felt like I should answer.

"Hello?"

"Hey, there, sis. Hope you don't mind me ringing you." Zora's voice was calm, friendly.

"Actually, I don't mind. You're probably the only person I'm willing to talk to right now."

"Good I called then. Dad said you might have some questions. He said you seemed upset. Thought I'd reach out and see how you were getting on."

"I appreciate that. I'm having some pretty major trust issues right now."

"I get that. You live with your aunt, yeah?"

"Yeah. Since I was 10."

"You said trust issues ..." She was clearly fishing for more details, but somehow, I didn't mind.

"She knew that Blair was my father, and she didn't ever tell me. I mean, my mother obviously knew, too, but I can't exactly be mad at her, because I was just a kid, you know? And my cousins might have known, too, right? It might have come up at some point ... some little family drama? I feel like they've been lying to me my whole life."

"And now that the cards has passed to you, they might be jealous as well, might feel like you don't deserve it. Like you're not a REAL member of the family."

"I never really thought about it that way, but now that you mention it, there just might be some of that, too. Certainly with Paul."

"Why don't you come hang with us for a little while? It's only the beginning of the summer. You could learn about your gifts, learn how to use them, you know?"

"I ... can't right now. There's some stuff I've got to do first." I strongly felt like I shouldn't tell her about the curse, but the temptation to go stay with her and Blair was strong.

"He really could use your help, if I'm honest. He's trying to bring all us kids together. I think he really feels like he wants a family around him, like he might have missed out on something."

"Really?" I felt like she meant it, but somehow it didn't sound right to me.

"Family's gotta be there for each other, am I right? Who else can you trust?"

"I'm the wrong person to ask right now."

I heard her mumble something unintelligible, and then she said, "Dad wants to talk to you. Here. Listen to what he has to say."

There was a pause as she handed the phone over. "Did I hear Zora offer for you to come stay with us for a while?"

Um, awkward. "Yes. She didn't ask you first?'

"No, but I think it's a marvelous idea. We have so much to discuss, and you have so much to learn."

"Well the thing is, I can't right now. I have ... unfinished business."

"How long do you think it will take? I think the idea of you coming to visit us is very exciting, and I do have a window right now where I don't have many other obligations. And there's so much you could learn! I think it's significant that Judgement was quiet for so long, and now it's becoming active again! It can't be a coincidence! Surely, there's an element of fate here, don't you think?" His insistence was freaking me out a little bit, to be honest.

"I can't just take off right now. My family needs me."

"Indeed we do."

"Look, I'm not against getting to know you, but now's just not a good time."

He paused, and I got the impression that Dorian Blair didn't get refused very often. "We both know you'll end up joining me sooner or later, my girl. Why wait?"

Something about the way he said *my girl* angered me. Until a few hours ago, I hadn't even known he existed. I wasn't *his* girl. In fact, it was becoming abundantly clear to me that I wasn't *anyone's* girl.

"Yeah, I don't think so. Not right now. But I'll call you again at some point." And before he could register his dislike of that response, I hung up the phone. A moment later, a text came through:

That was a rather rude way to end the conversation. I'll be coming by your house shortly so we can discuss this matter further. I'd advise you to meet me at the end of the driveway in an hour.

The message felt like a threat, though a threat of what, or to what end, I wasn't sure. What I did know is that I was furious with pretty much everyone right now, and I frankly didn't want to deal with any of them.

***

Though it was late afternoon and the heat of the day, and a rainy, muggy day at that, I needed to get out of the house and away from everyone. I packed a hiking bag, including my EMF meter, an umbrella, and the Judgement card.

I stopped in the kitchen to fill a water bottle and grab some fruit. I also grabbed a plastic sandwich bag, just to make sure the cards wouldn't get damaged if it started to rain. Then I scribbled an angry note to my aunt:

I know about Blair being my father. I know you knew and didn't tell me. I'm taking off for a while. I don't know who I can trust anymore.

I knew it sounded petulant. I knew it would make her worry. And I didn't care.

I also had no intention of meeting Blair as he had insisted. Who the heck did he think he was? Showing up out of the blue and making demands? No way. Not happening.

I headed out the back door and made sure to slam it heavily. Then I grabbed my bike out of the garage and pedaled down the driveway and out to the main road. I wanted to go somewhere that wasn't too far away, but also somewhere no one would think to look for me. Just past Laz's family's property, there were some thick woods off of Fort Lynn Road, and I decided that was my destination. Yeah, technically I would be trespassing, but when we were younger, Logan and I had hung out with the Danning twins, whose property abutted those woods, so I figured I could talk my way out of trouble if I needed to. I seemed to remember that the twins had wedged a platform in the crotch of a tree and nailed up some boards to create a makeshift ladder. That seemed like a good place to disappear and reexamine my life for the rest of the day.

Once I got to a relatively dense part of the woods, I pulled off the road and slid my bike under the barbed wire perimeter of the property. Then I pulled the two middle wires apart from each other and slipped through. Barbed wire is good for containing livestock, not so good for keeping out determined trespassers.

I pulled my bike into the woods so it couldn't be seen from the street, and skirted the edge of the woods just inside the treeline until I made it onto the Dannings' property. From there, it took a little trekking and backtracking, but eventually, I found the "treehouse" and climbed up to the platform to think. I wondered how long it would take my aunt to realize I was gone. I wondered what would happen when I ignored Blair's invitation. I wondered what would happen whenever I went home. I wondered how this would change my life.

I also wondered a lot about the cards ... not just Judgement, but the others, too. I didn't even know what Judgement's powers were, much less those of the rest of them. I pulled out my phone and looked up the meanings of tarot cards, starting with my own. I read a handful of different sites and came up with a common thread: the Judgement card was about reaping what you sow. It represented good coming back for the good you put out, but it also represented a reckoning if you'd done wrong. It represented karma. That seemed to make a lot of sense, and it occurred to me that the interpretation definitely fit in with the Sheffield curse.

Daniel Sheffield had been the holder of the card, and then the card traded hands to Robert's line, and with it came the curse. Pieces clicked into place. The curse began when Robert and his mother had killed William and Anne, when they had cut off Daniel's branch of the family tree, killing his child and his grandchild. And thereafter, all but one of the children in Robert's line were marked for death, leaving only one to each generation to bear the curse forward. Robert had killed Daniel's progeny, and his own progeny would pay for it for centuries.

My phone buzzed. It was Aunt Pam.

I got your note. Where are you? Let's talk.

I promptly ignored her message. Instead I left her on read, popped in some earbuds and put on some music. Several minutes later, it buzzed again. This time it was Logan.

Mom's freaking out. Where RU?

I considered answering, but then decided against it, because if I didn't respond, then he wouldn't have to lie to his mother about hearing from me. *Buzz buzz.*

It's unfortunate that you've ignored my invitation. Now I'll have to decide what to do about that.

Oof. That sounded ominous, but frankly, I didn't care much. Honestly, the petty side of me was deeply enjoying all these people trying to get ahold of me and having no idea where I was. *Buzz buzz.*

Ree, I'm not kidding. Mom's doing that phone search thing, and is coming looking 4 U. I'm coming w/ her. WTH is going on?

Ah, so she hadn't told him about Blair being my father. *Interesting.* *Buzz buzz.*

That weird guy from the FM is parked at the end of the driveway. We just drove past him. ANSWER ME. R U OK?

Okay, now I was pushing it too far. I didn't want Logan to be worried … not much, anyway. So I texted back.

I'm fine. I don't want to see your mother right now. She knows why.

UR being a jerk.

I have a good reason. Just ask her.

There was a pause before he responded.

UR right, it's messed up. But where RU? This guy is following us. Think he's looking 4 U 2.

Wait, what? *He's following you?*

Logan didn't answer.

I waited another minute or so. If this was payback for making him worry, I was going to kick his butt.

LOGAN, ANSWER.

Buzz buzz.

Your cousin is my guest for the time being. I've called 911 for your aunt. Text me when you've recovered your manners.

BLAIR. What had he done? I scrambled out of the tree and ran for my bike, this time heading directly for the Dannings' driveway rather than trying to navigate the fence again. If they saw me, I'd just have to deal with it later. I pedaled as fast as I could manage down Fort Lynn Road. Up ahead, I saw a flashing light, and it took a moment to register in my brain that it was my aunt's SUV nose-down in the ditch.

With a cry of despair, I leapt off my bike and threw it aside as soon as I was close to the wreckage. It certainly wasn't the worst accident I'd ever seen—the one Logan and I had been in at the beginning of the summer was far worse—but Aunt Pam lay slumped over the steering wheel and the remains of the airbag. I rushed to the driver's door and tried to pull it open, but it was locked.

Twilight was falling, and I hoped it wouldn't take the paramedics too long to get here. I went around to the passenger side of the car, where Logan's door hung open. What kind of strength must they have had to make my weight-lifting athlete of a cousin go with them? I hoped he was okay.

"Aunt Pam," I climbed into the seat and shook her arm gently, just in case anything was broken.

She groaned, and I exhaled heavily in relief. She leaned back in her seat and raised her arm to her bleeding brow. I fished a wad of fast-food napkins out of the glove compartment and dabbed at the blood. The cut wasn't as bad as it looked, but it also looked like her nose might be broken. "The paramedics are on their way," I told her, and hoped it was true. I wondered if maybe I should call again in case Blair had been lying, but then I heard sirens approaching.

"Aria," she mumbled, "it was Dorian. He ran us off the road. I'm sorry I didn't tell you about him ..."

"It's okay; don't worry about that now."

"Where's Logan?"

"He's okay; he's with Blair."

"He's WHAT? Ow!" She grabbed her side in pain.

"He's with Blair. It'll be okay. Nothing will happen to him. I promise. I won't let it."

"You don't understand. That's why your mom never wanted you to know about Dorian. He's ... he's not a good man."

"Yeah, I've figured that out. The ambulance is here. Just hang in there. They'll take care of you."

The EMTs filed out of the ambulance and set to work moving my aunt onto a gurney for transport to the Sentara South Medical Center. While they were loading her into the ambulance, I loaded my bike into the back of the SUV and locked it up. I climbed into the ambulance next to my aunt and watched the paramedics do their work. Her injuries appeared not to be too serious, thankfully. That didn't change the fact that I would find a way to make Blair pay. Father or no, he wasn't my family. What was left of my family was the three people at Sheffield Glen who had cared for me since I was ten. And this man was a threat to them. I called Paul from the ambulance, and he said he'd meet us at the hospital.

Paul was true to his word, and got to the hospital only ten minutes after we did. He called the car insurance company and had the SUV towed back to the house until we could figure out where we wanted to take it for repairs.

I sat in a chair beside my aunt's exam bed while doctors and nurses poked and prodded her, realigned her nose, took her insurance information, gave her pain meds, and finally told us we could go home. Even in the time in between all the staff's comings and goings, I couldn't bring myself to say anything. It was all too much. And I felt like it was all my fault.

By the time we piled into Paul's truck to go home, it was dark. I was the first to break the silence.

"I'm sorry."

"No, I'm sorry," my aunt replied. "I know I should have told you about Dorian when you first brought him up. But your mother had chosen not to tell you, and I never thought I'd have that conversation with you. I wasn't prepared. I didn't know what I should tell you. What I should NOT have done is deceive you."

I nodded. "I guess we both screwed up."

"I guess we did. But now we have a bigger problem. This guy has Logan."

"He doesn't want Logan. He wants me."

"That is also not acceptable. I'm calling the police."

"Let me see what he wants first," I urged. "We might be able to solve this peacefully. I know he wants something from me, I just don't know what."

Paul spoke up. "If he's willing to run Mom and Logan off the road so he can kidnap Logan, I think it's fair to say his intentions aren't honorable."

"I'm sure you're right about that," I said, "but involving the police might trigger him to hurt Logan. This isn't a normal person we're dealing with. He can make people think things, believe things. It's connected to his abilities as the Magician, I think. But he's more dangerous than some crackpot. And I don't even know what Zora can do."

Despite her obvious reservations, Aunt Pam nodded and relented.

"All right. Talk to him. But if we don't like what he has to say, we call the cops. Agreed?"

"Agreed."

Chapter 21

A good night's sleep was definitely in order, and for once, I was happy to sleep in the same room with everyone.

Everyone but Logan. Neither Blair nor Zora had responded to my repeated attempts to reach them. It was obvious they wanted me to "sweat it out" a little and think about my choices. I would have been frantic if I hadn't felt, down to my very core, that they wouldn't hurt Logan for now. They just wanted to throw me off balance, and it was working.

I couldn't believe that Aunt Pam and Paul had not chastised me for running off and thereby leaving my family vulnerable. I certainly felt responsible, and maybe they knew they couldn't possibly punish me more than I was punishing myself.

The next morning at breakfast, Paul announced that he had to take off for a day or two in order to get a couple of things we needed for finally laying our ancestors to rest. I didn't like the idea of him taking off, and neither did Aunt Pam, but he insisted that his errand was critical. As he was heading for his truck, I caught him outside the garage.

"Hey, Paul, can you at least tell me what's so important? I think it's a really bad idea for you to take off when we don't even know where you're going. What if Blair comes for you, too?"

He took a deep breath, trying to decide how much of his plan to reveal. At last, he looked me in the eye. "So listen, I've known for a while that there are other people and other cards who might be in play. I guess you need to know all this. I don't think anything's going to happen to me, but I'm going to share this with you just in case."

I didn't like how he said *just in case.*

"There's a monastery not too far from here, and there's someone there I need to see. I need to tell him what's happened, and who knows, maybe he can even help us. He doesn't ever use or check his phone, so it would be faster if I just go talk to him. I wouldn't do it if I didn't think it was important."

"This guy is another card holder?"

"Yeah," Paul continued. "The cards, and the people for that matter, are called Arcana. He's one of them, and he knew my dad back in the day. He told me that one day, I'd need to come see him, that I'd need his power when I lost my own. I think that time is now."

I had to agree. "So which card is he?"

He paused. "Death."

"Wait, what?" I asked, taken aback.

"It's not what you're thinking. He's not some homicidal maniac or something. But he knows things. And I think he saw some of this coming. I'll be in touch. See you in a day or two. Blair isn't going to hurt Logan, because he wants something from you. Don't do anything stupid."

And with that, he climbed into the driver's seat and backed out, made a messy three-point turn, and headed down the driveway.

He seemed pretty sure that Logan was at least relatively safe longer term, but I didn't share his uncharacteristic optimism. I went back inside and climbed the stairs to my room, determined to do whatever I had to in order to free Logan and set things right. I took a deep breath and dialed Blair's number. Again.

"It took longer than I expected for you to call, my girl. I was beginning to fear that you'd given up on your cousin here."

"First of all, you know very well that I've been trying to reach you since last night. Secondly, I need some proof that Logan is okay. Let me talk to him."

"Oh, I'm afraid he can't talk right now, but I can show him to you. Hold on." There was a pause and I heard the artificial camera shutter sound from a cell phone camera. A moment later, my phone buzzed, and when I pulled the phone away to look, I was greeted with a picture of Logan sitting in a chair, staring off into space.

"What's wrong with him?" I demanded.

"Nothing at all. He's merely ... daydreaming, I suppose. He's utterly unaware of where he is, nor does he realize he's in any danger whatsoever."

"What did you do to him?"

"Surely it hasn't escaped your notice that I have certain skills when it comes to people's thoughts. Well, let's just say that young Logan here feels as though he's intently watching a very important movie. It would certainly be a shame if he got any more ... dangerous ... ideas into his head."

"Enough with the threats, already. What do you want from me?"

"Ah, cutting to the chase. I approve. What I want is your loyalty. It became pretty apparent that I wasn't going to get it by winning your affection, but fear is equally motivational, I find."

"Loyalty for what?"

"For now, let's just say that your unique skillset as Judgement will be quite valuable to me."

I saw an opportunity, and decided to gamble. "I don't have all the powers of Judgment yet, FYI. I don't even know what they are yet."

He pondered that for a moment. "I do know that your cousins' bloodline was suffering from diminished powers, mostly likely from a magical blockage of some sort. I was rather hoping when the cards transferred itself to you that the curse, if that's what it is, wouldn't follow. That does present some difficulties."

"How do you know about the magical troubles in my family?"

"I know a great many things, my dear. All the more reason why you shouldn't toy with me."

His knowledge of my family was unsettling, but I had to buy some time, and maybe safety for Logan. "I'm pretty sure we've figured out how to break the curse, but we need Logan here to do it.

His voice was thick with skepticism. "Oh, do you now? How convenient for Logan."

I concentrated on feeling very sincere about what I was saying. I mean, it might even have been true. "You don't understand. I have to have ALL of Robert Sheffield's descendants present in order to break it. It won't work otherwise."

He considered that, and I felt like he was also trying to evaluate if I was lying or not.

"I'll consider what you've said and call you back with my terms," he said in a clipped tone, and then hung up without waiting for my response.

I went inside and reported my conversation to Aunt Pam. She agreed to wait a bit longer on calling the police, and I sent a message to Paul as well. He didn't respond, but I didn't really expect him to, since he was driving.

***

Since there wasn't anything more I could really do, I put my phone in my pocket and went out to the chapel to continue working, but I was having a hard time being motivated. I hadn't really made all that much progress when my phone rang with Blair on the other end.

"My gut tells me this may be a well-played gambit on your part, my girl," he began, "but I also sense there may be some truth to what you say. So here are my terms. I will return your cousin so you can do what you must in order to break your family curse. But then you will come with me so I can train you properly with your abilities. You cannot tell them in advance that you are leaving, as they would certainly try to stop you. You will simply pack a bag, slip out of the house, and leave with Zora and me. Step out of your old life into a new one. A better one, though I doubt you'll believe that just yet."

"You mean leave them? Like really leave and never come back? Never even talk to them again?"

He chuckled. "Nothing so drastic as that. I'm sure you could talk to them again eventually. After you've been trained, of course. And, naturally, should you back out of our deal, your family might develop some fairly ... self-destructive ... behaviors."

A chill ran down my spine at the implication of what he was saying. "So why don't you just force me to come with you?"

"Very clever, yes. I'd thought of that, of course, but I'm afraid that wouldn't work. Being a member of the Arcana gives you at least limited resistance to my *suggestions*, unfortunately. Terribly inconvenient, but there you have it."

"How frustrating for you."

He chuckled again. "Indeed. But we find work-arounds for these little problems. Sadly, it does occasionally require me to be a bit more ruthless than I'd like, but it's all for the greater good, as you'll see once you are with us."

"Us?"

"Well, as I told you, you do have a few siblings."

"And they're all with you? Like Zora?"

"It's a work in progress. These things take time. And while I'd love to continue this little chat, I do have a pressing matter which requires my attention. I'll return your cousin to you within the next 24 hours. Remember our arrangement."

I didn't recall actually agreeing to the *arrangement*.

"Ah, but you don't really have a choice, do you?" And then he hung up.

Holy craptoast. He read my mind.

I lay down on the grass and stared up at the sky. "What am I supposed to do?" I whined to no one in particular. There was no *right* thing to do here, and it seemed like (at least for me) every outcome was a negative one. It just didn't seem fair.

I turned my head toward the house that had been my home for the past five years, and for half a dozen summers before my parents died. The thought of leaving and potentially never coming back filled me with sadness. I looked up at my big window on the top floor, the one that had been put in just for me, the one where I spent so much time. And something moved. Someone was there.

It wasn't like Aunt Pam to go into my room, and with the way things had been lately, it was just as likely to be a spectral ancestor as a living one. I hopped up and headed into the house to find out.

I passed Aunt Pam in the kitchen on my way up, so I was pretty sure my instincts had been correct. I was strangely excited. Was Anne waiting for me with some important message, or perhaps the myling was growing impatient. Either way, it was something I'd rather focus on than the danger my cousin and my freedom were both in.

When I entered my room, there was a chill in the air, as I had expected, but I didn't see anyone. What I did see was that the Judgement card was lying on my bed where I'd left it.

"Okay, you have my attention," I said aloud. "I'm here. Tell me what you want." Was that rude? It sounded rude. I walked over to the card and picked it up, and as I did so, a faint breeze blew past me. I sat on the edge of the bed and held the card between my hands. *I'm listening,* I thought. I slowed my breathing and concentrated on the card. Maybe the mystery woman whose voice I had heard had some advice for me.

I tried to focus only on my breath, the way they'd taught us to do in the exactly three yoga classes I'd ever been to. I pictured the air coming in through the bottoms of my feet, rising through my body, and reaching the crown of my head; then I pictured it following the same pathway in reverse as I exhaled. I'd been doing that for maybe a minute when my mind began to wander, brushing on several of the things plaguing my mind: Logan, Blair, the cards, my ancestors. I imagined myself standing by the chapel ruins, not the half-excavated mess they were now, but the grassy mounds they had been a week ago.

As I watch, time seems to reverse itself, and I see the vegetation slowly fade away, and the walls of the small building repair themselves until the building I'd seen in my dreams is standing before me. The door is open, so I walk in.

A single person awaits me inside, sitting in the front pew. At first, I think it's Logan, but then he stands to face me, and I know that I am looking at William Sheffield.

"So you are the new Judgement?" he asks me.

I nod. "Sort of. My name is Aria."

"Welcome, Aria. I bring you a message from my father."

"From Daniel Sheffield?" This is unexpected.

"Yes. He was Judgement long before you, as I was meant to be. But he no longer resides on this plane of existence, so it is up to me to tell you what he needs you to know."

"Why haven't I seen your spirit before? I've seen Anne's ... and your son's."

His eyes grow sad. "I am bound to this ethereal plane, and also this physical place, but I cannot roam as they do. I am little more than a watcher, and what I can see is limited to the magical tapestry of fibers that weave into the lineage of Judgement. I can hear my father's voice from time to time, but I cannot ascend to be with him while his blood curse still stains our family. They are lost and wandering. She is searching for him. But that is not what I came to tell you. You must not turn to the Magician once you come into your Power, Aria."

"But he'll hurt Logan or one of the others if I don't. He can make them do things."

"I am aware of the Magician's power. But he is unaware of yours. He seeks to build an all-powerful family, but his arrogance will be his undoing. You not only carry Judgement's blood within you, you also carry the Magician's. His foolish plan has created children far more powerful than he is. He can only defeat you if he controls you. And Arcana children aren't inclined to be under anyone's control."

I let this sink in for a moment. "You mean I have his powers?"

"Not exactly, but you are resistant to his powers because you carry his blood. He did not count on that. And your own powers will be stronger than my father's were because you come from two magical lines, not one."

"Magical lines? Blood lines?"

"Yes. I do not know the entire history, but I do know that the cards were created hundreds of years ago by a cabal of magical families in order to bring order to the chaotic celestial powers in the Universe. They were divided among the families so that no one group could become too powerful, and then the cards are passed down through the generations to members of each bloodline."

"So what are my powers?"

"You won't know for certain until the curse is broken, but you will have the ability to enact Karmic Judgement on those you choose. You will also know when people are lying to you. The rest will be unique to you, and tailored to how the energy manifests itself in your case."

"What does that even mean?"

"I'm afraid my time with you is limited. You will learn, and you will be guided by a manifestation of Judgement as was my father. But you must remember this: you must not add your power to the Magician's. He is a Reversed Magician, bent on power and control, no matter what he tells you. You can find a way to protect your family, but if he gains your power, the

balance of energies in the world will be in peril. The same goes for the others he has fathered. You must find them, unite with them, and foil his plans. The balance must be preserved at all costs." The walls of the chapel begin to shimmer, and time starts moving forward again. *"William, I'll try, but I have no idea what I'm doing! How can I reach you?"*

"You cannot, my young cousin. I doubt I'll be able to reach you this way again. I lack the energy to create another vortex. But break the curse, unlock your abilities. Judgement will help to guide you. Farewell, cousin. I have faith in you."

The walls disappear and nature reclaims the rubble. The chapel soon looks the way I have seen it for most of my life.

I hadn't thought things could get any more complicated, but it turns out I was wrong.

***

As night fell, I began to worry that Blair wouldn't keep his word, but I was also afraid to text him, in case offending him was a sin for which my cousin would be punished. About an hour after the sun fell, I got a text message from Blair, saying simply, **REMEMBER.**

About sixty seconds later, I heard the front door open, and I flew down the stairs to find Logan standing in the front hall looking confused and lost. I threw my arms around him.

"Logan! Thank God you're alright!"

"Yeah, I'm fine," he replied distantly. "What's been going on?"

I pulled away and looked into his eyes. His pupils were contracted to being almost pinpricks in his hazel eyes.

"You don't remember?"

"Huh? No, I ... just got home."

"I know you did. Do you remember how you got here?"

He shook his head. "I was standing on the driveway by the road, and I walked."

I took his hand and led him to the couch in the living room. Once he was settled, I poked my head through the doorway and yelled toward the stairs. "Aunt Pam! Logan's back!"

I heard a gasp from the direction of the master bedroom, followed by the thundering of motherly feet down the hallway and stairs. Her eyes were wide and full of tears when she reached us. She flew to Logan's side, mumbling and cooing over him.

"I'll bring you something to drink, okay?" I said, feeling in the way and not knowing what else to do.

"Okay. That'd be nice," he mumbled from deep within Aunt Pam's hugs and kisses.

When I returned to the living room, Aunt Pam had backed off a bit and was contenting herself to hold his hand and gaze at him as if he might disappear if she looked away. He smiled up at me rather blankly, almost as though he was sleepwalking. "Everybody's so happy to see me!"

"We missed you, dorkus," I smiled.

He raised the glass to his lips and took a long swig, then nearly choked on it. His pupils dilated, then returned to a normal size. "What the hell?"

"Now there's the Logan we all know and love," I laughed.

"How did I get here? Mom, are you okay?" He looked pointedly at me. "That jerk and his enforcer ran us off the road."

"Yeah, I know," I told him. "That was yesterday, bud. But you're home now."

"And I'm okay," Aunt Pam added. "Just a few bumps and bruises."

"Dude, no wonder I'm so hungry!"

"Come on, hon. I'll make you both something to eat." My aunt led us into the kitchen, but waited for us to follow, clearly not willing to let either one of us out of her sight.

While we ate, I filled them both in on what I had learned from William, but tactfully left out the threat and *arrangement* I had tacitly made with Blair. I also told them what Paul had told me about where he was going and why.

"So, Paul went to get Death? That doesn't sound like a good thing." Logan chewed heartily on the PBJ his mother had handed him.

"I don't know that he's bringing the guy back. I just know he wanted to talk to him. He seemed to think Death would have some insight about all this."

"I still think it's weird that Blair just let me go."

"Yeah, well, we ... came to an understanding."

Chapter 22

Paul got home around dinnertime the next day. The first thing he did was grin and punch his brother in the arm, which was about the most affection you ever saw out of Paul.

"So what did you find out?" I asked. "I kind of expected you to bring some hooded figure home with you."

"Oh, ha ha," he said drily. "I actually did find out a few things and Karl had some theories about how we can go about breaking this curse."

"That's good news! Wait ... a monk named *Karl?*"

"Yes, Karl. That was his name before he joined the monastic order. Yeah, he thinks we're on the right track with the re-burial process, but that it's probably not enough. His theory is that if they were regular ghosts, that would be enough, but there's more at work here."

"I can't argue with that part."

"So what else do we have to do?" Logan chimed in.

"Well, Karl thinks we need to summon the spirits and bring them to-gether. We also need to make sure we consecrate the ground."

"How the heck do we do either of those things?" Logan asked.

"Karl helped me with the summoning part. It's actually not all that different from what I was doing for all those years, except in reverse, sort of. I was banishing, so this is the opposite. As far as the consecration, that's easy. I've got that covered. We just need to find those bones."

"I guess we'd better get an early start tomorrow, then," I replied. "We've made some progress, but there's still a whole lot to do."

"You're right about that, and we need to do the summoning tomorrow as well. If we do it tonight, that might not go well. We need to wait until we're almost ready for the new funeral or whatever. We don't want them just hanging around while we try to sleep. Especially not the myling." He shuddered involuntarily, and Logan drew his shoulders in slightly, remembering his terrifying brush with the creature.

"Okay, then. Tomorrow morning, we get after it."

***

I decided to sleep in my own room that night. I knew I was in no danger from the myling, and frankly, I was not sleeping very well, sharing a bed with my aunt and listening to my cousin snoring.

As I lay in the darkness, I thought about the work we would be doing tomorrow. Would we finally be able to put the Glen's spirits to rest? I certainly hoped so. The reality of how they had died weighed heavily on me. Clearly, William and Anne had not found a way out of the chapel, and no one had been able to rescue them. Most likely, they had died of thirst if they hadn't found some quicker, more merciful way to end their lives. I honestly couldn't imagine anything more horrible, and I found myself sobbing softly at the thought.

I rolled over and grabbed a tissue from my nightstand. As the covers slipped off my shoulders, I noticed that the temperature in the room was much cooler than it should have been. I knew I wasn't alone, yet somehow I wasn't afraid. Instead, I crawled out of bed and padded over to the wardrobe, and pulled the Judgement card out from behind the ancestry chart.

I pressed the card between my hands and tried to reach out to the presence in the room with me. From the brushes I'd already had with it, I knew it was the myling. The burning rage I'd felt from it before, the hunger that had rolled off of it in waves was still present, but another emotion was predominant now. It felt a bit like curiosity. Not the kind of curiosity you have when you start down the rabbit hole of learning something new and interesting; more like the curiosity a feral cat has when they see a human with food who seems willing to feed it.

Soon, I thought toward the angry spirit. *Peace soon. No more hunger. Only rest.*

I wasn't sure if it understood, but it didn't feel threatening. Just curious, waiting. I pictured what we planned to do, pictured us finding the bones of our distant relatives and carrying them gingerly to a new spot. I pictured us planting the new flowers, and saying our own private prayers for their souls. I pictured their spirits together, disappearing into sunlight as a family. When I finally opened my eyes, the room had returned to its normal temperature, and the myling was gone.

I didn't remember dreaming, but my sleep was fitful, filled with the anticipation of getting to work the next day. I awoke shortly after 7 a.m. (heresy for summertime) and quietly rose and dressed. I headed downstairs to the kitchen and made myself a bowl of cereal. It was frustrating to have to wait for the others to wake up, especially because it could easily be two hours before the next person made their way down to the kitchen, even though we'd said we would get started early. *Early* for this household in the summer generally meant around 9:30. Rather than waiting around, I decided to get started, and then they could join me whenever they got up. My progress would be slower working alone, but at least I'd be moving forward. I left a note on the refrigerator and slipped out the back door and into the dewy yard.

With July only a few days away, the mornings were already warm by the time the sun was up. I twisted my hair into a ponytail as I walked to the shed, where I grabbed a square-ended shovel, a pair of work gloves, and a small gardening trowel. The chapel ruins came into view, looking so different than they had only a few weeks ago. Rather than one large mound, there were now multiple piles of sorted material and a small-er-than-it-used-to-be mound which, I discovered, was plenty muddy and soupy thanks to recent rains. I was pretty sure I could count on being a whole new level of dirty when the day was over, but on the bright side, it might be a lot easier to dig in wet earth.

I focused my efforts on the area where I had found the remains of the door, and this time when I touched the handle, it was only a hunk of metal. No visions or shocks, no waves of cold. I used the hand shovel to dig what was left of the handle assembly out of the dirt and moved it over to the scrap metal pile.

I thought back to the vision I'd had two days before, and tried to approximate where Anne had been sitting. We had managed to find the wall, but at least 70 years of debris still covered what would have been the chapel floor. I figured the first thing I needed to do was to see how deep I was going to need to dig to find the bottom, so I took the square shovel and slid it vertically down the edge of the wall we'd uncovered. Even with all we'd done, there were easily two more feet of earth to sort through. I felt safe taking the top layer off with the large shovel, and maybe halfway down, I'd switch to the smaller one so I could be more careful.

The work was strenuous, and it didn't take me long to work up a sweat, even in the cool of the morning. I focused on an area six feet square, lowering the height a little at a time. Engrossed in the work, I lost all track of time, and by the time I was ready to switch tools, I was surprised to find that Paul had joined me and was moving stones around on the other side of the chapel.

"Hey," I greeted him.

"Hey," he said back. "Want some water? I brought bottles."

"Yeah, thanks." I set my tools down and pulled off my gloves. He handed me a bottle, and I chugged half of it. "So, I feel like we should focus over here," I said, indicating the area where I'd been digging. I explained my vision from a couple days earlier, and he nodded somberly. Without another word, we started removing more soil, but more carefully now, in case we should find the grisly prize we sought.

"I'll be over here." Paul pointed to an area about eight feet away from the area where I was digging. There was a relatively flat patch there, and all the vegetation had been removed, leaving an uneven patch of dirt. He set to work drawing a series of symbols in the earth, muttering in a language I couldn't understand, but which sounded a bit like Latin, if I had to guess. I couldn't really follow what he was doing, but his movements were practiced and confident from having performed them so many times, only now he was reversing them to call the myling to us rather than to banish it.

Late in the morning, Aunt Pam and Logan wandered out and chipped in with our efforts. There was something about all of us working together in silence that felt important. We were making good progress, even with our hands and small shovels. "Many hands make light work," as my mother used to say when I was small. The thought of her made me sad, and I stopped digging long enough to finish the bottle of water I'd started earlier.

As I was hydrating, I felt a coolness settle around me and goosebumps popped up on my arms and back. I shivered involuntarily and looked around me. I didn't see anything or anyone, but the faint scent of lavender floated in the air around me. *Anne.* I closed my eyes and thought of her, of all she'd suffered. "We're almost there, Anne," I whispered. She was here, and I felt like that meant we were close.

The humidity already made the air feel thick, but there was a heaviness in the air now. I didn't know if the others could feel it, but as I returned to my work, I left aside the shovel and began digging down with my gloved fingertips. I felt a new sense of urgency as I dug and I felt as though I was out of space and time, despite having my family around me.

I am waiting, came the female voice I had heard before. The woman in the woods. She was part of all of this. *Soon you will find the destiny that awaits you.*

I was too intent to form words, even in my mind, but her last sentence both confused me and piqued my curiosity. She seemed aware of this and answered my unformed thoughts: *At the end of the curse, you shall know it's beginning.* I had no idea what that meant, and it truly didn't matter to me at that moment. All that mattered was finding the bones of the lost souls who had been trapped here for so long.

The work gloves were thick and soaked with mud. It was like trying to dig with a towel wrapped around my fingers. I stripped them off, despite hearing distant warnings from my aunt, and plunged my fingers into the earth. I must have looked like a dog or a badger or something, but I didn't care. I pulled rocks and roots from the ground, searching for what I knew lay underneath them. So close. So close. And then, as my fingers reached in for the next load, they came against something smooth, concave, and I felt a wave of thick, icy air roll over me. I stopped digging long enough to follow the wind with my eyes, and I saw a shimmer in the air, and then the face of a boy who looked like Logan but wasn't Logan. *William.* He didn't react, but watched me, phasing in and out of my vision.

"Here!" I called. "I think I've found them!" My fingers continued their work, uncovering what looked to be a shoulder bone. Working together, we uncovered the rest of the skeleton, which I was sure was William's. The others would certainly be very close by.

Logan and Aunt Pam had stepped up behind us. We all stared at the bones, and I think we were all taking stock of what we were feeling. The macabre drama that had taken place so many generations ago became shockingly real in that moment, and instead of being grossed out or frightened, I think we all felt deeply sad, even traumatized by what we knew had occurred here. My eyes were wet with sweat and tears, and when Paul cleared his throat, I knew it was affecting him as deeply as it was affecting me.

"Let's finish this," he said softly. "Let's see if we can give them the peace they've been denied."

Aunt Pam began the task of gently removing the bones and arranging them on a cotton flat sheet she'd brought from the house. Paul and I continued digging gently outward from where we'd found William, and Logan took a shovel and moved over to a flat area among the hydrangea bushes and began to dig a proper grave. Each of us performed a grim and heartbreaking task, but all of us worked together to try and set right what had gone so wrong long ago.

Almost in unison, Paul and I found the next set of bones: he brushed dirt away from a femur just as I discovered the curved edge of Anne's skull. My eyes stung with tears as we cleared the earth from around her figure, lying on her side as if she'd fallen asleep rather than passed from her earthly life.

In the distant reaches of my mind, I heard a sound which broke my heart: the feeble cries of an infant. If you've ever heard a baby cry, you understand how that sound can fill you with a mild sense of panic, at least when you don't know how to pacify the need it communicates.

Find him, came Anne's voice in my mind. *Find my baby, my son!* I kept scraping and digging, and I could hear the baby's cries, but I couldn't find him. Why couldn't I find him? *Find him,* she begged. *Find James.* James. The baby's name was James. As his name rang through my mind, a desperation overcame me. My stinging eyes overflowed and my tears salted the earth as I exposed more and more of Anne's frame.

Emotions overtook me. Pain, loss, grief, and I knew that the feelings were Anne's and William's, but also my own. The grief of being separated, parents and child, the longing for a family forever denied, consumed me and I cried bitterly for the anguish that had become integral in our family's legacy. I felt, too, James's longing, the desperate yearning for the parents who could not answer him or satisfy him because as he cried for them, they were already gone.

Through my tears, I glanced over at Paul and was startled by what I saw. He, too, was clawing at the ground with his fingers, digging like a man possessed. He, too, was crying. Could he hear and feel them as I could? I reached out to touch his shoulder.

"No!" he howled. "I have to find him!" He became frenzied in his efforts, his hands bloody and filthy, but desperate beyond the pain. Aunt Pam came at the sound of his voice and, seeing his apparent distress, moved as if to stop him or pull him away.

"No, Aunt Pam," I choked, grabbing her arm with my muddy hands. "He has to do this. He has to do this part alone."

She looked at me like I was out of my mind, but saw something in my face that at least made her pause. In that brief instant, Paul wailed, a heart wrenching sound I'd never heard from anyone, but which echoed the despair welling within me. His head dropped forward and his chest was heaving with sobs, and the tips of his battered fingers rested on the edge of a tiny skull, smaller than my fist.

Unlike the cold breezes that had blown through me when Anne and William had appeared, the wave that hit me now was like a concussive blast, like when something explodes and sends shockwaves outward. I fell backwards, my head spinning, The air whooshed out of my lungs and I fought not to lose consciousness.

I took several deep breaths and struggled to sit up.

"What is happening?" Aunt Pam asked, visibly shaken and looking back and forth from Paul to me.

"It's broken," I gasped. "The curse. It's broken. They're together." I began sobbing again. "They've finally found each other. We just have to finish what we've started, and then they can be at peace."

Paul looked up at me through red-rimmed eyes and nodded.

We lifted the remaining bones out of the ground and laid them on the sheet. Then the three of us silently carried our precious cargo to the area where Logan had been digging. He had made a hole about three feet square and maybe four feet deep.

"Wait a minute," Paul muttered. We lay the sheet on the ground and he pulled three small bottles out of his pocket. "Holy water," he replied to our unspoken question. "We have to consecrate the ground."

Pulling the cap off of one of the bottles, he sprinkled its contents over the bottom of the newly dug grave. Then each of us took a corner of the sheet and lowered it carefully into the hole, and Paul sprinkled another of the bottles over the now intermingled remains of our ancestors.

We stood in silence, pondering the weight of the task we'd just finished.

"Wait for me. I'm bleeding," Paul said quietly, and walked toward the house. Several minutes later, he returned with bandaged hands. Logan, Aunt Pam, and I finished filling the dirt into the hole while he stood by somberly. When the task was done, he pulled out the final vial of holy water ... and the Judgement card.

I raised an eyebrow at him. "I hope you don't mind," he said quietly. "I went into your wardrobe and got it. I felt like it should be here for this." He handed the card over to me, not without reluctance.

"I think you're right," I told him, and took the card gingerly in my filthy hands. He sprinkled the last vial of holy water over the newly-made grave. "William, Anne, and James Sheffield, may you find the peace in the next world that you were denied in this one."

In the quiet that followed, I closed my eyes and listened, not with my ears, but with my mind, searching for some reassurance or confirmation that we had done all we needed to do. I heard the whimpering of a baby, just as I had before, but then I heard a new sound, the *sshh sshh* of a mother's soothing and then the deeper hum of a man's mumbled words of comfort to the son with whom he'd been reunited. I felt a lightness in my heart, and

I knew there would be no more single-survivor generations from Robert Sheffield's line. Judgement's curse had been broken, it's blood price paid.

Chapter 23

After a long, hot shower, I came downstairs to an announcement that we were going out to celebrate. I couldn't deny that today was a big day; my cousins could finally live freely, with no fear that one of them was destined to die young. Logan hadn't known about that, of course, but Paul had lived with that terrible knowledge for years. It certainly was cause for celebration, but the knowledge that I was going to have to pay the proverbial piper put a damper on my joy.

I decided, though, that Blair could wait until tomorrow. Surely he'd give me that much.

We went out to dinner, and ordered ridiculous amounts of food: appetizers, entrees, and even desserts. I didn't even want to consider what kind of calories we were talking about, and I felt Thanksgiving-stuffed by the time we piled back into Paul's truck (which, thankfully, had a back seat) to head home.

Logan joyfully gathered up his sleeping bag from his mom's bedroom floor and trotted back to his room, thrilled with the prospect of peaceful sleep in his own bed for the first time in two weeks.

I found myself unable to sleep, thinking about how I was going to handle Blair the next day. He wasn't likely to give me too long of a reprieve, and even though William had warned me against giving Blair what he wanted,

I couldn't bear the thought of someone in my family suffering because I was wrong about thinking I could protect them. I didn't even know how to protect myself, much less someone else.

I pulled my school suitcase out of the storage area in the attic, and hoisted it up on my bed. I didn't like the idea of giving Blair what he wanted, but getting my family out of danger was the top priority. I could figure out how to mess up his plans once I'd removed the threat to the people I loved. I packed the way I would if I were going away to school for a semester: clothes, toiletries, and a few key personal items I couldn't live without. Then I sat down to write the note I was dreading. I knew it would worry and scare everyone, but that was better than the looming danger Blair presented.

Dear Aunt Pam, Paul, and Logan,

I know you guys are going to be mad at me when you find this note and realize what I've done, but I have to do this to keep you guys safe. I am hoping that I'll be able to find a way out of this and return home soon, but Blair has abilities I don't understand, and can hurt you if I don't give him what he wants, at least for now. He won't hurt me. He just wants me with him because of whatever powers I'll get from being Judgement now that the curse is broken.

I promise I'll be careful, and I'll contact you when I can. In the meantime, please know that I love you. All of you.

Love, Aria

I took a deep breath and texted Blair.

OK, it's done. I'm ready.

A couple of minutes later, he replied. **Marvelous. I am glad to see that you are true to your word, though I'd expect no less. Zora will pick you up at the end of the driveway in 30 minutes. Do not keep her waiting. That would be ... unwise.**

Thirty minutes. That seemed like such a tiny amount of time, especially considering that I'd have to find a way to sneak this stupid suitcase out of the house. As many times as I'd left this house for prolonged stays elsewhere, it had never hit me like this, because who knew when I'd ever make it back?

I set my suitcase on the floor, and picked up my backpack, where I'd packed anything that I considered precious, immediate, or breakable. I set the note on my pillow, and reached behind the ancestry chart to grab the Judgement card.

Suddenly, it felt like my ears were popping the way they do when you change altitude in a plane.

At last! The woman's voice that I heard in whispers boomed in my ears. *I've waited so long for you, Aria! You have done well.*

"Who are you?" I asked aloud.

I am Ma'at, goddess of judgement and truth. You and I have much to discuss.

"We definitely do, and I swear I want to spend the next hour doing nothing but getting answers to the 468 questions I have about the Judgement card and my family legacy. But right now, I have to sneak out of this house."

I sensed her disappointment. *Ah, well, I suppose I can wait a little longer. You are doing the right thing, you know. You gave him your word, and you must keep it, though it was given under duress.* My ears popped again, and I knew that she was gone. I slipped the card into my backpack.

I started to roll my suitcase across the wooden floor, and it was pretty obvious from the racket it made that I was going to have to carry it, not roll it. I walked as quietly as I could down the attic stairs, and crept past Logan's and Paul's rooms. Both of their doors were closed, so that was easy.

As I made my way down to the first floor, though, I realized I had a problem. I could hear Aunt Pam chatting on the phone in the living room, barring my exit to the front door. I could slip out through the kitchen, but then I'd have to pass the big picture window in the living room while rolling my suitcase. That was no good, and she'd clearly be able to see me for at least fifty feet. The long driveway curved around to the right after that, and my exit would be obscured by hedges.

The only way to get out without walking right past her was to go out through the basement, which had an exterior door on the side of the house. The basement door made a loud *creeeaaak* as I pulled it open, but my aunt kept chatting away, so I slipped down the stairs and out the side door. I had to lug my bag through the grass and around the shed, but then I was able to pick up the driveway after the curve and roll it the rest of the way.

I was both relieved and saddened that no one had caught me and stopped me from leaving. I desperately wanted to turn around and try to achieve my escape in reverse, to creep back into my room, bury myself under the covers in my bed, and not come out for at least a week. I swallowed the lump rising in my throat and kept walking.

I spent about three minutes at the end of the driveway with my heart pounding, thinking with every beat about turning around and going back inside. I didn't, though, and I was sitting dejectedly on my suitcase when Zora pulled up in a black rental car. She arched an eyebrow and popped the trunk when she saw my enormous suitcase.

"Planning on movin' in, are ya? Did ya remember your jim jams? I'm not loaning you my stuff to sleep in, sis."

"I didn't know what I'd need, so I brought pretty much everything."

"Probably a good idea," she agreed.

"How'd he get you on his side?" I asked, genuinely curious. "What did he threaten *you* with?"

She made a sound somewhere between a chuckle and a derisive snort. "No one threatens me," was all she said.

"You're working with him by choice? You're cool with him just threatening people to get his way while he gathers all the children he spread around the globe?"

"Get over yourself, sis. He'd have been more patient if he could. We sorta have a timeline. But you'll see the wisdom in it eventually."

"Somehow, I doubt it."

"Give me your phone."

"Why?"

"So I can throw it out the window, ya git."

"No."

"Look, we can't have your cousins trackin' us through your phone."

"All my pictures are on my phone. You can't throw it out the window."

"Fine. Is that an Android?"

"Yeah."

"Give me your SIM card."

I wrestled with the back of the phone and used my earring to pop out the card. I reluctantly handed the card to Zora. "I'll be giving this to Dad, just so you know." She tossed it into the cup holder.

"Of course you will," I grumbled.

"It was that or your phone. Speaking of, hand it over. I promised you'll get it back eventually if you behave yourself."

She nodded curtly and tucked the phone into a pocket on her jacket sleeve.

After a few more minutes, we pulled into a bed and breakfast not far from the Japanese steak house where they'd approached me.

"Huh," I sniffed.

"What? Are you too good for the likes of this place?" She side-eyed me something fierce.

"No, I just didn't peg you for B 'n B people. You don't seem the *cozy* type."

"It's a practical decision, love. Dad rented the whole place. Much more private, plus the food is good."

"The whole place? But there are only two of you."

"Yeah, well, then you get the excitement of choosing your room for the night. But we'll be out of here tomorrow, so don't get too comfortable."

"Comfortable is one thing I'm definitely not."

She pulled through a portico and out back to a parking area. Then she popped the trunk and turned off the ignition. "Get your stuff, princess. Dad will be back soon."

"Oh, so he just had some other important business to attend to? So important he couldn't attend the kidnapping of his own daughter?"

"Quit being such a drama queen. You came willingly, even if ya aren't too pleased about it. And yeah, he had pressing business."

I retrieved my bag and followed her inside. I chose a room on the first floor, just in case there was an opportunity to escape and head home. It was quaint, decorated in a patchwork of antique styles, with bright yellow walls and a fireplace in the corner. Not that I'd be using a fireplace in mid-summer, but it was still pretty, and somehow that brought me a tiny amount of comfort. I rolled my bag to the foot of the bed and flung myself across the comforter to weep dramatically into the criss-crossing pattern of rosebuds.

Enough of that, child, boomed the goddess' voice in my head. *We have much to do, and a great deal of information to cover.*

I sat bolt upright. "Wha—?"

Prepare a bowl of water.

"A what? Water? Why?"

Just do it, child. Put water in a bowl.

I looked around the room. On the dresser sat the typical bowl and pitcher that you'd find in any room decorated to make you feel like you'd gone back in time 100 years. I filled the bowl about halfway with water and set it on the bed. "Now what?"

The card, child. Get the card, hold it, and focus your attention on the water.

I did as she instructed. I held Judgement between my palms as I'd done before and looked into the water. At first nothing happened, but the longer I focused on the water, the more I felt centered, drawn in. The surface of the water shimmered, and I could just make out the image of a female face.

Well, hello there.

"Any chance you know how to solve all my problems?"

Certainly not, child. But I'm certain that understanding your place in the universe will help you find a solution.

"So you can tell me what all my powers are?"

Perhaps I'd better start at the beginning. You need to understand who you are. Then your abilities will manifest themselves naturally.

"Okay, so who am I?"

You are Judgement, as am I. You are she who demands truth. She who balances the scales. You are the eye that sees into the soul, whose examination cannot be denied.

"How is that useful?"

I do not know about useful. I know that the wicked cannot hide from you when you fix the gaze of Judgement upon them. You can bring the truth into the light, and you can bring a reckoning to those who deserve it. Deceit is the poison of this world, and you are the antidote.

"I don't mean to be disrespectful, but what does that mean in practical terms?"

The surface erupted into ripples, and I wasn't sure if it was out of amusement or frustration. *Imagine the power that lies in never being taken in by deceit. Imagine the power of being able to expose it in all its forms. Imagine what a danger you could present to those who are hypocrites and pretenders to the throne.*

"So you're saying I'm a threat to him."

A great threat, yes, though even he probably doesn't realize how much. You must learn how your role in the Arcana will manifest itself so that you can learn to use it.

"How do I learn that?"

One way to begin is by focusing on conversations you have with those around you. Concentrate on whether or not they are being truthful. In this way you can hone your skills at detecting lies.

I nearly jumped out of my skin when Zora started banging on my door.

"Oy! I'm checking in on you. Unlock your door."

"Just a minute!" I poured the water down the sink with mumbled apologies to Ma'at, returned the pitcher and bowl to their place on the dresser, and opened the door. Zora was towering over me (which, to be fair, would be hard for her not to do), looking bothered.

"Took you long enough. What've you been up to in here, then?" She strolled in and plopped down on the bed.

"Wallowing in self-pity, naturally."

"Heh. That will pass in time."

I decided to try following the goddess' instructions. "So, did you grow up with your father?"

"*Our* father, and yeah, pretty much." As she spoke, I concentrated on her words. *Are you telling me the truth?* "I mean I lived with my mum for most of my life, but he was around a good bit." As she finished her sentence, the air in front of her chest began to glow. I set my attention on that glow.

"So your mother was an Arcana?"

She regarded me with guarded interest. "Yeah, she was Strength. I was lucky to have her around to teach me what I was." She paused, then added, "What WE are. There are members of the Arcana who will try and control us if we don't know how to use our abilities." The glow began to waver and took shape. Hanging in the air between us now was a ghostly set of scales. Above the scales, I could see a feather hovering, and as I watched the feather floated downward and landed on one side of the scales. They remained balanced. Somehow I knew that meant she was telling me the truth.

"And is *our* father one of those?"

"Of course not. He is trying to gather us so he can teach us." She looked away from me for a moment, and when she looked back there was something ... a trick of the light? For an instant, her eyes appeared lighter in color, almost gray. Then she blinked, and they were back to the deep, intense brown they had been before. The feather lifted slightly off the scale, but that side of the scale also dropped downward a bit, as though someone had placed a weight on it. I wasn't sure what that meant, but I was pretty sure that what she was saying wasn't the truth.

"So how many of us are there? His kids, I mean."

"I think six." The feather touched back down and the scales returned to balance. True.

"Have you met the others?"

"You're the second one I've met." True. But I could tell my interrogation was making her a bit wary.

"Sorry for all the questions, but you have to understand that this is all overwhelming for me. I need information so that I don't freak out. I need to know who and what to trust."

That seemed to satisfy her, and it was the truth, after all.

"So what, he just has all these children around the world?" Honestly, that didn't just sound shady, it sounded kind of disgusting. "And your mom knew this?"

"My mother understood the importance of what he was trying to accomplish. And he was around for us if we needed him. Plus, he was there for me when she died, and took me in and made sure I never had to worry about anything. You'll see when you get to know him." Throughout her speech, the scales never wavered. All of what she was saying was true. "He'll probably be back soon. Go back to being dramatic or whatever, but don't get any ideas of taking off or contacting your *other* family." She got up abruptly and left the room, closing the door behind her.

I quickly refilled the water bowl and stared into it, calling Ma'at. *Well done, child. A very successful first attempt. What have you learned?*

"Well, I learned that scales appear when I'm trying to figure out if someone's lying or not. And if the scales stay balanced, they're telling the truth."

Precisely. You are weighing their hearts against the feather of truth. This was done with all souls entering the afterlife in Egypt. They had to pass Judgement to enter the Field of Reeds.

"So what happened if the scales didn't balance?"

I would throw their heart to the demon goddess Ammit, who would devour it. Then they could not pass to the afterlife and their ka *would wander the earth forever.*

"Yikes. Harsh."

Deceit creates disorder and disharmony. Disorder and disharmony is a threat to all.

"Is this something Daniel Sheffield was able to do? But because of the curse, no one else could?"

Something like that, yes. But Daniel Sheffield did not perceive Judgement through my aspect. So it would have manifested differently for him. I believe he leaned more towards the Babylonians.

"So any powers I have are related to what the Judgement card means in tarot, right?"

Essentially. The Major Arcana of tarot represent different divine forces. Judgement is one of those forces, which is why nearly all religions have some sort of deity who renders judgement on the wicked.

"And each person who becomes Judgement sees a different god or goddess?"

That's one way of looking at it. You see me because I am the embodiment of Judgement which best aligns with you. But Judgement itself is a divine energy, not an individual deity. As Ma'at, I render judgement as a way of maintaining balance and harmony. Other aspects of Judgement may view it through the lens of punishment and vengeance.

"As in cursing the entire bloodline of someone who destroyed yours?"

Very much like that.

"Whoa." I thought about the implications of that, and started to see her point about what I might have the ability to do, and why I would be a danger to someone like Blair. "What are the Magician's powers?"

I do not know exactly what powers have manifested in this Magician. But his divine energy is that of individual power. The Magician is always persuasive and clever, confident and strong of will. You know that this Magician is reversed, and that means he seeks power for his own ends, not the common good. More than that, I cannot tell.

"Don't you deities talk or anything? Some sort of divine social network?"

There was a trilling sound that might have been laughter. *Perhaps in an earlier dawn of time, child. But when the cards were created by the Grand Mage and his Council, the chaos of divine energies was harnessed, sorted, and separated. So now we are apart from each other, relegated to only a tiny sliver of the Universe.*

"Why would they do that?"

I believe they thought it was best for humankind, but I was not consulted in the matter, so I cannot be certain of their motivations. This is enough information for you to meditate on for the moment, Aria. I will be with you, but this path is yours to travel, and some of the answers you seek are for you to discover on your own. Have faith in the balance of all things, for in that balance lies immense power.

Chapter 24

A couple of hours later, Zora came by to inform me that Blair would return in the middle of the night, and that we'd be leaving the next day. She wouldn't say where we were going, but I got the impression we'd be there for a while.

As I tried to fall asleep that night, I kept imagining my family panicking, searching for me, calling the police about Dorian Blair. I wasn't sure how the boys would react, except that Paul would be pissy, because he pretty much always was. Was it strange that I was going to miss his surliness as much as Logan's goofiness? I wondered if they'd be mad at me for the choice I made. Maybe if they were, it would be easier for them. They would be alright as long as they were together, though, and that was all that mattered. I knew they loved me, but I always felt like a plus-one, no matter how hard they tried.

It started with that weird pressure feeling you get in the front of your face, accompanied by a couple of tears sliding out of the corners of my eyes and onto the pillow, but before long, I was wracked with sobs. The sobs led to straight-up ugly crying. The ugly-crying gave way to sniffly-snorty hiccups, and the hiccups gave way to a dreamless sleep.

When I awoke, sunlight was streaming through the windows, and I had a blistering headache. I groaned and rolled out of bed. I may have spent an unreasonable amount of time in a hot shower. And when I had procrastinated as much as I could justify, I opened my room door and made my way to the breakfast room. The smell of bacon and syrup smacked me in the face. Rather than it being a comforting smell, I felt mildly sick.

Zora and Blair were sitting at a table eating. "You look like rubbish," she said to me around a mouthful of waffle.

"Well, well, look who's finally awake," he said pleasantly, but without looking up from his smartphone. "Slept well, I trust?"

"Great. Glorious. Never better."

"Not a morning person, I see."

"Nah, she's always like that, far as I can tell." Zora dug into a sausage patty with vigor. "One thing I'll say for you Yanks. You know how to do breakfast. I might lose my Brit card, but this is far better than a full English."

"We aim to please," I grumbled and pointedly sat at another table.

"Under the circumstances, I'll forgive your poor manners. Mostly, I'm pleased that you saw reason and didn't make things more difficult than they needed to be."

"He means he's chuffed he didn't have to club you over the head and drag you here. Of course, that woulda been my job, so I guess I should say thanks for saving me the effort."

"Don't tease her, Zora. This is a challenging transition and she'll need your help to adjust." There was just something about the way he said it, ever-so-casually. I could feel something itching at my mind that I couldn't quite pinpoint. But when the nice lady who owned the B-n-B showed up with a cinnamon roll the size of my fist, I decided I could spare them any more sarcasm for a few minutes. Apparently Zora had the same feeling, because she tapped the one earbud that was hanging in her ear and started humming along with her chewing.

***

Within the hour, we were piled into the car and heading south on I-81. When we pulled into Shenandoah Valley Airport, my heart nearly stopped. I don't know what I expected, but I guess it hadn't occurred to me that Blair might hijack me and take me away somewhere. We walked out onto a remote runway, where a sleek silver and blue plane awaited us. I felt a rising panic as I walked closer to the aircraft. This was very similar to the plane my parents had crashed in. I started walking slower as my breath came faster. Blair noticed my discomfort and put a hand on my shoulder. His reassurance was oddly calming, and I felt my heart rate slow. I still wasn't excited about getting on this plane, but I also wasn't on the verge of a panic attack, which somewhere in the back of my mind, I realized I should have been. No one would be able to track me or find me after this. And yet, I climbed the gangway almost passively. Zora tossed our suitcases into the cargo area, and we all climbed into the luxurious six-seater plane. Blair mumbled a few words to the pilot, and then we all took seats and buckled in.

I hugged my backpack to my chest as we started rolling down the tarmac and finally lifted into the air. If I had known which way was north, I'd have tried to look for familiar building shapes in Harrisonburg, or even a glimpse of Sheffield Glen. Nothing looked particularly familiar, though, without the context of knowing what direction we were flying. A little more than an hour later, I saw what appeared to be a sprawling city below us. I felt us descending and spotted another small airport, which was clearly our destination.

We pulled close to a building with the letters EPPS in large red letters on the side. After disembarking, we made our way through a small terminal and emerged into a parking lot. I rolled my suitcase behind me as we walked, listening to the rumbling noise of the wheels on the asphalt. To our left was a small playground empty except for two kids climbing on a blue-roofed play structure, and a mom seated nearby on a bench. I spotted a historical marker beside the playground, and just made out the word ATLANTA and the year 1941. Well, at least now I knew where I was.

It was hotter here than Harrisonburg, and there was no Shenandoah Valley breeze. The humidity was insane, but the plants must have liked it, because as we drove, there was greenery everywhere. It was early afternoon when we pulled into a secluded driveway with a wrought-iron fence in a very upscale neighborhood.

Somehow, this was not the kind of house I expected Blair to live in. I expected something dark and brick and mildly sinister, not impeccable gray siding with a dozen beautifully white-framed windows and azalea bushes everywhere you looked.

"Home, sweet home," Blair said smoothly. I looked at the house and caught myself almost smiling. What the heck was wrong with me? Zora hopped out of the passenger seat and unloaded the bags, and I climbed out while Blair drove the car around the side of the house to pull it into the garage.

"You're gonna have to get your own bag, princess," Zora quipped as she shouldered Blair's leather duffel and rolled her own small bag toward the double doors that led into the house. I grabbed the handle of my bag and followed her. My brain was itching again, like it had at breakfast that morning: like there was something I should realize, something I was missing that was right in front of me. As I crossed the threshold of the house, I was struck by its beauty: all sunlight and class. Wooden floors glowed golden, complemented by rich gray and white furnishings, and the entryway to each room was framed with smooth white pillars. I found myself *wanting* to be here, *liking* it here. *What in the world was going on in my head?*

Zora wasn't waiting around for me. She cut through the living and dining rooms, and started up a dramatic staircase that rose up out of the massive kitchen. "Hey," I called, "where am I supposed to put my stuff?"

"Any room that's not mine, sis," she called back. "Take your pick."

I watched her disappear up the stairs and heard a door close behind her just as Blair came up the stairs from the lower-level garage. "Well, now, you just take your time getting settled in." That smooth, velvety voice again, making me forget that I hated him. "There are three bedrooms upstairs other than Zora's, and it's first come, first served. So take a good look and see which one suits you."

"Yeah, okay, thanks." *Was I kidding? Okay, thanks? Really?*

He patted me on the shoulder and crossed the kitchen, disappearing through a doorway on the far side. He seemed pretty sure I wasn't going to make a run for it. And honestly, I didn't have any intention of it, so he had good reason for confidence.

I lugged my bag up the wooden stairs and abandoned it at the top. The door to the right was closed, so I surmised that was where Zora had disappeared to. In front of me was an office, and to the left stood four open doors. I peeked in each of them, and opted for one in the middle. The biggest one stood at the farthest end of the hallway, but as near as I could tell, it was directly over Blair's room, and that seemed like a bad idea.

The room was tastefully appointed with a four-poster double bed, a dresser, and a chair. I went and retrieved my bag and rolled it inside, unsure of whether I wanted to unpack or not. I mean, I knew I didn't *want* to but I wasn't sure if I *should.*

I decided not to, at least not yet. Instead, I thought I'd wander around and check out the rest of the house. As I wandered from room to room, I found myself wondering if Blair had furnished it himself, or bought it this way. I wondered how long they had lived here, and made a mental note to ask about that later. It seemed to me that it was roughly the same size as Sheffield Glen, though it was cool and gray rather than warm and brown like home. *Home.* I felt a pang of homesickness as I stomped down the stairs to the basement. Most of the basement was unfinished, and appeared to be empty storage space with a washer and dryer in the corner. There wasn't much in the fully finished section; just a table and chairs, a TV, and an exercise bike. I looked out the back door, and saw a heavily wooded back yard. Finally something familiar! I opened the door and stepped out onto a stone terrace that extended the length of the house.

At one end, I found the exterior garage doors. Around the other end, I found the holy grail for any kid seeking privacy: a wooden two-story playhouse half hidden by the tall pines that surrounded the property. I climbed the steps and sat down on the bare floor and stared back at the house. I pressed my back and my palms against the wood. Feeling the solidness of the pine made me feel grounded, real. I closed my eyes, thinking of home. Thinking about how these pines were just like the pines around the Glen.

Good. I heard Ma'at's voice in my mind, but it was so far away. Why was it so far away? *Ground yourself in the trees.*

"Where are you?" I asked her.

"On the patio, my girl," came Blair's voice from the side of the house. "Can you sense me? Remarkable. That's a very handy talent." He had heard me and thought I was speaking to him! Ma'at's voice fell silent. I scrambled down from the playhouse and walked around to the edge of the patio. Blair rose from chair and looked down at me. "Making yourself at home?" he inquired.

"That might be a bit of a stretch," I said, but not disagreeably. "This is a nice house, though. How long have you lived here?"

"Not long," he replied, confirming what I'd suspected. "I bought it about a year ago, actually. Good place for a family, don't you think?"

I decided that being direct was the way to go. "I have questions."

"No doubt you do, my dear. Quite a few of them, I'd imagine. But I'm not sure how many of them I'm prepared to answer just yet. Not sure how much I can trust you, you know?" He sounded amused.

I stepped closer to the patio and looked up at him. "I'm not sure how much I can trust you either."

He chuckled, and the sound was almost musical. "I'd imagine not. I know you probably think my methods are cruel, my girl, but I assure you that there's a greater purpose to all of this."

"You're trying to create your own private basketball team? Your own X-men?"

He chuckled again. "Something like that, I suppose."

"Why?"

"That, I'm afraid, is a conversation for a time when I know you better."

Somehow, I wasn't even offended by that. "So what am I doing here now then? Couldn't you have gotten to know me back in Harrisonburg over lunch?"

"A reasonable question. But, regrettably, that wasn't practical. I have time considerations. And it's rather important that you gain some skill in your abilities before we run out the clock."

"What do you mean by that? Are we under a time crunch?"

"Ah, another question I'm not quite prepared to answer." I was growing irate at his continuous refusal to give me straight answers, but then the rising anger inexplicably receded like the tide, leaving me with lingering questions, but only a mild sense of annoyance.

"But there will be others? You have more kids?"

"Indeed. We'll be bringing them all here eventually."

"Zora says she met one."

"One of your sisters, yes. She wasn't quite prepared to join us yet, but she'll be along eventually."

There was something about the way he said that that stirred something inside me, a deep kernel of suspicion, of rage. *Why am I not still angry?*

"I suspect that, as you get to know me, you'll find that I'm actually quite agreeable most of the time," he said, almost in answer to my unspoken question. That made the hairs rise on my arms.

"Yeah, I guess I probably will," I responded quickly. "I think I'm going to go unpack now."

"A marvelous idea," he smiled.

I returned to the back of the house and the basement door, my heart thudding in my chest. How could I possibly hope to find a way to prevail over someone who could read my mind? I was quickly coming to the conclusion that I was in way over my head.

Chapter 25

Despite what I had told Blair, I just couldn't bring myself to completely unpack. I put two or three outfits into the drawers, and took my toiletry bag into the en suite bathroom. I stared at the mirror and tried to figure out my next move. It sure felt like I didn't have one.

I closed the bathroom door and pushed in the stopper on the sink. I filled it about halfway, and then reached out, trying to call the goddess for help. I closed my eyes and heard nothing of the booming voice, more like psychic white noise. When I opened my eyes, I thought I could just barely make out facial features in the water, but they were so faint that I might well have imagined it. Why would she abandon me like this, just when I needed her help the most?

Frustrated, I drained the water and sighed. I walked back into the bedroom (it wasn't MY bedroom and I refused to think of it that way) and flopped down on the bed. My eye caught my backpack sitting on the chair where I'd dropped it when I first arrived. Of course! The card! Maybe I could reach Ma'at if I held the card and tried again. I leapt off the bed, fished the card out of my backpack, and darted back into the bathroom to try again.

This time, I held the card between my hands as I reached out with my thoughts. When I opened my eyes, I could see Ma'at in the water, but she was definitely fainter than she had been at the B-n-B.

"Well, THERE you are," I said, somewhat petulantly.

Her lips began moving, but I couldn't hear her voice; all I got was a louder white noise that resembled static.

"I can't hear you."

Her lips began moving again, and I really regretted the fact that I was terrible at lip-reading.

"Thousand walking? What does that mean?'

She moved her lips again, slower this time.

"Thousand water? The house is water?"

She rolled her watery eyes at me.

She repeated it again, ridiculously slowly.

"The house is ..." she nodded. "Wonder?" No. "Warty?" Definitely no. "Warded?" She nodded. "The house is warded?" Well, no wonder I couldn't hear her. "Is that why I could hear you outside?" Another nod. "So if I want to talk to you, I need to take the card and go outside." Emphatic nodding. I drained the water out of the sink and slipped the card into my back pocket. It poked out a little bit, but somehow, I didn't think it would strike Blair or Zora as strange that I would carry it around with me.

It actually made some sense that Blair would have protective psychic shielding around the house. He had no way of knowing what my abilities were, and trying to find a way to mute them just made sense. That was going to make it awfully difficult to try and hone my skills, though. I didn't even know what all of them were, and it seemed like this house was designed to make sure I didn't find out. That also explained why I was being so agreeable when I had essentially been coerced into leaving my home and family.

Blair was smart, and he was careful. That was a pretty dangerous com-bination. Zora was smart, too, but maybe she wasn't as careful as he was. Maybe she didn't even know about the wards. Maybe she was unaware that he had the ability to dampen our moods. Even now, I wasn't angry at him for his blatant manipulations. I was aware of them, but felt inclined to shrug them off as if they weren't really all that important.

Ma'at had told me that persuasion was a common denominator in any Magician, reversed or otherwise. There was no doubt in my mind that I was feeling the effects of that ability. I wasn't even this placid in my normal life; there's no way that my passivity was natural.

The afternoon was giving way to evening as I walked back out onto the terrace. At its center a small fountain, maybe three feet in diameter, bub-bled away. The terrace overlooked a heavily wooded area, and I couldn't help but wonder how far back those woods extended. I placed my hands on the wooden railing, and surveyed the land as far as I could down the hill. It looked like it must be a pretty sizable property.

I turned back to the fountain and knelt beside it, facing the house so that no one could sneak up on me. I slid the card out of my pocket and held it between my hands as I gazed into the burbling water. "Can you hear me?" I asked the goddess.

I can hear you, but not well, came a fair reply. I was going to have to get farther away. There was a flagstone walkway that circled the building and led to the playhouse I'd found earlier. I checked the patio to see if Blair was still there, but it appeared he had gone inside. I didn't want him overhearing me again. I didn't think I'd be able to explain away my constant habit of talking to myself. As it was, he thought I had sensed him. I was okay to let him think that for now; it would keep him on his guard thinking he couldn't sneak up on me.

This time I stayed on the first story of the playhouse and walked all the way to the back railing of the platform. It overlooked the woods just as the railing on the terrace had. I felt like that was likely to work in my favor. I didn't have any water here, but if I could hear Ma'at, I didn't really need to see her.

"Can you hear me now?" I asked quietly, feeling like an old cell provider commercial.

I can hear you. Well done.

"I need help. He's too strong."

You are stronger than you know. But you must learn to shield your thoughts from him.

"You got that right."

We don't have much time. You will be missed. Close your eyes and see yourself as though you are sitting inside an egg.

"That's gross. Why would I be inside an egg?"

An eggSHELL, child. Imagine you are surrounded by a clear eggshell.

I did as she instructed, though it was hard not to imagine it as a bubble.

Now, she explained, *slowly turn the shell opaque. Imagine you can see out of it, but no one can see inside. Good. Now imagine that eggshell shrinking and changing shape. See it take the shape of your body and cover you like a second skin. Imagine that the part of the shell that surrounds your head is twice as thick as the rest, and imagine it turning gray as stone.*

I did what she told me, and I noticed something surprising. The anger I had felt when I first saw the car accident he had caused when he hurt my aunt and kidnapped my cousin boiled up inside of me, though it had been all but forgotten moments ago.

Ah, well done. Now you have your OWN shielding against his magic. You will need to strengthen it by concentrating on it frequently over the next few days. After a while, you will become used to it and won't have to focus on it quite as much. It should shield your mind somewhat from his influence. Now you must go. Learn what you can about his motives, and develop your abilities. Only seek me out if it's absolutely necessary.

"But I feel so alone here."

It is a hard lesson, child, but the greatest growth occurs in solitude.

***

I 'd never been so bored in my life. I tried finding something to
binge-watch, but nothing held my attention. There was no way Blair
would let me go for a walk, and I had no one to talk to or hang out with.
I missed my room, the Glen, my family, everything. With Blair's influence
over me muted, the grief of loss hit me full force, and I was desperate to
distract myself, if only to keep my feelings hidden. There had been some
books in the formal living room, and I really hoped there was something
there that would hold my attention.

It didn't look too promising at first. There were some art books, which
might have been mildly interesting to look at if I knew anything at all about
art. There was a book about Atlanta's history, which was DEFINITELY
not going to do the trick. I ran my fingers down the spines of the books
until I came across a title which grabbed my interest: *Historia de Tarot.*

I flipped the book open. I had taken two years of Spanish! I could do
this!

Oh, wait. No I couldn't. The book wasn't in Spanish. It was in Latin,
and hand-written Latin at that. Big yikes. I checked for a publication date,
but couldn't find one. Well, I could look at the pictures ...

It turned out that there were a few pictures, which was lucky. There were
three images: the first image showed a world in chaos, a civilization at war.
It was pretty brutal, with pictures of humans being impaled, beheaded,
trampled ... all in brilliant color. The center panel showed a collection
of elaborately dressed people standing in what looked like a semi-circle
around a flaming bronzed bowl. Several of them were holding a bleeding
right hand aloft. In front of the bowl, there was a colorful arrangement of
small paintings; it rather looked like a weird game of Go-Fish.

The bottom part of the picture showed twenty-two glowing orbs raining light down onto what appeared to be children of varying ages. On closer inspection, each of the orbs bore a tiny symbol, some of which I recognized. I saw the symbols for male and female, a moon, and a smattering of what looked like astrological symbols. Two from the end, I found the symbol that had become so familiar to me: Libra. The twentieth position ... the twentieth card: Judgement.

I had a pretty good idea now of what the artwork represented generally. It explained the creation of the magical Arcana deck. As I flipped through the rest of the book, I saw that there appeared to be a section dedicated to each card. I was really wishing I had taken Latin instead of Spanish. If only I knew how to understand the book, I felt like I could learn so much. I was also willing to bet that Blair had studied plenty of Latin and had spent hours poring over this volume.

"A little light reading?" I yipped at the sound of his voice. I hadn't heard him come in from the other room.

"Not reading, exactly. My Latin is a little rusty."

"Yes, well, you'll find that a great deal of magical books are written in Latin, for some reason. I think that there were some rather cheeky monks out there who were desperately trying to decry the idea of magic, but were secretly fascinated by it. They certainly spent a ridiculous amount of time hand-copying these tomes. Are you able to learn anything from the book, despite your language difficulty?"

"Well, I think I may have learned a little from the big painting at the beginning of the book. It looks like the world was at war, so this group of people made the cards, maybe to try and bring peace, and then they passed the cards down to their children."

"Marvelous, yes. That's a fair approximation." He seemed genuinely pleased, and I felt like I had passed some sort of test. "The group of mages in the middle image did create the cards to try and bring peace, but as I think the last 500 or so years of history tells us, they weren't very successful."

I couldn't really argue with that. The world had never really been any-thing but a mess, largely of human making.

"So their plan didn't work."

"Exactly," he grinned. "It didn't work. Now, my dear, I am thrilled that you have an interest in trying to learn what you can from this book, but I would ask that you wear a pair of the gloves you'll find in that end table drawer whenever you want to peruse it. The book is several hundred years old, and skin oils are quite damaging, I'm afraid."

"Oh!" I whipped my hands back from the pages. "I had no idea."

"Quite alright. There's no way you could have known." He went over to the table he'd indicated, pulled out a thin pair of white cotton gloves, and handed them to me. I slipped them on.

"Like I said, I don't speak Latin. Can I possibly use the internet to translate some of this?"

He made a sour face, clearly disappointed that our lovely little conver-sation had hit a snag. "I'm afraid I just can't allow that yet, my girl. We haven't quite reached that level of trust yet. I can, though, bring you a Latin dictionary and you can try to piece things together."

I must have looked shocked at the notion (because I was. Who did things that way anymore?), because he laughed at the expression on my face. "There were thousands of years when people figured things out without the internet, Aria."

I bit back at least four caustically sarcastic comments. "Well, I guess I could give it a shot. I don't have a whole lot else on my calendar right now."

"Wonderful. Why don't you bring that book up to the office, and I'll fetch the dictionary for you. That will be a much more comfortable place to work, I think."

"Yeah, okay," I agreed, somewhat reluctantly.

I sat at the desk with the really really old book ... and also the book about the history of the arcana. I was pretty sure this Latin-English dictionary had been printed during the Great Depression. How did anyone ever learn this way?

Slowly. Very, very slowly.

Chapter 26

I decided to start by working on the section of the book dedicated to Judgement. It was maybe twenty pages long. The only picture, unfortunately, was on the very first page, and looked remarkably similar to the card I still had in my back pocket. Same image, different artist, probably. That was sort of interesting, though, because it meant that this book would allow me to see what some of the other cards looked like.

Without some knowledge of Latin grammar, I was really at a loss to translate more than a word here or there. But as I flipped through the Judgement pages, I came across a few lines that had been beautifully illuminated by a border matching that of the cards.

Altiora peto
Celeritas et veritas
Honor virtutis praemium
Etiem quod esse videris
Candor dat viribus alas

Something set apart like that was bound to be important, so I focused on just that section. I flipped back and forth in the ancient dictionary, searching for meaning in the lines. It took me about a half hour, but the results seemed to make some sense. While I was pretty sure I was still fudging the grammar a little bit, it almost sounded like poetry. I spoke the Latin aloud, followed by my best guess at an English translation:

I seek higher things
Swiftness and truth
Honor is the reward of virtue
Be what you seem to be
Sincerity gives wings to strength

The card in my pocket came to life, metaphorically speaking. It was like I was sitting on a cellphone set to vibrate. I pulled it out and held it in front of me. The buzz radiated into my hands and up my arms, almost like two walls of static moving toward each other. It spread through my shoulders, and toward my heart, where the two walls crashed together. I threw my head backward as the waves of energy flowed through me. The initial rush subsided, but I felt as though someone had turned on the electricity inside of me, and now it was crackling off of my skin.

I stood up at the desk and caught my reflection in the window. Only it wasn't my reflection, not exactly. I could see myself, but a glowing form of Ma'at surrounded me like an aura. Her long black hair hung down around my shoulders, and her dark eyes, heavily outlined with kohl, overlaid my own. A voluminous white strapless gown flowed over the tee shirt and yoga pants I was wearing, and atop my head rested a golden crown with a single, fluffy white feather adorning it. The feather of truth!

I raised my hands and I was now holding the glowing scales I had seen before. I alternated my hands up and down, and the scale plates on either side moved with them.

I would not do that, came the goddess' voice, loud and clear. *You hold in your hands the Scales of Judgement. You and I are now One.*

Wait, what? "What do they do?"

They render judgement, naturally. You must be very careful.

"What do you mean, 'we are One'?"

You have cast a spell to bind us. As long as you live, we cannot be separated from one another. We are One.

"Like 'till death do us part?'"

Your death. I cannot die.

"What? I don't want to die!"

All mortals die. I did not mean now.

"Oh. Okay, then. But the Scales?"

I told you it was my office to weigh the heart and render judgement. You and I are One. You can judge a soul just as I can. But do not do this lightly. We are not in the Underworld. Weighing a living soul comes with consequences.

"Consequences?"

When you judge a living soul, the feather of truth is an extension of you. If you carry any guilt in association with that soul, you are judging your own as well. You risk punishing yourself along with one who you would deem wicked.

"So what do I do now? I don't want to accidentally go around judging people!"

You summoned them; you must banish them for the time being. You cannot maintain this level of connection with me, at any rate. Your body would not be able to contain this level of divine energy for very long.

"How do I banish them?"

I do not know. They simply appear when I will it, and disappear when I will it. Perhaps it is the same for you.

It was worth a try, I guess. "Okay, Scales. You can go away now." Nothing changed. "I don't need you right now; you can go away." Again, nothing. Ma'at's energy crackled along my skin like electricity.

Electricity. I had an idea.

I closed my eyes and imagined myself reaching up and flipping a switch on my forehead. When I opened my eyes again, the scales and aura of the goddess were gone, and the charge I'd felt along my skin had resolved itself into a low hum.

Speaking of skin, I about jumped out of mine when someone knocked on the closed door behind me.

"Hey, sis! What's going on in there? Ya summoning demons or something?" She opened the door and entered to find me standing next to my two hours of self-imposed Latin homework.

"What's this then?"

"Oh, I, um, found this book downstairs, and Blair said I could look at it, but I don't understand Latin. So I was trying to translate some of it."

"Just a little swot, aren't you?""A what?"

"Very dedicated little student."

I didn't think she meant it kindly. "Only when it suits me," I replied. I turned to face her, and she looked startled. She looked me up and down with new appreciation, like maybe she knew that something about me was different.

"Right. Well, listen, sis. It's getting late, but we're going to get an early start tomorrow. Dad wants us to head over to his training facility so we can work on our skills a bit."

"By doing what? And why can't we do it here?"

"Quit asking so many bloody questions. You'll see tomorrow, unless you've got some other pressing appointment?" She was trying not to, but I could tell that she was staring at my forehead. There was no mistake about it this time. Her deep brown eyes faded to a stormy-sky gray. Just like Blair's eyes. Just like mine. I had always thought that I had my mother's eyes, but now I wasn't so sure.

My mind was flooded with questions: How were her eyes doing that? WHY were her eyes doing that? Why had I never noticed the color of my eyes was just like the color of his? I really wanted to ask her about the change in hers, but I thought I'd better play it cool for the moment.

"Sadly, no. My calendar is wide open."

"Right then. Breakfast is at half seven. Don't be late."

"Does that mean 7:30?"

"Obviously." She rolled her eyes, took one more look at my forehead, and then left the room, leaving the door open.

I couldn't help but wonder what she'd been staring at. I looked at the mess of paper on the desk, and decided I had had sufficient adventures in Latin for one night anyway. So I stacked everything together and laid it in an empty desk drawer.

I took a shower and twisted my hair up into a wet messy bun. What kind of training facility was he taking us to? I didn't like the sound of it, and I also wasn't too sure I wanted him knowing what all my new skills looked like. But I figured I'd better show him something, or he'd know I was sandbagging. I crawled fretfully into bed.

It wasn't my antique bed at home, but the sheets were fresh, and the mattress was soft. Within minutes, I was fast asleep.

Chapter 27

After the insane cinnamon rolls from the day before, boxed frozen waffles were a decided letdown. Still, I ate two of them and a couple of slices of bacon, because I wasn't sure what the day held in store, and I suspected I didn't want to face it with a growling stomach.

Blair had pulled the car around front, and by 8:15, we were on the road. I didn't really pay too much attention to where we were going, since I didn't know Atlanta and so had no context for the road names I was seeing, but it seemed to me we were basically back-tracking toward the airport. Eventually, we found ourselves in a commercial district and parked outside a small run-down building with a big roll-down warehouse door in the back.

We entered through a regular door to the left of the big one, and the building was not at all what I expected inside. It seemed to be set up into a series of stations, each set with a different type of task.

"It looks like kindergarten on steroids," I commented.

"That's actually not the worst analogy," Blair responded, "in that each station is designed to test whether you have an aptitude in different types of skills."

"How will I know?"

"Well, you'll be spending thirty minutes at each station. Zora will work with you, and I will observe, monitor, and record."

"So you'll be following me around with the clipboard while she barks orders in British?"

"Something like that, though my role is a little more high-tech than a clipboard." He nodded toward a small office located on the second floor of the warehouse. "I have equipment upstairs which will record and measure your efforts. Some skills, of course, might not fall into any of these categories."

As annoyed as I was at being treated like a guinea pig, I had to admit that this might actually be a useful exercise. I also noticed that the itching in my brain was gone, and I took that to mean that he had no magical dampening on this set-up. That was pretty logical, because how could he test my abilities if he was muting them?

"Alright, sis, let's hit it." Zora moved to the first station. It was a cubicle like you might see in an office building, maybe 10 feet square. A table with items of varying size sat in the center: a scrap of cloth, a pen, a rock, a dictionary (what was it with this guy and ancient reference books?), a gallon of paint. "Right. Now your first job is to try and move each object without touching it. Start with the velvet square, and if that works, move on up the line."

It didn't take long to realize that telekinesis was NOT one of my abilities. In fact, I'd argue that it was evident in the first five minutes, but Zora insisted on trying for the full thirty. She even brought other items of the same light weight, but which were made of other materials: paper, a coin, a flower. No luck on any front. Can't say we didn't give it the college try, though.

The second station started out similarly. She had me trying to draw energy from various elemental materials. I burned myself pretty nicely on the candle by holding my hand over it for too long. Then I idiotically stuck that same hand in the salt. Public service announcement: don't do that.

When she set a bowl of water in front of me, though, I got nervous. I wasn't sure I wanted her or Blair to know that I could summon Ma'at that way.

"Concentrate on the water, Aria," she told me. Within seconds, Ma'at's face appeared and though I didn't mention that fact to Zora, she immediately leaned forward. "What do you see?"

"I ... I'm not sure exactly. I think it's a woman's face." I didn't want to lie. I remembered what Ma'at had said about bearing guilt myself when rendering judgement, and I figured that dishonesty would definitely count against me.

"What is she doing?"

"I can't really tell. I can only see her face."

"Is she someone you know?"

"She's familiar. I think she's someone I've seen in spirit form."

Zora was staring at my forehead again and her eyes faded to gray. This time, though, they didn't fade back. "Is there anything else you can tell me about her?"

"No, I don't think so." Technically, that was true. I wasn't sure it was safe to tell her much else. And therefore no, I couldn't. *What was up with her eyes?*

She kept at me for another half an hour at the Elemental station, but only focused on the bowl of water. She kept asking me to focus on the outcomes of future events, trying to determine, I thought, if I had any ability to see the future. She typed some notes into the tablet she was carrying around, and I was pretty sure she knew I had more ability with the bowl of water than I was letting on.

The next station involved something called astral travel and remote viewing, which basically meant the ability of my consciousness to leave my body and go places or see things that weren't nearby. Big, fat zilch on that one.

When we sat down at the next table, Zora picked up a card and focused on it.

"Alright, focus on what I might be thinking. What shape am I looking at?"

I laughed out loud. "Okay, Dr. Venkman," I chuckled. She didn't seem to get my *Ghostbusters* reference, and I was genuinely disappointed. We tried with a bunch of cards, and I definitely wasn't showing any aptitude for this skill either. It occurred to me that being a total failure might give away that I wasn't telling them all I knew, so I decided to reinforce something she already knew.

"Look," I began, "I can't read your mind and figure out what's on the card, but I am pretty sure I can tell if you LIE to me about what's on the card."

That piqued her interest. "Right then, let's have a go. You tell me if I'm lying or telling the truth."

I closed my eyes and imagined the scales in front of her heart. It wasn't the big set I'd been holding back in the office, not the ones that would weigh her heart in judgement; just the smaller ones I'd used when we first arrived in Atlanta. When I opened my eyes, she was staring at my forehead again. She typed something into her tablet, then held a card up in front of her.

"I'm looking at a circle."

"True."

"Now I'm looking at a plus sign."

"True."

"Alright, a triangle."

"False."

"A check mark."

"True."

On and on it went until we had gone through the whole deck. She didn't share the results with me, but I knew I hadn't missed even one.

None of the other tests seemed to bear much fruit. I wasn't particularly strong, nor was I able to control her thoughts or actions with my mind.

I wasn't able to read "vibes" off of an object, or read the thoughts of the bunny rabbit she brought in at one point.

At the very last station, she pulled out her tablet and laid it on the table. "Last one," she began. "Now, I'm going to ask you a bunch of questions, and I want you to tell me your gut-reaction answer. I don't want you to think about it. Just answer. We're checking to see if you have any sort of gift of insight."

"I don't really know what you mean by that, but okay."

"Here we go: Question 1: Are you in danger?"

"If I don't make *him* happy, yes."

"Question 2: Are you in danger from me?"

"Oddly, no."

"Why is that odd?"

"I don't know; I guess because you could definitely hurt me if you wanted to."

"But I won't?'

"No."

"Interesting." She seemed strangely pleased by that.

"Do you trust me, then?"

"No."

"Do you trust our father?"

"No."

She hesitated here, and I got the feeling she was asking a question that wasn't on his list. "Am I in danger?"

"Maybe."

That gave her pause. "Can you explain?"

"Not really. But I think it's the same as me: If you make him happy, you're safe."

Zora spent about twenty minutes asking me more questions, some of which made sense to me, and some which didn't. But every answer checked some kind of box on the tablet. When we finally finished, I was both starving and exhausted, and that kind of combination made for a cranky me.

Blair came down out of the office, and we all piled back in the car. "So when do I find out the results of all those tests?"

"I should think the results are largely obvious," Blair replied. Seemed like I wasn't the only cranky one.

"Well, generally, yeah, but I don't know what some of them mean. Like all those questions at the end. I don't understand what some of them were even about."

"I'll need to go over all of it in some detail. I'll discuss it with you more tomorrow." And that, it seemed, was the final word. He did stop at a fast food joint and get me some nuggets, though, so at least he wasn't a total savage. I ate slowly just to be annoying.

By the time we got back to the house, it was nearly 3:00 in the afternoon. We'd spent about four-and-a-half hours at the warehouse, plus drive-time and nugget consumption. As we pulled up the drive and walked toward the door, I felt a now-familiar buzzing in my brain that told me I was walking through the warded perimeter he had set up. I could feel some of the sharpness I'd experienced while we were off the property ebbing away. Clearly these protective wards were intended to keep me, and maybe even Zora, pacified and agreeable. It irritated me that, even though I was aware of what they were, I wasn't able to completely nullify their effects. I concentrated on the protective "eggshell" Ma'at had told me to visualize, and my head got slightly clearer, but I was still feeling way too *nice*. I was also mentally exhausted from all the tests. I stomped up to the room where I had put my stuff (*not my room, not my room, not my room*), flopped down on the bed, and stared at the ceiling fan. I don't even remember falling asleep.

When I awoke, it was dark outside. I looked at my watch, and it was after 9:00. I really HAD been tired! And now, I had that really awful feeling when you nap for way too long, and you're completely screwed up afterwards. My head felt thick, and I think I might have just rolled over and gone back to sleep, had my bladder and my stomach not protested. I made a quick pit stop in the bathroom and then made my way down to the kitchen.

If I had to say one good thing about Blair, the man knew how to stock some snacks. Salty, sweet, spicy, whatever I might crave was there. Given my fast-food lunch, I thought I'd better try to eat something that at least somewhat resembled healthy food, so I grabbed a banana and some grapes out of a huge bowl on the kitchen island. I also spotted some snack bags of cheddar popcorn, so I snagged one of those, too. It's all about balance.

I was debating where to stuff my face when I heard Blair's raised voice coming through the wall. One side of his bedroom adjoined the kitchen, and I moved toward the sound, straining to hear what was being said. Right now, all I could hear was tone, and he didn't sound too happy. The small porch where I'd seen him the day before had an entrance off the kitchen, but if I slipped out there, I ran a decent chance of being spotted. I crept closer to the patio door, and noticed something I hadn't before. Right next to the patio door was a half-bathroom! I set my food on a nearby counter, slipped inside and closed the door as quietly as I could.

The sound was somewhat amplified, but it was like listening through water. While I could hear noise, the actual words were muffled and hard to decipher. I did recognize a few words: *New York, foster care, David, Zora,* and *leave.* His voice rose in clear agitation, and I caught one more phrase: *hold onto him!*

That sounded like the end of the conversation, so I zipped out of the bathroom. I grabbed my food and hoofed it across the kitchen to the family room. By the time I heard Blair's footsteps, I was surfing binge-watching options on TV. Blair completely ignored me and trotted up the stairs calling for Zora.

Her door opened, and I heard the back-and-forth of their voices, but couldn't catch any words. About a minute later, Blair came back down the stairs and went back into his room. I wasn't sure he'd even seen me. Something was definitely up, and I had a hunch I knew what.

I had a brother, and his name was David.

Chapter 28

The next morning, Zora came downstairs with her small suitcase.

"Where are you going?" I asked her.

"I have to go to New York."

"Why?'

"Always with the questions."

"Humor me." I was really curious as to whether she'd tell me.

She eyed me, glancing at my forehead as she'd done during the assessments the day before.

"Just tell me," I said.

She took a deep breath, as if she was deciding something. "There's another Arcana kid there. I'm going to pick him up."

I paused, then asked her very seriously, "Does he want to come here ?"

As she responded, her eyes faded to that gray color again. "I didn't ask."

Her response touched a nerve. "How could you not ask that?" Didn't it bother her that she was essentially kidnapping people? My anger flared, and without meaning to, I summoned the Scales. The BIG scales. "What could be so important that you're just cool with ripping people away from their families?" As I grew angrier, I pictured the Scales more clearly, like they were something physical. I felt like I wanted her to answer for my crying relatives, my loneliness, and my homesickness. I placed my hands underneath the plates, and was about to summon the feather of truth. I couldn't let this happen to another kid.

Her eyes grew wide. "What the hell are you doing with your hands?" She looked confused, but underneath the confusion I saw fear.

I didn't move my hands or call the feather, not yet. Could she see the scales? "It's not right, what you're doing," I told her. "You choose to be here, and that's cool. But you can't just go around collecting people who don't want to be here. That's *wrong*." There was a strange air of authority in my voice, and I could feel Ma'at's aura enveloping me.

Zora's mouth hung open. "Your chakras ... what are you DOING right now?" she demanded. I didn't answer, but she was definitely alarmed. As she stared at me, all the gray drained from her eyes. That seemed significant, but now wasn't the time to ask.

"What you are doing is WRONG."

"Look, he's basically homeless, alright? He doesn't have anyone to miss him, or anywhere to go." Gray, brown, gray, brown ... her eye color kept shifting between the two, and I began to wonder if she was even aware of it.

I hesitated, but didn't release the Scales.

"He's been bouncing around the foster care system up there. We finally tracked him down. We're going to give him a *home*." She was defensive and afraid, though she didn't know why.

"I already had a home," I said flatly.

"Yeah, well, I don't know what to say about that." She was definitely telling the truth about that, and she was shaken. "I have to go." She grabbed her bag and tried not to look terrified as she rushed toward the door. She was almost out the door when she stopped and shook her head as though she was trying to clear it. She looked at me over her shoulder with a furrowed brow, an emotion I couldn't identify in her brown eyes. She mumbled, "I'm sorry," and then she left.

***

Being alone in the house with Blair was definitely awkward. I guess I had expected that he'd be keeping a very close eye on me, but for most of the day, he was in his room, supposedly going over my results from the previous day. I wasn't really sure what there was to go over, but apparently it was taking awhile.

The day was a dull one, which just amplified how lonely I already was, and how much I missed my family. I rode the exercise bike in the basement, I watched six episodes of a TV show I'd decided to binge-watch, and I worked a little more on the Latin translation. Studying more of the book told me that each card had a foil ... sort of a companion card which could either enhance the abilities of each other, or maybe even cancel the abilities out if they were in opposition to each other. Sort of a psychic failsafe? A table in the back of the book, which had clearly been added sometime after the original text was written, since it was in English, showed the pairings:

O The Fool	I The Magician
II The High Priestess	V The Hierophant
III The Empress	IV The Emperor
VI The Lovers	XI Justice
VII The Chariot	XII The Hanged Man
VIII Strength	XIV Temperance
IX The Hermit	XVI The Tower
X The Wheel of Fortune	XXI The World
XIII Death	XVII The Star
XV The Devil	XX Judgement
XVIII The Moon	XIX The Sun

I wasn't sure how this information would be relevant, but it must have been important, or some ancestor wouldn't have written it inside a book that had already been hundreds of years old. I decided to copy the chart into the back of my legal pad, and just as I was finishing, Blair called up to me to say that we were going out to dinner.

***

It felt strange to be out to dinner with someone who was, essentially, my kidnapper. Yes, he was my biological father, but he had also forced me from my home. I eyed him over my steak salad, trying to decide whether or not I hated him. I decided I probably did. I could feel my brain itching again, though, and by now I knew that meant he was trying to influence me in some way. I figured that probably meant that I was even madder than I thought I was; it was just muted because of his psychic influence. I tried concentrating on my psychic eggshell, but I was having trouble concentrating in his presence. I wondered if that meant I needed to focus on it before being alone with him, but the thought seemed unimportant somehow.

The restaurant was much fancier than I was used to, and I felt awkward in my shirt and jeans. I took small bites and ate very slowly, afraid that I might drip salad dressing on the white tablecloth.

"Well," he said at last, "shall we discuss your assessments?"

I glanced around, paranoid that someone would overhear what would be a decidedly non-normal conversation. "Here?"

"Certainly. The booths here are designed to control the acoustics and facilitate conversation. Besides, no one will pay any mind to what we're saying."

"How can you be so sure of that?"

"Because they barely notice we're here. If they don't notice us, they won't listen to us." He smirked, and I realized that he was showing off. Apparently his skills at mind control and thought manipulation were not limited to one person at a time.

"Yeah, okay. What did you learn about me?"

"Well, for one thing, I learned that you either have very unusual skills, or you're very clever."

"What does that mean?"

"It means, my girl, that you showed almost no aptitude at most of the skills we tested. So either you have skills I cannot test, or you were misleading us during the evaluations. Possibly some of both."

I didn't respond; I just waited for him to continue.

"I suppose I couldn't really begrudge you that, but it would certainly benefit you to have a better idea of your own skills. That facility can also help you hone and control them."

"Assuming I have those kinds of skills, of course."

"Of course," he nodded curtly. "But here's what we did learn. You already know that you can tell when someone is lying. When the lie is obvious, and the person is not making an effort to simply mislead you, your success rate is 100%. That, in itself, is a very useful skill, and we can build on that. We can develop tests that are less obvious and see if you can also suss out deception and obfuscation as well as direct dishonesty."

"Definitely a useful skill," I agreed.

He continued, unfazed. "Zora thinks you might have some ability in remote viewing. At first we thought you might have the power of scrying, which would be *marvelous,* but it doesn't appear that that's the case. Remote viewing still holds some promise, however."

"What's scrying?"

"The ability to see future events with the use of some sort of viewing aid: a crystal ball, a mirror, a bowl of water."

"And remote viewing?"

"Essentially the same thing, but focused on the present, not the past or future."

"Seems like that's something you'd find extremely useful, too."

"If you're proficient at it, certainly."

"So you're really just trying to figure out how useful I'd be to you."

"Obviously."

I took a bite and chewed slowly. I felt anger rising, but I didn't want to play my hand too soon. I felt like I needed to figure out what he was planning. "Is that what you're doing with all of us? Your little magical spawn?"

"What a horrible term," he replied. "But I certainly would like to know how my *progeny* will fit into the world."

"Father of the Year."

"Tsk, tsk, my girl." He kept eating his salmon, looking completely unbothered. "And unless I miss my guess, your psychic sensitivities are growing more proficient."

"Well, I can see ghosts sometimes. And I've noticed that the house is warded. My mind is sharper when I'm not there."

He nodded as though he'd expected that answer. "Still, I suspect you have abilities that aren't really evident as yet." I could tell that he meant that they weren't evident to *him*. He knew I wasn't telling him everything. "As Judgement, you should have certain types of abilities. You have an ancestor who cursed generations. Now THAT is useful." There was something about the way he said it that made the hair on the back of my neck stand up.

"You want to curse generations? Whose generations?"

"You misunderstand. I don't necessarily want to curse anyone. I just want to know I can. Or, rather, that you can if needed."

"Why would I want to do that?"

"All in good time, my dear. We must get our little family together first."

"How did you manage it? Having a bunch of kids who are all Arcana?"

"That seems a rather indelicate question for a girl to ask her father."

My anger cranked up a notch at the casualness with which he said it, and anger sometimes damaged the filter between my brain and my mouth. "You may be my father, but you aren't my dad."

He had the audacity to look hurt. "I'm sure Steven Rush did an admirable job at that. Amanda always did have excellent taste in men." I hated hearing him say my parents' names. It put a lump in my throat to think of them.

"He did a great job. Especially considering I wasn't even his." My voice cracked. Suddenly, I wasn't hungry anymore.

Blair seemed not to notice. He shrugged nonchalantly. "I imagine he loved your mother a great deal. I'm sure he loved you, too."

I couldn't find words. I wanted to run away from this man who was so cavalier about the grief he had caused my family. "Did you? Love my mother?"

He raised his eyes and regarded me for a moment. "I was certainly fond of her. She was a brilliant woman, and quite lovely. Under different circumstances, I might have grown to love her. But there was too much at stake for me to stay with her."

I thought about what Zora had told me about her own mother. "Did she know? About the Arcana and all of this?"

"I think she did know about the Arcana generally. I didn't tell her who I was, of course."

"So you tricked her?" This man was disgusting. Interestingly, my anger made it easier for me to focus on my protective shell. The more I was able to concentrate, the more rage I felt, and vice versa.

"That's a coarse way to think of it. While it's true that my motive was not long-term romance, there was no guarantee you'd become Judgement one day."

I wanted to jump across the table and strangle him. "There was no guarantee she'd even go through with the pregnancy. Did you stick around for any of it?"

"I felt like that would be unfair to her. I never made her any promises of a long-term relationship, and when I sensed that she was pregnant, it was time to make my exit. I had no doubt that she would find someone who would give her a relationship worthy of her. I was quite fond of her, as I said. But I made sure that she would carry you to term."

"You make yourself sound so noble. Do you actually believe you are? You seduced my mother under false pretenses so you could make a magical baby, and then bailed on her. And from what I can tell, you did that to a half a dozen women." A part of me wanted to summon the Scales and Judge him. I wasn't sure what would happen if I did that, but I still wanted to. I held myself back, not wanting to show all my cards before I knew what he was really up to. He was pushing me to my limit, though.

He set down his fork and looked squarely at me. "I don't appreciate your tone, but I can understand your discomfort with the situation. The reality is that I am trying to create a path to a better world, and unfortunately, that means that there are other people who have parts to play whether they want to or not. I have always tried to treat the mothers of my children with respect, even though in most cases, they were not aware of my true intentions. I never said an unkind word to your mother, never mistreated her or belittled her. She did not require any financial or emotional support from me; she was a well-established geologist by the time we parted ways, and was strong and capable. As far as she was aware, I never even knew you existed, so she never felt I had abandoned her. We simply parted ways, and amicably at that."

His words did sound coldly reasonable, but I could also feel him itching at my brain.

"Stop trying to mind-control me."

At that he smiled genuinely. "Ah, so you CAN feel that. Marvelous." He went back to eating his salmon.

"What do you mean by *a better world*?"

"Now THAT is a worthy question. There are magical and non-magical people, Aria, and some of us who are members of the Arcana have a unique ability to see the better paths forward for our world ... a world that could move toward plenty, safety, and security for all. But non-magical leaders lack that vision. They only see what's in their limited perspective. If the Arcana can be united, we can do great good."

"With you at their head, no doubt."

He shrugged. "You're upset right now. This is difficult information to take in, I'm sure. But I am trying to be up-front with you. Everything I'm doing is for the greater good. Finish your meal, and then spend a day or two thinking about things. I think you'll see the big picture."

"And just out of curiosity, what happens if I DON'T see the big picture like you want me to?"

Blair raised an eyebrow at me, then turned his attention to a guy sitting at a table maybe 12 feet from us. The stranger looked like he was probably a businessman in his khakis and a blue dress shirt. He was having what looked like a friendly conversation with another man who was sitting across from him. Mr. Business picked up the fork from the side of his plate and looked at it curiously. He then grasped the handle of the fork in his fist and rammed the tines into his right thigh. He cried out in pain, and his companion leapt up from the table.

"Jack, what in the hell are you doing?" the man cried out in alarm.

"I ... I don't know!" He was staring at the fork which was now standing at a 90° angle in his leg. "I don't know why I did that!" He looked panicked and, frankly, I could understand why. A commotion started around him and the table. He pulled the fork out, and four small spots of blood appeared on his khakis and started to spread. He excused himself to go to the bathroom and clean himself up, and though he was clearly in pain, his leg would probably recover in a day or two. I couldn't help feeling, though, like his mind would take a lot longer. I imagined him trying to explain this episode to a therapist, and wondered how they would rationalize it.

Once the ruckus had died down, Blair looked at me matter-of-factly. He didn't have to say anything. His little demonstration had served as a very potent reminder that, while his mind control tricks had a limited effect on me, there was bound to be someone I love who was not so resistant, and might just get the sudden urge to fly if I wasn't giving Blair what he wanted.

1.

2.

3.

4.

5.

6.

7.

Chapter 29

T rue to his word, Blair essentially kept to himself for the entire next day and a half in order to let me consider his notion of the Brave New World Run by Magic People. His stunt in the restaurant was about the best insurance he could have devised to shut me up and keep me in line. I didn't care too much what he did to me, but I couldn't have lived with myself if my aunt or cousins suffered in retaliation for my attitude.

It seemed to me that the best course of action was to dedicate myself to working on translating more of that leather-bound book. From what I could piece together, the first part of the book seemed to talk about why the cards were made, and the other sections talked philosophically about each of the cards in turn. I couldn't find anything useful like a list of powers or how to use them, but there was an incantation at the beginning of each section. I was guessing that that incantation attuned each card to its holder.

I didn't dare mark up the book, but I had made a few key notes on my legal pad. In the section on Judgement, I translated a few lines that seemed particularly important: *gaudet tentamine virtus,* meaning *virtue rejoices in trial; culpam poena premit comes* meaning something like *punishment presses down upon crime;* and *furiosi solo furore punitur* which seemed to mean something like *madmen are punished by their own fury.*

After every half hour of translation work, I rewarded myself with an hour of TV, so the epic battle of Aria vs. Latin was going very slowly. But I felt like understanding the cards was key to figuring out a plan to get me away from this man and back with the people I loved, so the next time he strolled into the kitchen for a snack, I called down to him over the second-floor railing.

"Excuse me."

He looked up, surprised.

"What are the odds of me having Internet access to do research?"

"That would be exactly zero. You haven't shown yourself to be exactly trustworthy yet."

That was the answer that I expected, so I had a back-up question ready. "Okay, then, can you take me to a library to check out some books? You can watch me the whole time."

He considered that. "I suppose that would be acceptable. What are you working on?"

"I'm trying to learn more about the Major Arcana so I can figure out my abilities. I'm not having a lot of luck with the Latin."

"Latin grammar can be challenging, certainly."

"Can you read it?"

"Passably. I doubt I could compose anything, but I can get the gist of what I read most of the time."

"So you could tell me what some of this book says?"

He responded with a crooked smile, "You have but to ask, my dear."

Inside my head, I was screaming, *WHY DIDN'T YOU JUST SAY THAT INSTEAD OF LETTING ME KILL MY BRAIN CELLS FOR HOURS ON END?* But what I said was, "Oh, great. I have a few questions."

"About what?"

"The history part, mostly."

"Ah, yes, well, I can tell you a little about that. I have to make a couple of phone calls tonight, but I'll take you to the library in the morning, and we'll talk then."

***

Ma'at had been quiet for a couple of days, so I tried to connect with her while I was getting ready to go to the library the following day. I filled the sink about halfway with water and reached out to her. A moment later, her indistinct reflection appeared in the water. I was not surprised that her voice was inaudible. I exaggeratedly mouthed to her, *I'll try later,* and she nodded. Now that Blair was aware of some of my abilities, it appeared he had strengthened the wards somewhat until he was precisely sure what I could and couldn't do. I took the hint and spent a little time feeding energy to the shields around myself before we headed to the library.

I remained quiet on the drive, and when we pulled up to the most-ly-brick building, my attention was drawn to a collection of statues out front. A figure of a stag-headed man-creature with a human body sat facing several bronzed dogs, who watched him with rapt attention. There were sitting-stones encircling the figure as well, inviting passers-by to sit and listen to his story. I was fascinated by the art display. I felt like when I walked through the library doors, I'd pop out in Narnia.

Given that, the inside was a bit of a let-down. It looked like every other library I'd ever been in: bookcases with light wood sides and gray metal shelves, carpet that was really more like a fuzzy floor, low tables and tiny chairs in the kids' section. Blair went up to the circulation desk to fill out the paperwork or online form or whatever to get a library card. I started over to the computer to look up the types of book I was searching for. Blair eyed me warily, and hurried over to join me as soon as he'd finished at the desk. Clearly, he didn't trust that I wouldn't try to get a message to my family. He was right to doubt me. I'd been hoping to send a quick message to Logan on email or social media, but I didn't even have enough time to launch one of the sites before he started walking toward me. *Rats.*

I located the section for books on the supernatural and went and grabbed a few that looked promising. I sat down at a table to flip through them, and picked out two that seemed to have fairly thorough information on tarot. The lady at the desk booped the barcodes and told us the books were due back in two weeks. We were on our way out when I had an idea.

"Hey, I need to run to the restroom. Will you hold these for a second?" I dumped the books into Blair's arms and dashed off to the ladies' room.

I locked myself into the handicapped stall. Normally, I'd feel badly about that, but there were only a handful of people in the library, and I wouldn't be here for very long. I walked over to the sink and was distressed to find that there was no stopper. I glanced over at the toilet. Oh, man.

I stared into the water and sent my thoughts out to Ma'at, keeping one ear open for the bathroom door. Her face appeared in the water.

"Blair wants to bring the Arcana together. He says he's trying to make the world a better place or something."

Uniting the Arcana would increase their power, certainly. If they were working toward the same goal, they would amplify each other. That would make him more dangerous.

"That's what I thought. What do I do?"

That is for you to decide. But I believe it would be unwise to grant this Magician any more power than he already has. His heart is heavy with misdeeds.

I sighed in frustration. "Yeah, I can kinda tell that, even without the Scales."

I am not omniscient, child. I cannot give you answers I do not have. We are One, but you must understand who you are and who you wish to be. Only then will you know what path to follow.

"So we're doing riddles now? Can't you just magic something up to help me?"

Not all magic works that way; you should know that by now. Our energies have specific applications. You must work within that. His goal is to Reverse you, as he is Reversed. To twist your power to his ends rather than your own. This is what you must not allow.

I knew I didn't have much time before Blair would become suspicious. "So you can't really help me here?"

I can help you within the scope of Judgement's powers, but those are powers you already possess. The divine energy of Judgement is yours to wield. I can help you understand it.

"Can you get a message to Paul? He was Judgement for three years. Are you still connected to him?"

His time as Judgement was hindered by the curse. He never bonded with the energy within the card. He was merely its caretaker, as was his father. Had it been otherwise, you would not be Judgement now.

There was something about that statement that felt important, but I couldn't take any more time. I felt pretty cheated. I had my very own goddess, and she couldn't help me with my problems. That just didn't seem fair. I flushed the toilet and went back out to join Blair, who was waiting impatiently by the exit. He handed me the books without a word and we got in the car. Ma'at had told me that he would try to reverse me; was that what he had done with Zora?

"So Zora said she's known you pretty much her whole life."

"That is, indeed, true. When I was younger, I wondered who the other Arcana were. My father had told me they were spread all over the world and that no one knew who they all were anymore. I set out to find them, and Zora's mother, Aretta Bello, was among the first I met. Remarkable woman."

"And she was Strength when you met her?"

"She was, yes. She was a barrister in London. Sort of what you might think of as a public defender."

"How did she die?" It seemed like a rude question, but I didn't feel like I had to worry too much about hurting Blair's feelings.

"Cancer, I'm afraid. By the time she was diagnosed, things had already progressed beyond where treatment could be effective."

"And that's when Zora became Strength?"

"Actually, the changeover happened before Aretta passed. In some ways, Zora was very fortunate; she had the benefit of a parent who could help her understand what the Arcana were, and how to access her own power." He seemed surprisingly sincere.

"Did you love Aretta?"

"In a way, I suppose I did. We did not remain romantically involved, as you know, but we did remain close, and I tried to be active in Zora's life when I could."

"But you didn't do that with all the children you fathered." There was a definite accusation in my tone.

"Heavens, no. I can't imagine any of them would have been able to accept and appreciate what I was trying to do. Most women just aren't wired that way."

"So Aretta is the only one who knew the truth. About you being The Magician, about you fathering other kids, all of it."

"In fairness to me, Aretta wasn't interested in a lifetime commitment to me, either. She was fiercely independent. She liked the idea of being a mother, but wasn't particularly interested in being a wife. Mine or anyone else's for that matter."

"Sounds like you two were quite the pair," I replied sarcastically.

He smiled, a real smile, as though recalling something. "If anyone has ever truly understood me, it was Aretta." I felt as though I was seeing a different man from the arrogant, manipulative person I'd been living with for almost a week. I still didn't like him, but at least he didn't seem fake.

"This is going to sound like a weird question …" I began.

"That's alright; I'll answer if I can."

"Why did you bother with my mother? She wasn't in line to become Judgement, so there's no reason to think a child of hers would, either."

He hesitated, just for a second, and I sensed that I had struck a nerve. "That is true. Your mother was a bit of a gamble. It was clear from the information I had collected that Judgement had been largely inactive for some time. But the Sheffield name was one of the few that appeared in my records, so your family was easy to search up. This sounds awful to say, but I simply felt there was nothing to be lost. Your uncle had no sisters, of course, but he did have a female cousin of the right age. That's really all there was to it."

Even without the Scales, there was no doubt that this was the truth as he saw it. Something was nagging at me, though. There was a piece of this puzzle that I was missing. We arrived back at the house, and I took my library books up to the office to continue my research.

According to Ma'at, each card had its own set of energies, and therefore its own set of abilities within a certain scope. I thought if I studied the meanings of the cards, that would give me some insight as to what powers Zora, Blair, and I all had. I laid the books out in front of me: two books on tarot, and one book on different gods and goddesses from around the world. I spread them out with my legal pad, then dove in. Two hours later, I had more notes on the legal pad than I'd taken my entire sophomore year. I grabbed highlighter and marked the parts that seemed most important:

Judgement: conscience, doing the right thing, reaping what you sow, truth, spiritual progression, liberation

Judgement reversed: regret, reckoning, imbalance, loneliness, self-pity

Judgement Deities: Anubis, Ma'at (Egyptian); Kings Minos, Aeacus, and Radamanthus (Greek), Yama (Hindu), the Judeo-Christian God,

Nemesis and Poena (Greek), Praxidice (Greek), Takhar (Serer), Vidarr
(Norse), the Greek Furies, Tyr (Norse)
Known powers: Lie detection, knowing if someone's guilty?
Possible powers: Curses, remote viewing

The Magician: willpower, authority, confidence, strength of purpose, re-
sourcefulness, manifestation of desires
The Magician reversed: cunning, trickery, deception, selfishness, abuse of
power
The Magician (possible) deities of authority: Zeus/Jupiter/Mercury??
(Greek/Roman), Marduk (Mesopotamia), Odin (Norse), Shiva (Hin-
du), Amun (Egyptian), Dangun (Korean), Olorun (Yoruba), Jade Em-
peror (Chinese), the Judeo-Christian God
Known powers: Mind control
Possible powers: ???

Strength: strength, courage, determination, moral fortitude, willpower,
overcoming obstacles
Strength reversed: temptation, abuse of power, base instincts
Strength (battle?) deities: Kratos (Greek), Thor (Norse), Bast/Sekhmet
(Egyptian), Durga, Shakti (Hindu), Ishtar (Babylonian), Bellona (Ro-
man), Athena (Greek)
Known powers: some mind thingie, intimidating, chakras?
Possible powers: what is the mind thingie?, super strength?

I did a quick search on chakras, since I'd heard the term, but didn't really
know much about them. Chakras, according to what I read, are energy
centers in the body, and though there was some disagreement on how
many there actually are, there are definitely seven main ones that run in a
vertical line parallel to the spine. Each had a different function, but the one
on the forehead, the one Zora seemed to study when I used my abilities,

was the *third eye* chakra, the one most closely aligned with intuition. That made sense, and this was definitely a subject worthy of more research. Just then, Blair poked his head into the office.

"How goes the research?"

"Slowly. Would certainly go a lot faster if I could use the Internet."

He plowed over that comment. "Can I see what you've found?'

I sensed that this was a trap to see if I was trying to be sneaky. On the bright side, though, it probably meant that he couldn't read my mind anymore. I handed him the legal pad. He flipped through, looking first at the attempts at Latin translation, then paging his way forward to the tarot notes I just took.

"You've been very productive," was all he said, and handed the paper back to me.

"You said you could tell me about the history?"

He made a quick nod. "In summary, the early years of human history were filled with violence and chaos. In the mid-to-late 1500's, a group of mages representing magical families theorized that this chaos was caused by a constant clashing of cosmic divine energy. These families cast a spell to divide up and harness these powers in order to limit them and bring order to the human world. This spell is what created the cards. Each family took a card, and went their separate ways across the globe. Over the years, even the names of some of the families were lost to time."

"But you know some of them?"

"Some of them were well-documented, some I was able to track down through my own research ..."

"Which, no doubt, included the ability to use the internet."

"No doubt."

"So if they did all of that to try and split the energies up, why are you trying to bring some of them back together?"

"Clearly, splitting the energies up didn't do much to fix the chaos in the world, I think we can agree. Those of us with magical insight, the Arcana, can make a difference, make things better, as I mentioned to you before."

"But wouldn't that only work if the Arcana share a common vision?"

"That would certainly help."

And with your mind-control abilities, you think you can ensure it, I thought to myself. *Then you can start re-creating things in your own vision.*

"And what, exactly, is your vision? I mean, it's not like you're in a position of power or anything, are you?"

"Not myself personally, but I have allies. Everything would have to start slowly, of course, and there are ... timing issues. That's why it's important that I bring us all together in the next few months. It's a difficult task, two decades in the making. It would be much easier with your help."

"It's hard to want to help you, given that you ripped me away from my family."

"I *am* your family. I don't understand why you can't see that. Pamela and the boys certainly care for you, but has it never occurred to you that they were already a family when you arrived? Haven't you ever felt like you didn't quite fit?"

I didn't like that he was right. "I don't feel like I fit here either."

He laughed, but it was mirthless. "Of course you don't. You've only known me for a week. But I'll be able to help you learn about the use of magic, and it won't be long before you find that your life will never be the same now that you have power. You aren't an ordinary teenager anymore. This is where you belong."

"Why did it have to be like this, though? I'm only here because you've threatened to hurt people I love, and now you've even hurt innocent people just to prove that you could in order to intimidate me into doing what you want. How do you think that will build loyalty and trust?" I couldn't keep the anger out of my voice, no matter that I knew it was unwise.

"I told you, I don't have time to do this at a snail's pace. I'm already behind schedule." I could sense that there was great frustration behind this, and I got the feeling it didn't have anything to do with me. I knew it was stupid and risky, but I pushed back harder.

"You've been working on it for twenty years, and you could have tried getting to know me at any point in the last fifteen. You could have built a relationship with me instead of pretending I didn't exist. If you didn't want me at Sheffield Glen, then you could have stepped up when my parents died." I put extra emphasis on *parents* to remind him that I didn't see him as my father, no matter whose genetics I shared.

"Well, what good would you have been to me then? Judgement was under a curse and still in the hands of your uncle."

"What *good* would I have been? Being your daughter isn't enough?"

"Agh!" He threw up his hands in frustration. "You're as stubborn as Amanda! All the more reason why she'd have been useless to me as Judgement. I'd hoped you would be more reasonable if the card ever came down to you." He stormed out of the room and down the stairs. A few seconds later, I heard his door slam.

There it was again, that little something I was missing, wiggling around at the back of my consciousness. I started thinking about all the events that had had to line up for me to become Judgement (and therefore useful, apparently), and started working my way backwards. I snatched up my legal pad and started writing.

1. The curse had to be broken, which could only be done by someone outside of Robert Sheffield's line.

2. My mother and I were the only members of the Sheffield bloodline that didn't come down from Robert, which meant that one of us had to break the curse.

3. Since Uncle MJ was Judgement, there was no way it would pass

to my mother if he died; it would go to Paul or Logan as long as
the curse stood.

4. That meant that it had to be me, but that would never happen as
long as I was living with my parents. I had to be living at the Glen.
Just being there for the summers wouldn't have been enough.

5. Even living at the Glen hadn't done the trick. I only started tap-
ping into the magic at the Glen once I'd whacked my head.

6. That meant two events had to have happened to make my becoming Judgement even a possibility. My parents had to die so
that custody would fall to the Sheffields, and I had to have a
concussion/near death experience to "activate" my brain.

7. How far was Dorian Blair willing to go to add one more member
to his weird, dysfunctional family?

***

Sleep that night was troubled and filled with dreams I couldn't remember on waking. I just knew that I felt a renewed sense of dread creeping
up my spine as I considered the collective possibilities that had occurred
to me the night before. I wasn't sure if I should try and have it out with
Blair, or if I should play nice and back off. If my dawning suspicions were
right, my family and I were in much worse danger than I had realized. I
desperately wished I could find out the truth; if I threw accusations at him,
I knew he'd just deny them, or be cryptic.

The truth.

Wait a minute.

I was Judgement. The truth was my specialty.

Chapter 30

I grabbed a cup of water from the kitchen and slipped down the basement stairs. I let myself out, hoping I could get a few words in with Ma'at before Blair realized I was gone. It was early yet, but the day was already in the 80's, and the humidity was stifling as I crossed the flagstones. I climbed the ladder into the playhouse carefully, so as not to spill too much of the water, and I strategically positioned myself so that I would be able to see Blair if he came out onto the porch or the terrace.

I held the glass between my hands and pressed my back against the wood. Ma'at's face appeared almost instantaneously. I was getting pretty good at this.

"Do I have the power to force people to tell the truth?" I spoke in low tones, just in case.

An interesting idea. It certainly seems like that should be within your power.

"Do you have that power?"

I have never had a need for such a power, but if such a power exists, it will manifest when you are in control of the Scales. They are your spiritual talisman.

I had an idea.

Have you considered, child, what you would do with the truth if you found it?

I had not. "One thing at a time," I replied. "If I'm right ..."

If you are right, then you put your own life in great danger.

"Maybe. But he can't kill me. If he does, then Paul or Logan would become Judgement, and they would be totally useless to him because they don't share his blood."

Be careful, child. Think and plan before you act.

"Oh, I'll be planning. You can count on that." I drank the water and made my way back into the house. I went upstairs and packed my toiletries back into my suitcase; I didn't have to repack any of my clothes, because I'd never unpacked to begin with. I did shove all the dirty clothes to one side and left the clean ones on the other. If this went the way I'd hoped, I'd be going home one way or another.

Once I was packed, I walked across the upstairs landing and into Zora's room. I wasn't sure why, but I hadn't expected it to be so *tidy*. Nothing was just laying around; it looked like something out of a model home, except for a random anime poster on the closet door. Neatly-made queen sized bed with throw pillows, desk, matching dresser and nightstand, a comfy chair, and a wooden trunk at the foot of the bed. The upscale "genericness" of the decor led me to believe that Blair had, in fact, bought all the furnishings along with the house. I hated to go through her things, but I had every intention of being out of this house by nightfall, and she had something that belonged to me. I was hoping she hadn't taken it with her.

Thinking of Paul and his possessiveness over the Judgement card, I started by checking the desk drawers. There were a few papers and things in it, but I wasn't sure what they were, and I wasn't going to take the time to figure it out. I wasn't here to snoop, after all. I gave up on the desk and started on the nightstand. Luckily, I struck gold this time. There was my phone, sans SIM card, but otherwise intact. I snatched it up and slipped it into my backpack. Now, onto Blair himself.

His mind was strong, but I had managed, with Ma'at's help, to hide most of my strength from him. I had played his game for long enough. I thought carefully about what I needed to do, what I needed to know. Then I closed my eyes, took a deep breath, and concentrated on making my shield impenetrable.

It was time for a showdown.

***

I came down to find Blair at the kitchen table reading an investment magazine. His eyes narrowed when he looked up at me, and I knew he was still mad about our argument the night before. Well, his mood wasn't going to get any better this morning.

"I think it's about time you and I cleared up a few things and came to an understanding," I began. I had rehearsed this speech a dozen times in my head so that I wouldn't panic and say something stupid or show weakness.

He set his magazine down, but said nothing.

"I need to level with you about a couple of things, and I think you need to do the same."

"Is that so?" He seemed to be trying to decide whether he was amused or annoyed by my boldness.

"Yes, it's *so,*" I quipped, imitating his tone. "I'll go first. I do have at least one ability that I haven't told you about." He raised one eyebrow, interested. I took a deep breath and summoned the Scales before me. I started with the smaller ones, the ghostly lie detectors with the feather of truth hovering above them, waiting to tell me what I wanted to know. He raised an eyebrow and looked me over from head to toe. He didn't appear to see the Scales, but he knew my energy had shifted. The next part was sort of a guess. Zora had seen the Scales when I wanted her to, when I was angry. So I willed for him to see them, then waited for a reaction. There wasn't much of one.

"I can see you're doing something there," he said smoothly, "but I can't tell exactly what. I can feel the power you've called, though. I'm intrigued."

"I want you to tell me the truth," I said simply. I steadied my breath and launched into the sequence of questions I'd mentally prepared. I knew I had to ask them just the right way, play on his arrogance, and then blindside him with questions he didn't expect. I couldn't afford to let nerves get the best of me. "Let's start easy. I've felt you trying to influence my mood. Do you influence Zora's?"

"I influence everyone's." The feather floated down to the right side of the scale and the sides remained completely balanced. He was telling the truth, and the truth was a bit scary.

"Okay, thanks for the honesty. How about this one: did you cause my car accident last month?"

Both of his eyebrows went up this time. I had clearly surprised him. He hesitated ever-so-slightly before responding. "No, I did not cause your accident."

The scales didn't move, but the feather floated upwards until it hovered over the center.. That had happened once before, and I was guessing it meant that he was both telling the truth and lying at the same time. It was all in the wording of the question.

"Let me rephrase. Did you have any hand in causing the accident?"

His face darkened. "Whatever gave you that idea? What a horrible thing to suggest."

"Yes or no?"

"Certainly not." The feather floated down onto the scales, and the empty side grew heavier. He was lying. He may not have caused the accident, but I was betting he made Zora do it. It made me wonder what she'd be capable of when under his influence.

"Alright," I said, not showing him that I was aware of his lie, "have you known about me my whole life?"

"More or less. I knew your mother was pregnant when we parted ways, even though she didn't. But I didn't actually see you until you were about four. Pre-school dance recital. You were Susie Snowflake, I believe." Absolutely true. And a little creepy, though I think he was going for sweet.

"Interesting. And you didn't contact my mother even once in all that time?"

"No, there was no reason to." True.

"Did you ever have contact with my father?"

"No." True, though the feather did rise a little bit off the scales. Perhaps the question was too vague.

"Did you have any influence on my life before you and I met?"

"Yes." True.

"Like what?"

"An extra present here or there that I may have influenced someone to buy you. Remember that pink bike with the banana seat and the tassels? That sort of thing. I may have had some hand in influencing your aunt and uncle to send you to Lockridge instead of public school. Of course, Logan had to go, too, but they could afford it." True.

"Wait, why would you do that?"

He sniffed. "Superior education, naturally." Also true.

"Did you have any influence on me going to live with Aunt Pam and Uncle MJ?"

"Of course, though it was the natural order of things when your parents died. You'd already spent summers there, which was also my influence, before you ask."

"So you don't even have to be close to someone to influence them?"

"No, not if I've met them. Once my energy has crossed theirs, they carry sort of a signature, if you will. With enough concentration, I can reach my will outward for miles," he replied smugly.

There was one more question I needed to ask. I took a deep breath, not sure I'd want to know the answer. "Did you cause my parents' death?"

"I beg your pardon? Surely you're joking." The feather floated above the scales, and my heart began to pound.

"Yes or no?" I struggled to keep my voice even.

"No," he replied flatly, but the feather remained in its uncertain position.

"Did you," I took another deep breath, "have any hand or influence at all in the death of my parents?"

He stood in affected offense. "Absolutely not!" The feather settled on the scale, and the empty side dropped with the weight of his guilt.

I felt the grief and rage I'd shuttered up for so long rising to the surface, and as it rose, the small scales grew and morphed into Ma'at's Scales of Judgement. His eyes grew wide, as Zora's had, only instead of my forehead, he was looking at the rage in my face, rippling off me in waves. He could see the Scales now ... and deep down, he was afraid!

"LIAR!" I screamed. "Tell me the truth!" I placed my hands under the plates and held them in balance. "Were you in any way involved in my parents' death?"

He was clearly trying to deny it, but couldn't get the words out. I willed harder for him to tell the truth; I would not let him lie to me. Not now, not ever again. Finally, he hissed, "I influenced a maintenance man and a pilot at the plane hangar."

"To do what?"

"To misread the amount of fuel in the tanks."

"Which caused the plane to crash?"

"Essentially."

"You are responsible for their deaths! YOU KILLED MY PARENTS, YOU BASTARD!" Without even realizing what I was doing I reached out my hand, and I could see Ma'at's aura around my arm. She plunged her hand into his chest and pulled out a spectral image of his beating heart. He looked above me, and I knew he could see her flowing through me, above me yet a part of me, my true power revealed in terrible clarity. He stared at the superimposed image of the goddess and me, and he was frozen in horror. "You must face Judgement!" Ma'at and I placed the hazy blue heart opposite the Feather of Truth on the Scales, and the side with his heart sunk like we had placed a brick on it.

"What are you doing?" he gasped.

"Your heart is heavy with evil and deceit." The voice came from me, but it wasn't quite mine. "The punishment is mine to choose."

He clutched at his chest, not in pain, but in fear. He stumbled backward, knocking the chair over and nearly falling himself. "Get out," he gasped.

"Gladly," I growled at him. "And if I sense your influence anywhere near me or my family, your own wickedness will destroy you. Remember that."

I had my bags waiting at the top of the stairs, and without another word, I retrieved them and walked out the front door.

I was going home.

Chapter 31

Being fifteen has definite drawbacks, and one of them is a fundamental lack of ability to think several steps ahead. My brilliant plan had worked, but there were several things I hadn't accounted for. The first was that I now knew that my biological father had essentially murdered my parents in order to get to me. I hadn't accounted for the weight of that knowledge, or how it would deepen the grief that had always made me feel isolated.

I also hadn't figured out how to get home.

I rolled my bag down the street, which is not something you normally see in a swanky neighborhood like this one. I realized that I had no idea where to go. I knew that even without a SIM card, I could use my phone to call 911, but then I'd have to explain everything to the cops, and I had a feeling I'd end up Baker Acted if I did that. I remembered that there were a couple of schools nearby, because I'd seen them when we were driving, but that wouldn't do me much good during the summertime.

I reached the end of the residential street and spotted a street sign that told me I'd found Highway 41. I looked across the highway at the elementary school, and sure enough, it was deserted. To the right though, there was a parking lot full of cars, and when there was a break in the traffic, I made my way across. I found myself staring at a retirement community, and I made a beeline for the automatic doors.

It looked like I was in the lobby of a fancy hotel, only much quieter. There were only a few residents seated in the lounge area. One lady was reading, and another couple was talking quietly by a large window. Behind the desk, a man of about 35 eyed me, looking from me to my suitcase and back again with unconcealed surprise.

"Are you here to visit someone? I didn't get word that anyone would be using one of our guest suites this week."

I rolled up to the desk. "Actually, I need some help. I came to Atlanta with someone, and, well, it didn't work out." He leaned forward, clearly hoping for a sordid story. I let the tears that were so close to the surface pool into my eyes. "I just want to go home. But *he* took the SIM card from my phone, and I can't call anyone to come get me. Can I please use a phone?" I didn't even have to try and look pathetic.

"Well, bless your heart," came a voice from behind me. The reading lady had somehow managed to sidle up behind me, sensing a dramatic tale of woe, no doubt. "Jeffrey, give that poor girl the phone."

He reached for the phone but hesitated as he extended the receiver toward me. "Is it a local number?"

"No, I'm afraid not. Virginia."

"I'd love to help you, miss, but it's against regulations for me to be making long-distance calls from the desk phone."

"Oh, Jeffrey, for Pete's sake. The girl's in distress here."

"I'm sorry, Ms. Hopkins, it's regulations."

"Lord a-Mighty," Ms. Hopkins fussed. "can't you see this girl is in need, Jeffrey? Follow me, honey. My grandson gave me a cellphone. You can use that to call your family, and you're my guest until they come to get you."

"Now, Ms. Hopkins," Jeffrey called after us as we padded down the soft latte-colored carpet toward Ms. Hopkins' apartment, "you know it's against regulations to have overnight guests without approval in advance."

"Put a sock in it, Jeffrey," she called cheerfully over her shoulder. "I swear, he's a good boy, but none too bright." We reached a door marked 116, and she unlocked it and let us in. A Yorkshire terrier came prancing up to the door, wagging its tail so hard that I thought its butt would fall right off. "Prince William, you keep our guest company while I go get my phone." She hung her key on a hook by the door and disappeared into a room on the right.

I bent down to scratch the tiny dog, and he was elated. He licked my fingers and rolled all over my feet. Then he trotted off and brought me an athletic sock that had clearly been converted into a tug-o-war toy. We were engaged in fierce battle when Ms. Hopkins came back into the room.

"Here you go, honey. It's all charged up. You call your family, and I'll make us some snacks and then you can tell me all about your problems." She handed me a flip-phone that had clearly been designed for senior citizens, complete with large numbers and special buttons for immediate connection to emergency services. My hands were shaking with excitement as I dialed Logan's number.

He didn't pick up, but I didn't really expect him to, since he wouldn't recognize the number. I hung up and texted him.

Hey, jerk. It's Ree. I'm going to call you again. Pick up this time!

I gave him a minute to read the text, then called again. He picked up immediately.

"Ree? Is it really you?"

"Yeah, it's me." Without warning, tears filled my eyes and I was wracked with sobs. I tried to keep it in to save Ms. Hopkins from the awkwardness, but I was so relieved to hear his voice that I couldn't control myself. "I got away from him."

"Holy crap, we've been freaking out! Are you okay?" I could hear his breath quicken and his feet pounding either up or down some stairs, probably toward his mother.

"I'm okay. It's been a crazy week. I just want to come home," I said between hiccups of weeping.

"Mom! It's Aria! She's safe!"

In the background, I could hear my aunt's voice. "What? Oh, thank God! Put her on speaker! Aria, can you hear me?"

"Yes, Aunt Pam, I can hear you." My heart ached in my chest.

"Where are you?"

"I'm in Atlanta. He flew me here. He has a house not far from where I am."

"Is he after you?" Logan chimed in.

"No, I don't think so. I'll tell you all about it, but right now, this nice lady is letting me use her phone." I was hoping they'd realize that I couldn't tell the whole story in front of her.

"Don't worry about my minutes, honey, I never use them all," she called from the kitchen.

"Who's that?" my aunt asked.

"When I left Blair's house, I walked to this retirement home. Ms. Hopkins is letting me use her phone to call you."

"Tell her we owe her the world," Aunt Pam said. "Did you say Atlanta? Can you get to an airport? I'll book you on the first flight home."

"I probably can, I'd just have to figure out how to get there. Blair took the SIM card from my phone, so I can't use any of those apps until I get a new one."

Ms. Hopkins came into the room with a tray of cheese, crackers, and grapes. Prince William was scurrying around her feet barking, clearly wanting his share. She took a piece of cheese off the plate and set the rest in front of me. "Come on, Princey. Give her some privacy now." She lured him away with the cheese and went back into her bedroom.

"Alright," my aunt said. "I'm going to check on flights. Are you safe where you are?"

"Yes, I think so."

"Good. Can I reach you at this number?"

"Probably. Ms. Hopkins said I was her guest until I could go home."

"Okay, I'm going to try and book something for later today. Do you have ID?"

"Yes, he didn't take any of that." I couldn't believe it. I might be sleeping in my own bed tonight.

"Great. Give me a few minutes, and I'll call you back."

"Okay. Aunt Pam, I'm so sorry to have worried you like this. I had to go with him. I'll tell you all about it when I see you, but believe me, I wouldn't have left if I didn't think I had to. I'm so, so sorry."

"I'm just so grateful you're safe," she replied.

"Yeah, well, I'm still mad at you, doofus," Logan chimed in, but I could hear in his voice that he was smiling. "You've got me to answer to when you get home,"

"I'll deal with it," I smiled back.

We said our temporary good-byes and I hung up. Ms. Hopkins came back into the room so quickly that I could tell she'd been eavesdropping. I couldn't blame her. This was like a freaking TV drama. I couldn't tell her the whole story, of course, so I just told her that I had come to stay with a relative who lived nearby, and he had turned out not to be a very nice person. He had thrown me out, I said, and now I just wanted to go home to Virginia. She looked at me with sympathetic eyes, and I suspected she had some doubts about my so-called "relative" actually being a relative, but she kept them to herself.

"I'm just so glad you'll be going home. I'm sure your family misses you. I'd consider it a great pleasure to drive you to the airport and see you off safely."

"Oh, that's so nice of you," I gushed, "but I don't want to put you to so much trouble."

"No trouble at all," she assured me. "If it were my granddaughter in trouble, I'd sure want someone to help her out. I'd feel a lot better if I could be sure you got onto a plane headed for those who will look after you." She patted my hand.

"Thank you so much. You can't imagine how much I appreciate it."

My aunt called back and told me she had booked me a direct flight into Charlottesville, leaving in three hours. She spoke briefly to Ms. Hopkins and solidified my travel plans. I couldn't believe it. The nightmare, at least this part of it, was nearly over. I'd be sleeping in my own bed tonight.

Ms. Hopkins, Prince William, and I loaded into her car and, after a quick stop at a grocery store so I could get cash and buy a SIM card for my phone, we braved the Atlanta afternoon traffic. Miraculously, I made it to the airport with a half an hour to spare, which is to say that I was there two hours before my flight was scheduled to be wheels-up. I hugged Ms. Hopkins fiercely and thanked her repeatedly.

"Promise me you'll call me when you're home safely," she told me. "That's all the thanks I need."

"I promise," I told her, and hugged her again. I checked my suitcase at the desk and headed for my gate. I was giddy with joy.

***

When I stepped out of the security area at Charlottesville, I was instantly swarmed with hugs. Aunt Pam was sobbing, and Paul and Logan ribbed me endlessly after an initial proclamation that they were glad about my return. In the car on the way home—*home*—I filled them in on all of the events from the week I was gone. Paul asked a dozen questions about Ma'at and my newfound abilities; he was genuinely curious, but also a little jealous. Aunt Pam asked questions about our on-going safety, and what kinds of risks we might face. Logan mostly listened. When I told them what I'd discovered about Blair's hand in Logan and my car accident as well as the plane crash that had killed my parents, the car filled with a heavy silence. No one knew what to say, though our hearts were full of the same grief and fear.

By the time we pulled into the familiar driveway, it was well after dark. I hadn't even realized how tense I still was until I felt my jaw unclench and my shoulders relax as I took in the sight of the house that had been my home for the past five years. I couldn't wait to set foot in my room, flop down on the bed, just see my familiar possessions rather than the tidy alien environment I'd been in for the past week.

Logan offered to carry my bag and followed me up the three flights of stairs, lugging my suitcase with him. "Did you take literally everything you own? Maybe a few bricks and books?"

"Shut up, jerk." I punched his shoulder as he set the bag down.

"I'm glad you're home, doofus."

"Me too."

He gave me a big hug and then went downstairs, leaving me in my sanctuary. I walked over to the big window and stared out into the darkness. So much had happened since the last time I had looked out over the Glen from this window. I wondered about Anne and William ... and James. I wondered if they had found peace. I glimpsed my own reflection in the glass, then closed my eyes, took a deep breath, and reached out to Ma'at for the first time since fleeing Atlanta.

You have done well, child, but you have made a great enemy.

"What will happen to him now that I've Judged him?"

For the moment, nothing. You held back on punishment.

"Nothing will happen?"

When I weighed hearts, those who were deemed unworthy would be thrown to Ammut. You weighed his heart, but did not pronounce his unworthiness. You correctly assumed that you would retain that power.

"So I literally hold his heart in my hand?"

You hold his worthiness up to this point in his life. Remember, his is a living soul, not one which has pierced the veil of life. He could redeem his future life, but his sins up to now have been Judged.

"What does punishment look like on a living soul?"

I can only guess. I do not Judge the living.

"Would it be a curse, like what Daniel Sheffield cast on Robert's bloodline?"

I would imagine it would be whatever punishment you design that befits his wickedness. You should probably give that some thought in case you ever have occasion to pronounce a punishment.

"Do you think he knows that?"

Based on his reaction, yes. But I also think it would be foolish to assume that he would give up his quest. Magicians are notoriously stubborn creatures.

"So it's not really over. I need to plan for whenever he shows up again."

It would be wise, but I suspect he will need a little time to recuperate and do planning of his own. Rest now. Once you feel ready, I will teach you how to place a shield around others the way I taught you to place one around yourself.

I nodded, and felt her presence melt away, leaving me in solitude to ponder the darkness and the future.

Chapter 32

The next week passed quickly, and our family spent nearly every minute of it together, even Paul. There was little talk of Dorian Blair, only a meaningful return to normalcy, which we'd been denied all summer.

Gramps and Laz had created a beautiful memorial on the new burial site, and had moved several flagstones from the chapel over to create a sort of paved patio surrounded by the hyacinth bushes and all the plants we had bought at the farmers market. Off to each side, he had placed stone benches; it was now a place of beauty, serenity, and reflection. The aura of despair that had surrounded the chapel was gone.

I'd made it a routine to come out to the memorial garden every morning and center myself in the peace and quiet. I pulled out my EMF meter and walked through the whole house, the yard, and the chapel area. I felt no chill in the air and had no visions, so I felt confident that my ancestors had moved on to whatever next world had awaited them. The knowledge filled me with a profound sense of accomplishment. Not only had my abilities as Judgement helped to keep my living family safe, they had also helped bring peace and rest to those who had already died.

For the first time since this insane odyssey had begun, it seemed to me that being a member of the Arcana could have a real impact in the world.

I could see the allure of it, and if he had not been a total psychopath, Blair might have been able to win me over to his cause. One thing was sure, though, no good could come of putting him in a position of power.

I returned to the house and trekked up the stairs to Logan's room. He was surrounded by laundry baskets full of folded clothes.

"I can't believe the summer is almost over," I sighed.

"Feels like we hardly had one," he agreed.

"Did you actually fold all those clothes?"

"Heck, no. Mom did it. Not complaining. I stink at folding shirts."

I slid a couple over and sat on the foot of his bed. "I hear you. But it's kind of nice to see you doing something as mundane as chores for a change. How exactly am I supposed to survive two years at Lockridge without you?"

He shrugged. "You'll manage. Just don't take any crap from Mr. Reeves. He picks on the weak."

"Good advice. I'm wondering if I should go back. Blair told me he influenced Aunt Pam's decision to send us there."

"So what if he did? It's a good school, and it's where your friends are. Don't let him make you second-guess your whole life. Make your own decisions."

"I guess so. I mean, he can't influence me without me knowing, but he can influence people around me. I'm pretty sure I haven't heard the last of him; he'll probably just get more creative. He knows that if he does anything to you guys, he'll pay for it, but that doesn't mean he won't try something more subtle."

"I hear you, Ree, I do. But you've gotta live your life."

"Yeah, I know."

"Did Gramps tell you about Laz?"

I raised an alarmed eyebrow. "What about Laz?"

"Well, as you know, Gramps' kids don't have any interest in becoming caretakers here at the Glen. But guess what? Laz does. He loves it here."

"He does show up a lot."

"Yeah, well, Gramps is going to start training him, and Laz is going to take over when Gramps can't do it anymore. He asked Mom about it when you were gone, and she said yes."

I thought about that for a minute, and it seemed very right. "I think that's a good idea. I feel like Laz belongs here."

"We all felt the same way. Listen, you want to go for a hike when I finish this? It's hot out, but we can go down by the creek. We can even fish if you want."

My face brightened. "That sounds great. I'll go find the gear."

I went up to my room and changed into a tee shirt and water-resistant shorts, and grabbed my wading shoes. I tucked my phone (now fully functional and with all files restored, thankfully) into a waterproof cross-body bag and threw my hair up into a messy ponytail which I pulled through the back of a baseball cap. I was about to tromp down the stairs, but at the last minute, I spun around, opened my wardrobe, and reached behind the hanging clothes to touch the edge of the Judgement card. In my heart, I could feel that there was a fight ahead, but I just hoped that real family, not just biology, would win out.

As I walked back toward the stairs, I felt my phone buzz and pulled it out to check my message. My breath caught in my throat as I read the text:

Hey, sis. The game has changed, and so have I. We need to talk. -Z

Thank you for reading Rise of the Moon by JB Caine. The Arcana Trilogy continues with STRENGTH OF WILL.
If you enjoyed this book, please consider leaving a review on Amazon.

www.ingramcontent.com/pod-product-compliance
Lightning Source LLC
Chambersburg PA
CBHW060628260626
47161CB00008B/2834